Harry Castlemon, Richard H. Wilmer

Sailor Jack

the trader - Vol. 1

Harry Castlemon, Richard H. Wilmer

Sailor Jack
the trader - Vol. 1

ISBN/EAN: 9783337325275

Printed in Europe, USA, Canada, Australia, Japan

Cover: Foto ©Andreas Hilbeck / pixelio.de

More available books at **www.hansebooks.com**

CASTLEMON'S WAR SERIES.

SAILOR JACK, THE TRADER

BY

HARRY CASTLEMON,

AUTHOR OF "GUNBOAT SERIES," "ROCKY MOUNTAIN SERIES,"
"FOREST AND STREAM SERIES," ETC., ETC.

Four Illustrations by Geo. G. White.

PHILADELPHIA :
PORTER & COATES.

CONTENTS.

SAILOR JACK, THE TRADER.

CHAPTER I.

TOM RANDOLPH, CONSCRIPT.

"WELL, by gum! Am I dreamin'? Is this Tom Randolph or his hant?"

"I don't wonder that you are surprised. It's Tom Randolph easy enough, though I can hardly believe it myself when I look in the glass. There isn't a nigger in the settlement that isn't better clad and better mounted than I am."

"Well, I have seen you when you looked a trifle pearter, that's a fact."

"And what brought me to this? The Yankees and their cowardly sympathizers. I don't blame the boys in blue so much, for brave soldiers always respect one another, even though their sense of duty compels them to fight under different flags; but the traitors we have right here among us are too mean to be of any use. And the meanest one among them is Rodney Gray."

The first speaker was Lieutenant Lambert, who, by his zealous efforts to serve the cause of the South, brought about the bombardment of Baton Rouge, and the person whom he addressed was the redoubtable Captain Tom himself, who had just returned to Mooreville after undergoing two months' military disci- pline at Camp Pinckney.

The last time we saw these two worthies was shortly after the Confederate General Breck- enridge made his unsuccessful attempt to capture Baton Rouge, and the conscripting officer, Captain Roach, disappeared so com- pletely that no one had ever heard a word of him since, and the veteran Major Morgan, backed by fifty soldiers who hated all Home Guards and other skulkers as cordially as they hated the Yankees, came to take his place. Knowing that Captain Roach had been very remiss in his duty, that he had spent more time in visiting and eating good dinners than he had in sending conscripts to the army, Major

Morgan hardly gave himself time to take possession of the office in Kimberley's store before
he declared that that sort of work was going
to cease entirely, and that everyone in his district who was liable to military duty, Home
Guards as well as civilians, must start for the
camp of instruction at once or be taken there
by force. The news spread rapidly, and in a
very few hours everyone in the settlement had
heard it. The wounded and disabled veterans
of the Army of the Centre, of whom there
were a goodly number in the neighborhood,
were overjoyed to learn that at last there was
a man in the conscripting office who could not
be trifled with, and some of the civilians, who
came under the exemption clause of the Con-
scription Act, secretly cherished the hope that
Captain Tom and his first lieutenant might be
sent to serve under Bragg, who did not scruple
to shoot his soldiers for the most trivial offences.

As to Tom and his Home Guards, they did
not at first pay much attention to the major's
threats. It was right that civilians should be
forced to shoulder muskets, since they would
not do it of their own free will, but as for

them, they were State troops, and the government at Richmond could not order them around as it pleased. Besides, they had great confidence in Mrs. Randolph's powers of persuasion. She would never permit her son to go into the army, and having managed Captain Roach pretty near as she pleased, the Home Guards did not see why she could not manage Major Morgan as well; but when it became noised abroad that the latter had curtly refused Mrs. Randolph's invitation to dinner, intimating that he was not ordered to Mooreville to waste his time in visiting and nonsense, they were terribly frightened, and demanded that Captain Tom should "see them through." When they enlisted in his company, he promised to stand between them and the Confederate authorities, and now was the time for him to make that promise good ; but Tom was as badly frightened as they were, and did not know what to do. When his mother suggested that it might be well for him to put his commission in his pocket, and ride to Mooreville and talk the matter over with the major, Tom almost went frantic.

"Go down there and face that despot alone," he exclaimed, "while he has fifty veterans at his back to obey his slightest wish? I'd about as soon be shot and have done with it. Besides, what have I got to ride? The Yankees have stolen me afoot."

Captain Tom knew well enough that he was not telling the truth. It wasn't Yankees who "stole him afoot," but men who wore the same kind of uniform he did. You will remember that we compared the short visit of Breckenridge's army to a plague of locusts. Everything in the shape of eatables in and around Mooreville, as well as some articles of value, disappeared and were never heard of afterward; and among those articles of value were several fine horses, Tom Randolph's being one of the first to turn up missing. His expensive saddle and bridle disappeared at the same time, and now, if Tom wanted to go anywhere, he was obliged to walk or ride a plough mule bare-back, which was harrowing to his feelings. He wouldn't appear before a Confederate officer of rank in any such style as that, he said, and that was all there was

about it. But, as it happened, the conscripting officer had a word to say on that point.
On the morning following his arrival in the
village a couple of strange troopers galloped
into Mr. Randolph's front yard and drew up
at the steps with a jerk. Captain Tom's heart
sank when he saw them coming, for something
told him that they were after him and nobody
else; and paying no heed to the earnest en-
treaties of his mother, who assured him that
he might as well face them one time as another,
for he could not save himself by flight, he disappeared like a shot through the nearest door,
leaving her to explain his absence in any way
she thought proper. But after taking a
second look at the unwelcome visitors, Mrs.
Randolph knew it would be of no use to try
to shield the timid Home Guard. The trooper
who ascended the steps, leaving his comrade to
hold his horse, was a rough-looking fellow, as
well he might be, for he had seen hard service.
The little pieces of metal on his huge Texas
spurs tinkled musically, his heavy cavalry sabre
clanked against his heels as he walked, and
Mrs. Randolph thought there was something

threatening in the sound. He lifted his cap respectfully, but said in a brisk business tone :

"I'd like to see Tom Randolph, if you please."

"Do you mean Captain Randolph?" corrected the lady.

"No, ma'am. He was given to me as plain Tom Randolph, and that is the only name I know him by. I'd like to see him, if you please."

"Will you step in while I go and find him?"

"Thank you, no. I have no time to sit down. I am in a great hurry."

"You can spare a moment to tell me, his mother, what you are going to do with him, can you not?"

"All I can say is that the major wants to see him at once," was the short answer.

"Do you know what the major wants of him, so that I can explain——"

"Pardon me if I say that no explanations are necessary. It is enough for him to know that Major Morgan wants to see him without a moment's delay."

The tone in which the words were spoken satisfied Mrs. Randolph that the impatient trooper could not be put off any longer, so she turned about and went into the house. She knew that Tom had gone straight to her room, and when she tried the door she found that he had locked himself in.

"Who's there?" demanded a husky voice from the inside.

"It is I, my dear, and I am alone," was the reply. "Let me in at once. Now, call all your courage to your aid, and show yourself the brave soldier you were on the night you knocked that Yankee sentinel down with the butt of a musket and escaped being sent to a Northern prison-pen," she continued, as she slipped through the half open door, which was quickly closed and locked behind her. "Major Morgan wants to see you at his office, and, my dear, you had better go at once. The man at the door will not wait much longer."

"I don't care if he won't," shouted Captain Tom, who was terribly alarmed. "If he gets tired of standing there, let him go back where he came from and tell that major that

I—what business has that fellow got out there?"

Tom chanced to look through the window while he was talking, and when he saw one of the troopers ride down the carriage-way as if he were going to the rear of the house, it flashed upon him that the man was going there to watch the back door. At the same moment the jingling of spurs and the rattling of a sabre were heard in the next room, the door knob was tried by a strong hand, and something that might have been the toe of a heavy boot was propelled with considerable force against the door itself.

"Open up here," commanded a stern voice on the other side. "Do it at once, or I shall be obliged to force an entrance."

This threat brought Captain Tom to his senses. In a second the door was unlocked and opened, and the soldier stepped into the room.

"By what right does Major Morgan——" began Tom.

"I don't know a thing about it," was the quick reply. "It is no part of my duty to

inquire into my superior's private affairs. All
I can say is that I am commanded to bring
Tom Randolph before him without loss of
time. You are Tom Randolph, I take it.
Then saddle up and come with me."

"But the Yankees stole my horse and I
have nothing to ride except a mule," whined
Tom.

"Then ride the mule or come afoot. Make
up your mind to something, for I am going to
start in half a minute by the watch."

"You will give my son time to exchange
his citizen's clothes for his captain's uniform,
of course," ventured Mrs. Randolph.

"Sorry I haven't an instant to wait, but the
color of his clothes will make no sort of difference to Major Morgan," was the reply. "Now
then, will you order up that mule, or walk, or
ride double with my man?"

"Are you an officer?" faltered Tom.

"Not much of one—only a captain."

"Well, that puts a different look on the
matter entirely," said Tom, who up to this
time thought he was being ordered around by
a private soldier. "Since you are an officer

I expect to receive an officer's treatment from you, and I don't wish to be addressed——"

"That's all right. But hurry up, for the time is precious."

Being satisfied at last that his meeting with the dreaded conscript officer could not be delayed any longer, Captain Tom hastened to his room after his commission, while his mother sent a darky to the stable-yard to bring up the solitary mule that had been left there when the few remaining field-hands went to work in the morning. And a very sorry-looking beast it proved to be when it was led to the door—too decrepit to work, and so weak with age that it fairly staggered as Tom threw his weight upon the sheepskin which the thoughtful darky had placed on the animal's back to serve in lieu of a saddle. A sorry picture Captain Tom made, too, when he was mounted ; but he had no choice between going that way and riding double with a private, and that was a thing he could not bring himself to do.

While they were on their way to town Captain Tom made several fruitless attempts to induce his captors—for that was just what they were—to give him some idea of what he might expect when he presented himself before the major; but although he could not prevail upon them to say a word on that subject, he was able to make a pretty shrewd guess as to the nature of the business in hand, and if he had known that he was going to prison for a long term of years he could not have felt so utterly wretched and disheartened.

"If I were going to jail I might have a chance to get pardoned out," thought Tom, "but the only way to get out of the army is to be killed or have an arm or leg shot off. I'd be perfectly willing to go if Jeff Davis and all his Cabinet could be compelled to go too. I'm afraid I am in for trouble this time, sure.".

If Captain Tom had any lingering doubts on this point they were dispelled in less than half a minute after he entered the enrolling office. He had never before met the grizzly veteran who sat at Captain Roach's desk with a multitude of papers before him, and when their short interview was ended Captain Tom hoped from the bottom of his heart that he might never meet him again. He proved to be just what he looked—a thorough soldier, who had come there with the determination to perform his disagreeable duty without fear or favor. Every man in the office was a stranger to Tom. There were stacks of carbines and cavalry sabres in all the corners, horses saddled and bridled were hitched to the rack in front of the door, and there were a few tanned and weather-beaten soldiers standing around ready to start at the word, but there was not a Home Guard to be seen.

"This is Tom Randolph, sir," was the way in which one of the guards brought the new-comer to the notice of the conscript officer. "Don't sit down," he added a moment later, as Tom drew a chair toward him. "Take off your hat."

Captain Randolph was amazed, for this was not the way he had always been treated in that office. Hitherto he had been a privileged character, and had had as much to say as Captain Roach himself; but now things were changed, and for the first time in his life Tom was made to see that he was not of so

much importance in the world as he had supposed himself to be. He took off his hat, but
noticed that the soldiers in the room did not
remove theirs, and that nettled him. So did
the manner in which the major acknowledged
the introduction, if such it could be called.
He did not offer to shake hands as Tom thought
he would, but merely looked over the top of
his spectacles for a moment. Then he pulled
a sheet of paper toward him, ran his finger
down the list of names written on it until he
had found the one he wanted, and made a short
entry opposite to it; after which he pushed
away the paper and said :

"Report at one o'clock this afternoon.
That's all."

"But, major," Tom almost gasped, "what
am I to report for?"

"What for? Why, marching orders, of
course."

"Well, will you tell me where I am to
march?"

"Along the road that leads to the camp of instruction. Where else should a recruit march
to, I'd like to know. You're conscripted."

"But, major," protested Tom, drawing forth an official envelope with hands that trembled so violently that he could scarcely control them, "I really don't see how you can conscript me. I am a captain in the State troops, and there's my commission from the governor."

"It isn't worth straws," answered the major, snapping his fingers in the air. "Don't want to see it. Besides, you have resigned."

"But my resignation has not been accepted."

"That doesn't matter. It will be, for there are no such things as State troops now, I am happy to say. You're liable to military duty easy enough, and—that's all."

"I retain my rank, don't I, sir?" said Tom.

It was astonishing what an effect this simple question had upon the occupants of the room. Some quickly turned their faces to the wall, others tiptoed through the nearest doors, and all shook with suppressed merriment. The major jerked his spectacles off his nose, looked hard at Tom to see if he were really in earnest, and cleared his throat before he replied:

"No, sir; you will begin as Private Randolph, but will be given every opportunity to show what you are made of, and to win a commission that is worth something more than the paper it happens to be written on. Don't worry about that. Well, sergeant, where are the men I ordered you to bring before me?"

Hardly able to tell whether he was awake or dreaming, Tom Randolph yielded to the friendly hand that was laid upon his arm, and suffered himself to be led away from the desk, his place being immediately filled by four brawny soldiers, who raised their hands with a military salute. The first words one of them spoke aroused Tom from his stupor and interested him.

"We didn't find Lambert and Moseley to home, sir. They must have had warnin', I reckon, for they've took to the bresh."

"They needn't think to escape me by resorting to any such trick as that," said the major grimly. "They owe a duty to their country in this hour of her peril, and they've got to do it. I'll have a detail watch their houses night and day till they come back."

Tom Randolph could hardly believe that the soldier who laid his hand upon his arm and conducted him to a remote corner of the room, so that they could talk without danger of being overheard, was the same captain who had been so impatient and peremptory with him and his mother a short time before, but such was the fact. Having performed his duty and brought his prisoner to the office, as he had been told to do, the captain had thrown off his soldier airs and was as jolly and friendly a fellow as one would care to meet.

"You see you are going to have good company while you are in camp," said he.

"I don't know what you call good company," snarled Tom. "Lambert is nothing more than a common overseer, while Moseley is a chicken and hog thief. Good company, indeed!"

"But we heard that they are officers in your company of Home Guards," said the captain in a surprised tone.

"They were chosen against my earnest protest," replied Tom, "but they have never been commissioned by the governor. Their election

2

was not legal, and so I didn't report it. But, captain, I don't think your major has any authority to ride over the governor in this rough way."

"Hasn't he a right to conscript everyone who does not come under the exemption clause?" answered the captain. "If you have read that act I will venture to say that you did not see the words 'Home Guards' in it. Come now."

"But I am my father's overseer," said Tom, switching off on another track.

"Since when?"

"Since long before Breckenridge made his attack on Baton Rouge."

" Where are you employed?"

" On the home plantation."

" Your father doesn't need two overseers on the home plantation, does he? He has claimed exemption for—what's his name?—Larkin."

" And didn't he say a word about me?"

"The records of the office don't show it. Now let me tell you something. If your father wants to claim exemption for you instead of Larkin no doubt he can manage it with General Ruggles, who is in command at Camp Pinckney. Major Morgan has no authority to act in such cases. Just now your duty is to go home and make ready to report at one o'clock sharp. Don't be a second behind time unless you want to get the rough side of the major's tongue.''

''What shall I do to get ready?''

'' Why, pack up a suit or two of your strongest clothes, an extra pair of shoes and stockings, and a few blankets, which I assure you will come handy for shelter tents when you take the field.''

''And you don't think of any way in which I can get out of it?'' said Tom in a choking voice.

'' Oh, no. *That's* a dead open and shut. You've got to go to camp and stay there while your friends are working to get you out, if that is what you want them to do. But I wouldn't let them make any move in that direction if I were you. Why don't you go with us and make a man of yourself? We are whipping the Yankees right along, and you will have plenty of chances to distinguish yourself. We're bound to gain our independence, and don't you want to be able to say that you had a hand in it?"

The captain's earnest words did not send any thrill of patriotism into the heart of Tom Randolph, who just then wished that the Yankees would sweep through Mooreville in irresistible numbers, put an end to the war in a moment, and so keep him from going to Camp Pinckney. He turned sorrowfully away from the captain, who had really tried to befriend him by giving what he thought to be good advice, mounted his aged mule, and set out for home. His mother's face brightened when he dismounted at the foot of the steps, but fell instantly when Tom told her that she had better take a good long look at him while she had the chance, for after that day was past she would never see him again. Of course there was mourning in that house when he told his story, and the gloom that rested there was but partially dispelled by Mr. Randolph's promise to discharge Larkin without loss of time and claim exemption for Tom in his stead.

"If you could do it this minute it would

not keep me from going to the camp of instruction," whined Tom, "for the major has no authority to do anything but conscript everybody he can get his hands on."

"Has he warned Ned Griffin and Rodney Gray?" inquired Mrs. Randolph.

"That's so," exclaimed Tom angrily. "What a dunce I was not to speak to the captain about those fellows! But I was so taken up with my own affairs that I never once thought of it. However, I'll think of it when I go down to the office at one o'clock, I bet you. And, father, if you get on the track of Lambert and Moseley, don't fail to let the major know it. If I've got to be disgraced I want them to keep me company."

"I will bear it in mind," answered Mr. Randolph. "And since one o'clock isn't so very far off, hadn't you better get ready?"

The conscript thought this a very heartless suggestion and so did his mother; but they could not deny that there was reason in it, and so preparations for Tom's departure were made at once. The parting which took place an hour or so later was a tearful one on Tom's part as well as his mother's, but there was not very much sorrow exhibited by the black servants who crowded into the dining-room to shake his hand, as they were in duty bound to do, and Tom made the mental resolution that, when he returned from Camp Pinckney to take his place as overseer on the plantation, he would see them well paid for their indifference. He rode in his mother's carriage this time, accompanied by his father and a bundle of things that would have filled a soldier's knapsack to overflowing. When the carriage turned into the street that ran past Kimberley's store, Tom thrust his head out of the window, but instantly pulled it in again to say, while tears of vexation filled his eyes and ran down his cheeks :

"There's a bigger crowd of people in front of the office than I ever saw before. No doubt some of them will be glad to know I have been conscripted ; but if you have the luck I am sure you will have, I shall be back to turn the laugh on them before many days have passed over my head. Just look, father, and remember the name of every one who has a slighting word or glance for me, so that I may settle with him at some future time. I hope Rodney and Ned Griffin are there."

"You've got your wish," replied Mr. Randolph, after he had run his eye over the crowd, which extended clear across the street to the hitching-rack. "Rodney and Ned are there, but they seem to be standing on the outskirts."

Tom mustered up courage enough to look again, and then he saw what his father meant by "the outskirts." There were three distinct classes of people in that gathering. In the middle of the crowd and in front of the office stood two score conscripts, who were closely guarded by half as many of Major Morgan's veterans. Some of the conscripts seemed resolved to make the best of the situation, and joked and laughed with their friends and relatives who had assembled to see them off, and who formed the third class that stood outside the guards; but Tom noticed that most of their number looked very unhappy indeed. Tom did not see Rodney and Ned, but he discovered several disabled veterans of

Bragg's army with whom he had a speaking acquaintance, and they in turn discovered him and sent up a shout of welcome.

"Hey-youp! Here comes another, and I do think in my soul it's Captain Tommy Randolph," exclaimed one. "It's him, for I know that there kerridge."

"An' they tell me that you might jest as well be in the army to onct as to be in that camp," chimed in a second veteran. "There aint no sich thing as gettin' away when they get a grip onto you."

"Not by no means," cried a third. "Kase why, don't you know that they keep a pack of nigger hound dogs there that aint got nothin' in the wide world to do but jest chase deserters?"

The tone in which the taunting words were uttered was highly exasperating to Tom, whose face grew red with anger.

"I wouldn't mind them," said his father soothingly. "That's only soldiers' fun. They don't mean anything by it."

"I'll try not to mind them now, but I'll get even with every one of them when I come back," said Tom savagely.

Stepping out of the carriage, and showing himself to that little mob of laughing, jeering soldiers, was one of the most trying ordeals that Tom Randolph ever passed through, but there was no way to escape it. As he hurried through their ranks toward the guards, who stood aside to let him pass, they sent a few more words of advice and encouragement after him.

"Where's all your purty clothes, Tommy?" inquired one. "Go home to onct an' get 'em. If you don't, them fule Yanks will think you are nothin' but a dog-gone private."

"Don't listen to him, Tommy," said another. "The Yanks always pick for officers in battle, an' they're dead shots, I tell you."

"You're mighty right," chorused a dozen voices. "I never did see anybody who could shoot like them Yanks. I'm glad I aint got to face 'em agin, tell your folks. I wouldn't do it for all the money the Confedrit gov'ment is worth."

"It's a disgrace the way those fellows are allowed to go on," said Tom to the first soldier he met when he entered the office, and who turned out to be the captain whose acquaintance he had made that morning. "Why don't you put a stop to it?"

"Aw! They want some sport, don't they?" was the answer. "Let them go ahead with it until they get tired, and then they will stop. Besides, you might as well get used to such talk one time as another, for you will hear plenty of it in the army."

"But you mustn't permit them to force me into the army," whispered Tom to his father. "If you do, you will always be sorry for it, because you will never see me again."

In a dazed sort of way Tom reported to the major, and then tried to hide himself in a corner of the office where he would be out of sight of his tormentors, but he was quickly routed from there by one of the major's men, who told him to go outside where he would be under the eye of the guard. Of course his appearance was the signal for another outburst from the veterans, but he wisely tried to drown their gibes by entering into conversation with a conscript who looked as disconsolate and wretched as Tom himself felt. His father had given the bundle into his keeping, and taken his place outside the guards with the rest of the exempts, and Tom began to realize how it seemed to be alone in a crowd. Rodney and Ned did not come near him, and that made him angry and threaten vengeance. They might at least shake hands with him and assure him of their sympathy, Tom thought, but if they had been foolish enough to attempt it, it is more than probable that he would have turned his back upon them. More than that, Rodney Gray was not a hypocrite. Having had the most to do with the breaking up of Tom's company of Home Guards, he would have uttered a deliberate untruth if he had said he was sorry to see him conscripted. He wasn't; he would have been sorry to see him stay at home.

"And when he reaches the camp of instruction I hope some strict drill-sergeant will put him through an extra course of sprouts to pay him for the mean trick he tried to play on Dick Graham," said Rodney to his friend Ned. "I could have told things that would have got all the Pinckney guards down on him if I had been so disposed, and now I am glad I didn't do it. There he goes. Good-by, Tom Randolph."

"Fall in!" shouted a stentorian voice. "Not off there, but here, with the right resting where I stand. Haven't you Home Guards been drilled enough to learn how to fall in in two ranks? Face out that way toward the hitching-rack. Now listen to roll-call!"

In ten minutes more the conscripts had answered to their names and were headed toward Camp Pinckney, marching in a crooked straggling line with their bundles on their shoulders and armed guards on each side of them. There were forty-five in all, and two-thirds of them were Home Guards. There were many sober and tearful faces among the spectators when they moved away, and even the discharged veterans must have taken the matter seriously, for they did not utter one taunting word.

CHAPTER II.

A FEW of Tom Randolph's fellow-sufferers had repeatedly declared in his hearing that they never would be taken to Camp Pinckney alive ; but when the roll was called inside the stockade at sunset the following day, their dreary, toilsome march having been completed by that time, every one of them answered to his name. Not one of their number had made his escape, and indeed it would have been foolhardy to attempt it, for the guards were alert and watchful, and it was whispered along the line that they had strict orders to shoot down the first man who tried to break away.

Not to dwell too long upon this part of our story, it will be enough to say that Tom Randolph remained in the camp of instruction for two solid months, during which time he suffered more than he thought it possible for

mortal man to endure. He was given plenty
to eat, such as it was, but scarcely a night
passed that he was not aroused from a sound
sleep to go on post or to repel an assault that
was never made, and during the day-time he
was drilled in the school of the soldier and
company, and in the manual of arms, until all
the muscles in him ached so that he could not
lie still after he went to bed. Every hour in
the day indignities were put upon him that
caused his blood to boil, and he made matters
worse by resenting them on the spot, the result
being that he did more police duty than any
other man in camp. Time and again he
sought an interview with the commandant,
intending to complain of his treatment and
ask when he might look for his release, but
he never saw the general except from a distance, and then was not permitted to approach
him. All this while his father, who visited
him at irregular intervals, bringing news from
the outside world, was doing his best; but
there were so many difficulties in his way, and
so much red tape to be gone through, that he
found himself balked at every point, and it is

a wonder he was not tempted to give it up as a task beyond his powers.

"You see Roach's books show that I claimed exemption for Larkin, and I'm afraid that's against us," he said to Tom one day, after talking the matter over with General Ruggles.

"But you have as much right to change your mind as other folks, I suppose," replied Tom.

"Of course I have, but that isn't the point. If Larkin were here to take your place in camp the work might be easier; but you see he isn't. He has skipped."

"Skipped where?"

"Out in the woods, to keep company with Lambert and Moseley, I suppose. And when he went he left word with some of the neighbors that if anything happened to my buildings during the next few weeks, I might thank him for it. He put out as soon as I told him that I couldn't pay the beef and bacon the government demanded as the price of his exemption."

"Did you tell Major Morgan that you wouldn't pay it?"

"Certainly, and I told General Ruggles so; but that didn't scare them at all. If they want beef and bacon they'll just take it."

"Well, now, if that isn't a pretty way for a common overseer to treat a gentleman I wouldn't say so," declared Tom, who really thought that Larkin ought to have stayed at home and been conscripted in his place. "What difference does one man make in the size of an army, anyway? The general could let me go as well as not."

"But he won't, unless certain forms are complied with. Be as patient as you can, and remember that I shall leave no stone unturned."

"Get an honorable discharge while you are about it, so that I shall not be called upon to go through with this performance a second time," said Tom.

It is true that a single recruit made no great difference in the strength of an army, but for some reason that no one but General Ruggles could have explained it made all the difference in the world so far as Tom Randolph's release from military duty was concerned. One day, about six weeks after the conversation above recorded, Mr. Randolph walked into camp and told Tom that he was a free man—or rather that he would be in a few hours, for Larkin had been captured by Major Morgan's scouts, and was now on his way to camp to take Tom's place.

"And am I to have an honorable discharge?" inquired Tom, who was so overjoyed that he could hardly speak.

"No ; and I was foolish to ask for it," said his father in disgust. "The general laughed in my face and said you hadn't done anything worthy of it. Don't say a word about it, but thank your lucky stars that you have escaped being ordered to the front."

When the man Larkin and a few other conscripts were brought in under guard, Tom Randolph was standing as near the big gate as the camp regulations would allow him to get, waiting impatiently for somebody to come out of the commandant's office and tell him he could go home. He was mean enough to try to attract Larkin's attention when the latter tramped wearily into the stockade, but the man was so wrapped up in his troubles that he

3

could hardly have recognized his best friend, if he had had one among the curious crowd that was gathered about the gate. Tom was a little disappointed, but quickly dismissed Larkin from his mind when he saw his father approaching with an expression on his face that was full of good news.

"Come right along," said he. "It's all settled now. There stands the officer who has orders to pass us out."

"So the general has consented to do me justice at last, has he?" exclaimed Tom, who was not half as grateful as he ought to have been. "And he kept me here all these weary days and allowed me to be insulted and abused on account of that man Larkin, did he? Thank him for nothing. But I'll fix some others who are as much to blame for my being here as General Ruggles is. I haven't wasted all my time since I have been in jail, I tell you."

"I brought a mule for you to ride," continued his father. "But don't you think we had better bunk with the guard to-night? It will be as dark as a pocket in an hour, and besides it is going to rain."

"I don't care if it rains pitchforks. I'll face them rather than remain in this dreary hole a moment longer," declared the liberated conscript. "And I am not going to the barracks after my clothes or blankets. I will them to the first man who can put his hands on them."

Tom reached home in due time in spite of the rain and other discomforts that attended him on his journey, and it is scarcely necessary to say that his mother welcomed him as one risen from the dead. Her husband had told her doleful stories of Tom's life in camp, and she was afraid that he would sink under his many hardships before his release could be effected. But Tom was not as badly off as he pretended to be. A few days' rest made him as uneasy and full of meanness as he had ever been in his life ; but it is fair to say that his uneasiness was due to an unaccountable delay in the carrying out of a certain little programme which he had arranged while living in the stockade. This was what he meant when he told his father that he had not wasted his time since he had been in jail.

During the month of September it became known to the guards and conscripts at Camp Pinckney that a meeting of cotton and tobacco planters had been held in Richmond "to consider the expediency of the purchase by the Confederacy, or of a voluntary destruction of the entire cotton and tobacco crop," to keep it from falling into the hands of the Union forces. It is hard to tell why the news was so long in coming down to Louisiana, for the meeting, which was described as "one of the largest, wealthiest, and most intelligent that had ever assembled in the city," was held as early as February. Among the other resolutions acted upon by this patriotic assemblage was one calling upon the Southern people to destroy all their property in advance of the invading armies, even to their homes, so that the conquest of the United States should be a barren one. Of course this resolution met the hearty approval of those of the Camp Pinckney guards and conscripts who had no property worth speaking of, and some of them declared that if General Ruggles would let them have their own way for twenty-four

hours they would destroy thousands of bales
of cotton which the owners would never burn
themselves so long as they saw a prospect of
selling them to the Yankees. This set Tom
Randolph to thinking, and with the aid of
some of the Pearl River Home Guards who
were still on duty at the camp, he made up
a nice little plan to revenge himself on several
of the Mooreville people who had incurred his
enmity. It might have been successful, too,
if Tom had not allowed his unruly tongue to
upset it. As soon as he reached home he
began waiting and watching for some signs of
activity on the part of the Pearl River vagabonds, but up to this time the clouds that
hung over the swamp, and which he watched
every night with anxious eyes, had not been
lighted by any signal-fires.

The life that Tom Randolph now led was
dreary and monotonous in the extreme ; no
healthy boy could have endured it for a week.
Did he take Larkin's place as overseer and do
his work ? Well, hardly ; and he never had
any intention of doing it. The field-hands did
the work as well as the overseeing, and Tom

spent his time in loafing or in riding about the
country on a bare-back mule.   It is true that
Major Morgan's "drag-net" had not cleared
the neighborhood of everyone who was subject
to military duty, for a few of the desperate
ones, like Lambert and Moseley, had taken to
the woods, and a few others had joined the
Yankees in Baton Rouge, where they were
safe from pursuit; but it had caught the most
of the able-bodied men and boys of Tom's
acquaintance, and now he found himself
almost alone.   He saw Rodney and Ned now
and then, but never spoke to them if he could
help it, or visited them on their plantations;
for since they, with Mrs. Griffin's aid, kept
him from being sent to a Northern prison, he
disliked them more than he did before.   He
had never got over being surprised at Mr.
Gray's action in standing between Ned and
the conscript officer, while he permitted the
other telegraph operator, Drummond, to take
his chances.   Mr. Gray must be Union at
heart or else he would not have done that;
and if he was Union he ought to be driven out
of the country.   Tom found a world of conso-

lation in the reflection that he would soon be
even with him.

It was while the returned conscript was taking his usual morning ride on his mule, with a
gunny-sack for a saddle, that he met his old
first lieutenant, as described at the beginning
of the last chapter.   He knew that the man was
living in the woods, otherwise he would have
had him for company at Camp Pinckney, and
he was surprised to find him riding along a
public road in broad daylight.   Lambert was
also mounted on a mule, the property of his
late employer, which he had appropriated to
his own use without troubling himself to ask
permission.   He remembered that Tom had
once drawn a sword upon him, and flattered
himself that in Camp Pinckney his tyrannical
captain was being well paid for that and other
indignities he had put upon his Home Guards ;
consequently he was not a little astonished and
vexed to find him breathing the air of freedom
on this particular morning.

"How did you manage to get away from
them fellers, anyhow ?" inquired Lambert,
nodding in the direction of the camp.

"I have influence with the governor," replied Tom loftily. "I did not want to stay, and consequently I didn't."

"Afeared of the Yanks, was you?" continued Lambert with something like a sneer.

"No more afraid than yourself. You took to your heels and are in danger every moment of being caught and sent to camp, while I faced the music at once and will never have to do it again. I am discharged from military service for all time to come."

"Well, by gum! I won't do none," said Lambert fiercely; and Tom noticed that every time he spoke he looked behind and on both sides as if he were in constant fear that Major Morgan's men might steal a march upon him. "I say let them that brung the war on do the fightin'. I didn't have no hand in it, an' nuther am I goin' to holp 'em out. Yes, I'm livin' in the woods now, me an'—an' some other fellers; but I have to come out once in a while to get grub an' things, you know."

"Then why don't you come at night?" asked Tom.

"Kase it suits me better to come in the daytime. I aint a-skeared. There's plenty kiver handy."

"But if you dismount and take to your heels you'll lose your mule."

"Who keers? 'Tain't my mu-el, an' if they take him I can easy get another. What you drivin' at now?"

"I am my father's overseer."

"Shucks! You couldn't tell to save your life if a corn row was laid off straight or not."

"No matter for that," said Tom sharply. "As long as I hold the position I can live at home and show myself openly; and that's more than you can do. Have you seen that converted Confederate and his Yankee friend lately?"

"Who's them?" inquired Lambert.

"Why, Ned Griffin and Rodney Gray."

"Oh, yes; I see 'em every day 'most. They're livin' down there snug as you please, an' as often as I——"

"Go on," said Tom, when the man paused suddenly. "As often as you what?"

"As often as I want to see 'em I see 'em," added Lambert.

"That isn't what you were about to say at first," replied Tom. "I hope you are not a friend of theirs?"

"Look a-here, cap'n, wasn't I first leftenant of the Home Guards?"

"You were, and a very good officer you made, except when you took it upon yourself to act without waiting for orders from me; and then you always brought yourself into trouble. Can you be trusted?"

"If I can't, what's the reason I was 'lected to that office?" asked Lambert in reply. "What do you want of me?"

"The members of the Randolph family are not quite as poor as some people seem to think, I want you to understand," said Tom in a mysterious whisper. "We have several little articles hidden away that our neighbors know nothing about, and next week we shall have some store tea and coffee and salt to hand around to those who need them. Your shoes are full of holes, too. You ought to have a new pair."

If Lambert had given utterance to the thoughts that were in his mind, he would

have said that his old commander would miss
it if he hoped to bribe him in this way.
There were few people in the settlement who
did not stand in need of the articles Tom
mentioned, but Lambert knew where he could
get them for the asking. Still he wanted to
know what Tom wished him to do, and said
so.

"You fought the conscript officers offen me
long's as you could, an' I aint likely to disremember it," he replied.

"I kept you out of the army for more than a
year, and now is the time for you to pay me
for it," replied Tom impressively. "Now
listen while I tell you something. You know
that our government has ordered every planter
who owns cotton to burn it so that it will not
fall into the hands of the Yankees, don't
you?"

"No!" answered Lambert. He was surprised, for this was news to him; but he saw
what Tom was trying to get at.

"Well, it is the truth, and those who do not
comply with the order will be punished in some
way, and their property destroyed by our own

soldiers.   Now there's old man Gray ; he has cotton."

"And he won't never burn it," exclaimed Lambert.

"That's the idea exactly.   He'd rather sell it to the Yankees for sixty cents a pound ; and so far as I can see there is nothing to hinder him from doing it."

"Less'n some of our fellers slip up an' burn it for him," put in Lambert.

"You've hit it again," exclaimed Tom, who told himself that he wasn't going to have any trouble at all in bringing the man to do the work he had suddenly laid out for him.   "He can sell his cotton if nobody stops him, but my father can't sell his because he is known to be a loyal Confederate.   Do you think that's fair or right ? "

"I know it aint," answered Lambert. "Gray is Union, and oughter be sent amongst the Yanks where he b'longs ; but your paw is Confedrit and so am I.   Do you want me to tech off that cotton ? "

"Well, no ; not exactly that.   You know where it is, I suppose ? "

"There aint much of anything in the woods in this country that I don't know something about," said Lambert with a grin. "I reckon I might find it if I took a notion."

"That is what I thought, and now I come to the point. While I was in camp I learned that a squad of our soldiers is coming here some day to look after the very cotton we are talking about," said Tom, who did not think it would be just the thing to say that he had proposed the expedition himself, and accurately described the bayou in which Mr. Gray's four hundred bales could be found. "Now if you happen to see that squad while you are riding about the country——"

"I'll take leg-bail mighty sudden, I bet you," interrupted Lambert.

"Without offering to show them where the cotton is hidden?" cried Tom.

"You bet! I aint got no call to go philanderin' about the woods with a passel of soldiers, an' if you was the friend you pertend to be you wouldn't ask sich a thing of me."

"Why, man alive, they are Home Guards," began Tom.

"Then I wouldn't trust none of 'em as fur as I could sling a church house," replied Lambert.

"And besides, they don't know that you have been conscripted, for they belong to the Pearl River bottoms, miles away from here."

"No odds; Major Morgan's men can give me all the dodgin' I want to do, an' if them Pearl River fellers don't find that cotton till I show it to 'em they'll never find it. I jest aint goin' to run no fule chances on bein' tooken to that camp."

Tom Randolph wished now that he hadn't broached the subject to Lambert at all, for what assurance had he that the man, whom he knew to be vindictive and untrustworthy, would not go straight to Mr. Gray and tell him all about it?

"I thought you were a friend of mine, but since you are not it's all right," said Tom, intimating by a wave of his hand that Lambert's refusal was a matter of no moment whatever. "But come with me to the house, and let me see if I can't find something for you." And as he spoke he looked down at the man's broken shoes and bare, sunbrowned ankles.

"Shucks!" exclaimed Lambert. "I don't need to go beggin' shoes an' stockin's of nobody; an' as for the salt an' store tea that you've been talkin' about, I have them in the woods every day."

"I don't believe it," said Tom bluntly.

"It don't make no odds to me whether you do or not, but it's a fact."

"Where do you get them? You haven't the cheek to go to Baton Rouge, after the part you played in having the place bombarded by the Union fleet. You wouldn't dare show your face there, and I don't believe you have any friends to bring goods through the lines for you. I haven't forgotten that old man Gray wanted that mob to thrash me as if I were a nigger, and I hope you remember that he was strongly in favor of hanging you. Ned Griffin warned you, and you jumped out of bed and ran for your life."

"Do you reckon I've disremembered all the things that happened that night?" said Lambert with a scowl. "I aint, I bet you, an' mebbe you'll find it out some of those days. I aint nobody's coward, an' I dast do a good many things when I make up my mind to it. You jest watch, an' you'll see fire some of those nights. But when you see it you may know that no Pearl River Home Guards didn't have a hand in it."

"Will you do it yourself?" said Tom gleefully.

"I aint a-sayin' who'll do it, but it 'll be done. I've been mistreated an' used like a dog all along of this war, an' I'm a-goin' to even up with somebody to pay for it."

"And when the work is done come to my house; ask for anything I've got and I will give it to you. Where are you going now?" asked Tom, as the man began digging his heels into his mule's sides and tugging at one of the reins in the effort to turn the beast around.

"I reckon I'd best be joggin' along back. I've been out from under kiver 'most long enough. You watch out an' you'll see that fire; that's every word I've got to say about it."

The two separated and rode off in different

directions—the one in a brown study, and the other shaking his head and muttering angry words to himself. Lambert was very well satisfied with the result of the interview, for it had suggested something to him that he never would have thought of himself, but Tom could not drive away the thought that perhaps it would have been better for him if he had turned his mule's head down the road instead of up when he left his father's gate that morning.

"I know that Lambert was awfully angry at me because I shook my sword in his face, but what else could I do when he acted as if he were about to rush up the steps and lay violent hands upon me in mother's presence?" soliloquized Tom. "Perhaps I talked too much and at the wrong time; but if Lambert plays me false, I'll put every Yankee scouting party that comes along on his trail. I'll keep a bright lookout for that fire, as he told me, but I shall not draw an easy breath until I see it. Then I shall feel safe, for of course if he fires that cotton he will not tell on himself."

Tom went up to his room at his usual hour

4

for retiring, but instead of going to bed he drew a big rocking-chair in front of a window that looked out toward Rodney Gray's plantation, and seated himself in it to watch for Lambert's signal fire—the light on the clouds which would tell him that one of Mooreville's most respected citizens was being punished because he, Tom Randolph, didn't like him. He had no assurance from Lambert that he would see the blaze that night, but he hoped he would, and he resolved that he would sit at that window for six months, if necessary, rather than miss the sight and the gratification it would afford him.

"Lambert's face grew as black as a thundercloud when I reminded him that Mr. Gray was one of the mob who wanted to hang him for bringing about the bombardment of Baton Rouge," thought Tom, "and I know he will have revenge for that if he gets half a chance."

Tom had not yet made up for the sleep he lost at Camp Pinckney, and in less than half an hour he was slumbering heavily. It was long after midnight when he awoke with a start and a feeling that there was something

unusual going on. His eyes rested on the
window when they were opened, and the sight
he saw through the panes sent a thrill all
through him and brought him to his feet in an
instant. The glare on the sky told him there
was a fire raging somewhere in the depths of
the forest, and that it must be a big one, for
the whole heavens in that direction were
illuminated by it.

"He's done it; as sure as the world he's
done it," said Tom, who was highly excited.
"It's all the proof I want that I am not so
much of a nobody as some people make me
out to be. But I had no idea that baled cotton
would give out such a blaze as that. However, four hundred bales, if they were all
in one place, would make a pretty good-sized
pile."

Tom's first impulse was to rush downstairs
and tell his mother the good news, but he was
afraid she might not keep it to herself. She
would be likely to call his father's attention to
the light in the sky, and that was a thing Tom
did not care to have her do. Mr. Randolph
had changed wonderfully of late—ever since

he missed salt from his table and learned that
cotton was worth sixty cents a pound in
Northern markets—and Tom had not failed
to notice it. He wasn't half as good a Confederate as he used to be, and even showed
a desire to be friendly with Mr. Gray and
Rodney, who belonged to that unpatriotic
class of planters spoken of by the Southern
historian who "were known to buy every
article of their consumption in Yankee markets," that is to say, in Baton Rouge. This
being the case Tom did not go downstairs and
tell what was going on in the swamp for fear
his father might have something sharp and
unpleasant to say about it. He sat in his
chair and watched the light until it began to
fade away before the stronger light of the rising sun, and then went to bed, happy in the
reflection that there was one traitor in the
neighborhood who would not make a fortune
out of the unholy war that had been forced
upon the South by Lincoln's hirelings.

It was almost noon when he opened his eyes
again, and the first move he made was for the
window that looked toward the swamp that

inclosed Rodney Gray's plantation on three sides. Of course all signs of the conflagration had long since disappeared, but it had left gloom and anxiety in the house below, as Tom found when he went down to eat the late breakfast that had been kept warm for him. His mother seemed to have grown a dozen years older since he last saw her.

"What is the matter?" he demanded. "Your face is as long as my arm."

"O Tommy, did you see it last night?" she asked in reply.

"See what last night?" faltered Tom, who began to have a faint suspicion that it would be a wise thing for him to make his mother believe, if he could, that he had slept soundly through it all.

"Why, the fire. Someone's cotton has been destroyed. Mr. Walker, who lives on the plantation below, saw the light and came up this morning and told your father about it, and together they have gone to the swamp to look into the matter."

"Oh! the swamp," repeated Tom with a chuckle. "That's all right, and father need not have troubled himself to ride so far without his breakfast. Please tell the girl to give me a bite of something. Old man Gray has some cotton in there, I believe."

"But, my dear, we have two hundred bales in there, too."

The tone in which the words were uttered struck Tom dumb and motionless for a moment. Then he groped blindly for the nearest chair and dropped into it. It was true that his father had a fortune hidden not more than half a mile from the bayou in which Mr. Gray's four hundred bales were concealed, and up to that moment he had forgotten all about it. It was also true that all the cotton that had been run into the swamp was plainly marked with the initials of the owners' names, but Tom didn't know whether Lambert could read or not. He had never thought to ask him, and now he blamed himself for his stupidity. If it was the Pearl River vagabonds, and not Lambert, who applied the torch, there was the same trouble to be feared. Tom took particular pains to tell the men with whom he conspired to destroy Mr. Gray's property that every bale of it was marked R. W. G., but he now remembered, with a sinking at his heart that almost drove him crazy, that these Home Guards were as ignorant as the mules and horses they rode on their plundering expeditions, and perhaps there was not one among them who knew one letter from another. The fear that the wrong pile might have been committed to the flames threw him into a terrible state of mind.

"I don't wonder that you are sadly troubled," said his mother, in a sympathizing tone. "But I suppose it is about what we can look for in times like these. I never did expect to save that cotton. I was sure that if the Yankees did not steal it the rebels would destroy it."

(Mrs. Randolph called them "rebels" now. A few months before she would have spoken of them as "Confederates" or "our own brave soldiers.")

"Take it away," yelled Tom, addressing the girl, who just then brought his breakfast in from the kitchen. "I don't want anything to eat. I never want anything more as long as I live.

How many thousand dollars was that cotton
worth ? "

" You'll fret yourself sick if you give way
to your feelings like this," protested his
mother. "We are not sure that anyone has
troubled our cotton ; we only fear it."

"It would be on a par with the luck that has
attended me all through this miserable war if
every pound of it was gone up in smoke," said
Tom in a discouraged voice. "It's some con-
solation to know that we are all poor together,
for of course the men who knew where to find
our cotton knew where to find Gray's and
Walker's also."

With these words Tom snatched his hat
from the rack in the hall, and went down the
steps and out to the gate to watch for his
father's return. The latter was a long time
coming, and his face wore so dejected a look
when he rode up and passed into the yard, that
Tom could not find it in his heart to speak to
him. He simply turned about and went into
the house to wait, with as much fortitude as
he could command, for his father to come in
and tell the terrible news that was so plainly

written on his face.   His wife, who met him at
the door, did not say a word until he had
seated himself in the chair he usually occupied by the front window, and then she whispered the question :

"Is it all gone, George ?"

"Every bale," replied Mr. Randolph with a
groan.   "In the first place, nearly three hundred thousand dollars' worth of niggers ran
away and left us with barely a handful to do
our work for us, and now the cotton I was
depending on to start me afresh when the
war ended has run away too ; or gone up in
the elements, which amounts to the same
thing."

"Of course Mr. Gray's cotton——" stammered Tom.

"Wasn't touched," said Mr. Randolph, fin-
ishing the sentence for him.   "You may believe it or not, but it is a fact that our cotton
alone was destroyed.   Walker and I found Mr.
Gray and Rodney and Griffin and a dozen or
so others in the swamp when we got there, and
they had been trying to drag some of my bales
out of reach of the flames; but they didn't go

there until morning, and of course were too late to be of any use."

"The cowards!" exclaimed Tom bitterly. "If they saw the fire when it was burning, why didn't they go at once?"

"Would you have done it?" replied his father. "They thought the fire had been set by soldiers and were afraid to go out in the dark; but if the soldiers had had a hand in it they would have burned other cotton. It was the work of someone who has a spite against us, and he has made beggars of us. I haven't a dollar of good money, or a thing that can be turned into money; and even if I had, you and your Home Guards have made yourselves so obnoxious to the Baton Rouge people that I wouldn't dare go there to trade. Oh, yes; we're fit candidates for the poorhouse if there was one in the county."

Tom Randolph covered his face with his hands and trembled violently. He could not speak, but told himself that the world would not have held half so much trouble for him if that man Lambert had never been born into it.

CHAPTER III.

WHEN Tom Randolph and the man Lambert brought their interview to a close and rode away in different directions, as we have recorded, the latter turned into the first lane he came to, and finally disappeared in the woods. For three or four miles or more he rode along the fence that separated a wide corn-field from the timber, passed in the rear of Mr. Gray's extensive home plantation, and at last came out into the road again opposite the house in which Ned Griffin and his mother now lived. Having made sure that there were none of Major Morgan's men in sight (he feared them and the Baton Rouge people more than he did the boys in blue) Lambert crossed the road and threw down the bars that gave entrance into the door-yard. The noise aroused Ned's hounds, whose sonorous yelping quickly brought their master to the porch.

"Oh, it's you, is it?" said Ned, when he saw who his visitor was. "I don't know how to explain it, but I have been looking for you all day. Have you done anything for your country since I seen you last?"

Ned's manner would have made Tom Randolph open his eyes, and might, perhaps, have aroused his suspicions, there was so much unbecoming familiarity in it. More than that, his words seemed to imply that there was some sort of an understanding between him and the ex-Home Guard. The latter seated himself on the end of the porch, pulled his cob pipe from his pocket and tapped his thumb-nail with the inverted bowl to show that it was empty, whereupon Ned went into the house and presently came out again with a plug of navy tobacco in his hand. The sight of it made Lambert's eyes glisten.

"I aint seen the like very often since the war come onto us," said he, as he proceeded to cut off enough of the weed to fill his pipe; "an' this here nigger-heel that we uns have to put up with nowadays aint fitten for a white man to use. Do you know, I think Rodney

Gray is jest one of the smartest fellers there is a-goin' ?"

" I've always thought and said so," replied Ned. " But what has he done lately that is so very bright?"

" Hirin' me to watch that cotton of his'n so that I could tell him if I see anybody castin' ugly eyes at it," said Lambert, settling back at his ease on the gallery so that he could enjoy his smoke to the best advantage. " When you told me that Rodney would take it as a friendly act on my part if I would do that much for him, I didn't think there was the least bit of use in it, but now I know there is. I run up agin somebody a while ago, an' who do you think it was ?"

" I'm sure I don't know, but I hope it wasn't anyone who had designs on that cotton."

" It was that Tom Randolph," answered Lambert.

" You must be dreaming ! " exclaimed Ned.

" Them's the very same words I axed myself when I first see Tom comin' t'wards me on his mu-el, kase I couldn't b'lieve it was him till I listened to him talk ; then I knowed it was

Tom, for almost the first thing he said was meanness. He's made it up with some of the Home Guards at Camp Pinckney."

"Gracious!" cried Ned, becoming frightened. "They're the worst lot of ruffians in the world. They shoot their prisoners."

"So I've heerd tell," said Lambert indifferently. "Well, them's the fine chaps that Tom has made it up with to burn old man Gray's cotton, an' he wanted to know if I would sorter guide them to the place where it was, an' I told him I wouldn't, kase I aint going to take no chances on bein' tooken to that camp. I'm scared of them Pearl River chaps."

"You'd better be, for they would just as soon shoot you as anybody else, simply to keep their hands in. Now, how are we going to keep them from finding that cotton?"

"That's the very thing that's been a-pesterin' of me ever since Tom spoke to me about it," answered Lambert.

"If you don't act as their guide they can easily find somebody else who will do it rather than be shot," said Ned in an anxious tone.

"I don't believe Rodney has enjoyed a night's sound sleep since he had his first talk with the Federal provost marshal at Baton Rouge. But he is bound to save his father's property if he can, and you must do all in your power to help him."

"Do you remember what you said on the night you rid up to my door an' warned me that the citizens allowed to hang me for what I done down the river?" replied Lambert. "You said that old man Gray was tryin' to talk 'em out of it by tellin' 'em that if they done it they would be sorry in the mornin', didn't you? Well, I don't forget a man who does me a good turn any more'n I forget one who does me a mean one." And when he said this he scowled fiercely, for he was thinking of Tom Randolph.

"Well, have you any plan in your head?" continued Ned.

"Nary plan. I jest rid down to get some good tobacker an' to tell you to warn Rodney to look out for breakers. What's the reason you don't want me to go nigh his house for a few days?"

"That's my business—and Rodney's," said Ned shortly.

"'Taint mine," laughed Lambert, "but if you asked me to make a rough guess——"

"But I don't ask you to make a rough guess," interrupted Ned. "Or a smooth one either. Did Tom Randolph tell you how he got out of Camp Pinckney?"

"——a rough guess, I should say that Rodney's got one of two things in hidin' down there; either a deserter from our side, or a Yankee pris'ner that he is waitin' for a chance to send to Baton Rouge. But 'taint none of my business, an' I won't tell," said Lambert with good-natured persistence. And then he stopped, for when he looked up into Ned's face he saw that it had suddenly grown very pale. "I aint said a word about it to nobody, an' aint goin' to ; but you tell Rodney that when he wants friends, as most likely he will, they'll be around. Me an' Moseley an' the rest didn't want to go into the army, an' we're bound we won't ; but for all that we're not the cowards that some folks take us to be."

"You have something on your mind, and I

am sure of it," said Ned, as the man touched
a match to his pipe and arose from his seat on
the porch. "If you will tell me what it is, so
that I can carry it to Rodney, I'll give you a
pair of shoes for yourself and Moseley."

"Them's jest the things that Tom Randolph
offered to give me if I would guide them Home
Guards to Mr. Gray's cotton," said Lambert
with a grin, "an' now I'm goin' to get 'em without goin' to all that trouble an' risk. Beats
me how Rodney can fight the Yanks the best
he knows how for fifteen months, an' then
turn square around an' buy shoes an' salt
an' things of 'em. Looks to me as though
the Yanks would 'a' shot him the first thing
they done."

"They are not savages, to shoot a man after
he quits fighting," said Ned impatiently. "It
takes Confederate Home Guards to do that.
What do you say? Do you want the shoes or
not?"

"Bring 'em out, an' I will tell you all I had
in my head when I rid into this yard," was
the answer, and Ned turned about and went
into the house. When he returned he brought

5

the shoes, which Lambert received with the
remark that he knew some planters in the
neighborhood who had willingly paid fifty
dollars for footwear that wasn't half as
good.

"But if they had had greenbacks instead of
rebel scrip they could have got their shoes for
a good deal less," replied Ned. "There isn't
a Confederate in the country loyal enough to
refuse Yankee money when it is offered to
him. Major Morgan wouldn't do it. Now,
what are your plans?"

"The only thoughts I had in my head when
I rid into the yard, was that I would come
here an' get a bit of good tobacker, an' tell
you an' Rodney that Tom Randolph was tryin' to have your cotton burned," replied Lambert, placing the shoes under his arm, and
backing away as if he feared Ned might try
to snatch them. "That's all, honest Injun."

"And haven't you hit upon any plan to
head those Home Guards off?"

"Nary plan, kase they aint found the cotton
yet. When they do, like as not I'll think up
somethin'."

"Then it will be too late to save the cotton," said Ned in disgust. "If you are going to do anything, you want to move before they get into the swamp."

"They'll be some cotton burned, most likely; I aint sayin' there won't," observed Lambert, placing one hand on his mule's neck and vaulting lightly upon his back. "But you can tell Rodney that his paw's will stay on the ground as long as anybody's. That's the onliest plan I've got in my head. When I get time to think up somethin' else I'll let you know."

Lambert rode out of the yard, stopping on the way to put up the bars behind him, and Ned Griffin went in to his unfinished supper. His mother, who had overheard every word that passed between him and his visitor, looked frightened.

"I can't imagine how the thing got wind," said Ned in reply to her inquiring glances, "but Lambert seems to know all about it. I am not afraid that he will lisp it, but I *am* afraid it will get to the knowledge of some enemy who will set Morgan after us."

"O Ned, that would be dreadful," said Mrs. Griffin with a perceptible shudder.

"I believe you. I don't know what the penalty is for helping a deserter, but I believe the major would send us to the front to pay us for it."

"I think you ought to tell Rodney," said Mrs. Griffin.

" He knows it as well as I do and is quite as anxious; but the man can't walk or ride, and how are we going to get him inside the Yankee lines? We can't take him there in a carriage, for the roads are too closely watched. Of course I shall stand Rodney's friend, but my 'rough guess' is that we'll wish that friend of ours had gone somewhere else for the help he needed."

That night Ned Griffin was aroused from a sound sleep by his mother, who rapped upon the door of his room, and told him in a trembling, excited voice that either Lambert had proved himself a traitor, or else the Pearl River ruffians had stumbled upon some enemy of Mr. Gray who was willing to act as guide, for they had certainly found the cotton and fired it. Ned was thunderstruck. He hurried on the few clothes he could find in the dark conveniently, and ran out to the porch ; but when he had taken one look at the bright spot on the sky, which seemed to be growing brighter and larger every moment, and compared its bearings with those of well-known landmarks in the range of his vision, he drew a long breath of relief.

"I almost knew that Lambert did not tell the truth when he assured me he had nothing on his mind," said Ned to his frightened mother, who had followed him to the porch. "Go back and sleep easy. That isn't Mr. Gray's cotton."

"Are you quite sure of it? How do you know?" inquired Mrs. Griffin. "It must be cotton, for there is no house in that direction."

"Stand here in front of me and I will show you why I know it is not Mr. Gray's," answered Ned. "Now, squint along the side of that post that stands on the edge of the gallery, and bring your eye to bear on that low place in the timber-line. Do you see it? Well, there's where Mr. Gray's cotton is.

The pile that's burning is half a mile farther off and a mile farther to the right."

"Do you know who owns it?"

"It belongs to Mr. Randolph, who has nobody to thank for it but his dutiful son Tom."

"Ned, do you know what you are saying?" said his mother somewhat sharply.

"I am quite sure on that point. Tom was too handy with his sword in the first place, and with his tongue in the second. He ought to have had better sense than to put such an idea into Lambert's head. That man can do as much damage of this sort as he likes, and those who don't know any better will blame the rebel guerillas or the Yankee cavalry for it."

"Do you think Lambert started that fire?"

"I am as well satisfied of it as though I had stood by and seen him strike the match that set it going. Half an hour more will tell the story at any rate. Now you run back to bed, and I will stay here and watch that low place in the trees I showed you a moment ago. If no blaze appears in that direction I shall know that this is Lambert's work."

Mrs. Griffin retired, and Ned sat there on the porch with the hounds for company, and looked first at the bright glow on the sky and then at the low place in the timber, until day dawned and Mr. Gray and two or three of his neighbors rode up to the bars and accosted him.

"Have you been in there?" asked his employer anxiously.

"No, sir," replied Ned emphatically. "I saw the fire, but not knowing what sort of men I might find around it I thought it best to keep away from it. But I don't think it was your cotton."

He did not say that he was as certain as he wanted to be that the loss was Mr. Randolph's, and that it had been brought upon him by Tom's insane desire to be revenged upon some members of the Gray family, for he knew there were one or two men in the party who would not rest easy until they had seen Tom severely punished. So he awaited an opportunity to say a word to Mr. Gray in private.

"I am sorry it was anybody's cotton, but of course I should be glad to know it was not mine," said Ned's employer, with an effort to smile and look as cheerful as usual. "But if mine didn't go last night it may go next week, so I don't know that it makes much difference. Between Yankees and Confederates we planters stand a poor show of selling a pound of this almost priceless commodity."

"Sixty cents a pound!" groaned one of Mr. Gray's companions. "Good money, too, worth a hundred cents on a dollar, and now it has vanished in flames and smoke."

"It wasn't your cotton either, Mr. Randall," Ned hastened to assure him. "Rodney and I have spent two weeks locating the cotton hidden in our swamp, and we can tell within two points of the compass the direction in which every planter's property lies from his gallery and mine. The pile that was burned last night was half-way between yours and Mr. Gray's."

"Whose was it, then?"

"Mr. Randolph's."

"I am very sorry to hear it," said Mr. Gray earnestly. "If it is the truth, Mr. Randolph will be left in very bad shape."

"Not worse than the rest of us, I reckon," said Randall impatiently. "He did all he could to help on the war, and now he's afraid to go to the front and help fight it out. It serves him right."

Mr. Gray might have retorted that there were others in the same boat—that Mr. Randall himself had been a fierce secessionist when the war first broke out and the Union armies and gunboats were far away, but now professed to be a strong Union man because he was anxious to save his cotton from being confiscated ; but he said not a word in reply. He turned away from the bars, and Ned Griffin hastened to the stable-yard to put the saddle on his horse. His riding nag and Rodney's were among the few that had been left to their owners when Breckenridge's army retreated after the battle of Baton Rouge, and the reason they were left was because the boys had done so much hospital duty both before and after the fight. The rebel soldiers repaid their kindness by doing as little stealing as possible under the circumstances; but when the rear-guard disappeared from view the two friends could not

find any bacon and meal for breakfast. But
their flocks of chickens and the few scrub cows
that were relied on to supply the plantations
with milk and butter were not molested, and
Ned and Rodney were thankful for that. The
former came up with Mr. Gray and his party
before they had gone very far, and when they
reached Rodney's place they were joined by
Rodney himself, who seemed to be on the
watch for them. He waved his hat in the air
when he saw his father and Ned approaching,
but put it on his head quickly when he discovered that they were not alone. In a moment
more he would have said something to be sorry
for, because he knew whose cotton had been
burned and who was responsible for it. After
greeting his father and exchanging opinions
with him and his friends, he fell back to the
rear and rode by Ned's side, but could find
no opportunity to compare notes with him.
However, each understood what the other would
have said if he could.

Half an hour's riding brought them to the
pile of smoking cinders and ashes that covered
the spot where Mr. Randolph's cotton had been

concealed inside a dense thicket of trees and bushes whose interior had been cleared away to receive it. The road made by the heavy four-mule wagons in passing in and out of the woods had been so carefully filled with logs and tree-tops that scarcely a trace of it could be seen now, and its owner had indulged in the hope that, with the exception of a few neighbors and faithful servants, no one knew the hiding-place of all that was left of his once abundant wealth; but some enemy had found it out, and he was a ruined man. This was the opinion expressed by every one of Mr. Gray's party, for when they came to examine the ground, which they did immediately upon their arrival, they did not find a single hoof-print save those that had been made by their own riding horses.

"There's no cavalry been in here," said Mr. Randall, who was the first to give utterance to the thoughts that were in the minds of all, "and, according to my way of thinking, that proves something."

There were a few half-consumed bales on the outside of the smoking pile, and it was while

the party was engaged in pulling these farther
out of reach of the fire that Mr. Randolph and
his neighbor appeared on the scene. Mr.
Walker looked somewhat relieved, but remarked in an undertone that there might have
been more than one fire even if he didn't see
it, and rode away at a rapid pace to assure
himself of the safety of his own cotton, while
Mr. Randolph sat on his mule and gazed
mournfully at the blackened pile before him.
There was no one who could say a word to
comfort him, for by this time the planters were
all satisfied in their own minds that someone
with whom they were well acquainted had
done the work; and if that was the case, it
might not be a great while before their own
cotton would disappear in the same way.
They gradually drew away and left him to
his gloomy reflections, and then it was that
Rodney and Ned had a chance to compare
notes and say a word to Mr. Gray in private.
When the latter had listened to Ned's story,
all he had to say was that it would have been
better for the community if Mr. Randolph had
not been so persistent in his efforts to have

Tom released from military duty. Of course he and the boys did not fail to satisfy themselves that the cotton in which they were most interested was still safe in its place of concealment, and Mr. Randolph did the same; that is, he spent all the forenoon in visiting the different localities in which his neighbors' cotton had been hidden, and when he found, as he had suspected from the first, that he was the only sufferer, his thoughts were bitter and revengeful indeed. To make matters worse Mr. Walker said to him while they were on their way home :

"If you were the only Confederate in the settlement I could easily explain this business; but why you should be singled out among so many is something I can't understand, unless it is because your son Tom has served the cause with too much zeal."

"Tom hasn't done any more than others, nor as much," replied Mr. Randolph. "Rodney Gray served fifteen months in the army, and here he is living in perfect security and entirely unmolested by our conscript officers, although he is known to be hand-and-glove

with the enemies of his country. I believe he
has assisted escaped Yankee prisoners, even if
others do not."

"Perhaps he has," said Mr. Walker, who
was one of those disbelieving ones who laughed
the loudest when Tom told of his desperate
fight with "Uncle Sam's Lost Boys," who had
been chased by bloodhounds while they were
terrorizing the country between Camp Pinckney and Mooreville. Mr. Walker knew, of
course, that there were four escaped prisoners
somewhere in the woods, who ran when they
could, and killed their pursuers as often as
a fight was forced upon them, but he did not
believe that Tom Randolph had been a cap-
tive in their hands as he pretended, or that he
had escaped by knocking his guard on the
head with the butt of a musket. He knew
Tom too well to put faith in any such story.
He did not believe, either, that Rodney Gray
would go back on his record as a loyal Confederate by helping runaway Yankees inside
the lines at Baton Rouge.

"Perhaps he has, though it is a hard tale
for me to swallow," continued Mr. Walker.

"But if you'd said that Rodney was given to helping deserters I'd believe you. He's got one in hiding this very minute."

"How do you know that?" demanded Mr. Randolph, now beginning to show some interest in what his companion was saying.

"You can't keep anything from the niggers these times, and yesterday I overheard two of my house servants talking about it when they thought they were alone," answered Mr. Walker. "It seems that Rodney and young Griffin found the man in the woods half dead from wounds and hunger and exhaustion, and took him home to nurse him back to health. There wouldn't be anything so very bad about that, and I don't suppose Major Morgan would object to it if he knew it; *but* the man doesn't want to go back to camp, and as soon as he is able to travel Rodney allows to take him to the river. There's something wrong in that, I reckon."

"I should say there was," exclaimed Mr. Randolph, who told himself that now was the time to make his more fortunate neighbor suffer as keenly as he was suffering himself in losing his valuable store of cotton. "Such work as that must be against the law, and the conscript officer ought to do something about it."

"That's what I think," said Mr. Walker; and then the two relapsed into silence, for neither was willing to speak the thoughts that were passing through his mind.

When they reached the cross-roads they separated, Mr. Walker keeping on toward home, while Tom's father, believing it to be a good plan to strike while the iron was hot, turned his mule in the direction of Kimberley's store. He found Major Morgan there; in fact he was always there, for it was his place of business, and wasted not a moment in conveying to him the startling information he had received from his friend Walker: but to his unbounded surprise the major took it very coolly. He listened until Mr. Randolph had told his story and then broke out almost fiercely:

"Do you for a moment imagine that I would have been ordered here if I had not been thought capable of attending to affairs in my district ? That news is old. I knew all about it a week ago."

"Then why didn't you arrest Rodney Gray a week ago?" said Mr. Randolph hotly.

"Because I am tired of working on evidence that is furnished me by tale-bearers. You've got something against that young Gray or you would not tell me this. I am satisfied to let that deserter stay where he is for the present. He's getting well there ; he would die at Camp Pinckney."

"You ought to be inside the Yankee lines," declared Mr. Randolph, his rage getting the better of his prudence. "There's where you belong."

"And there's where you will start for if you don't leave my office this instant," roared the major, rising to his feet and upsetting his chair in the act. "Captain !"

But Mr. Randolph did not linger for the captain to present himself. He hastened through the door, glancing nervously at the soldiers he passed on the way for fear they might stop him, swung himself upon his mule,

6

and started for home, lost in wonder. It seemed that in some very mysterious manner Rodney had gained an influence with the crusty conscript officer equal to that which he exercised with the Federals in Baton Rouge. Well, he had; but there was no mystery about it, only a little strategy. Rodney had been intrusted by the major with a few gold pieces which he had exchanged in Baton Rouge for greenbacks, and it wasn't likely that the officer was going to be hard on the boy who kept his pocket filled with good money. Even inside the Confederate lines greenbacks passed at par, and would buy more than rebel scrip, on which there was a heavy discount. But Rodney did not carry news; that is to say, neither side could wring from him a word of information concerning the doings of the other side. The Federal provost marshal knew this and so did Major Morgan, and the consequence was they were both willing to trust him. To quote Rodney's own language, he had fought for fame and didn't get it, and now he was working for money. All he had in prospect was wrapped up in his father's cotton, which was the source of no little anxiety and trouble to him.

Rodney was not aware that the major knew he was harboring a rebel deserter, who had been badly wounded while escaping from the stockade at Camp Pinckney, and was careful to keep the fact from the knowledge of all except those who could be trusted. He did not care to receive callers, for fear there might be a spy or mischief-maker among them, and relied upon his hounds to give him warning when anyone rode up to the front bars. They acted so savagely when they rushed in a body down the walk to meet a stranger, that the latter, whoever he might be, usually thought it prudent to hail the house before venturing to dismount, thus giving Rodney time to get the deserter into some inner room where he would be out of sight. But one morning, about two weeks after the occurrence of the events we have just recorded, he had visitors so many in number that they stood in no fear of the hounds, nor did they hail the house. They simply threw down one or two of the top bars, jumped their horses over the rest, and

came up on a gallop, their leader drawing rein
in front of the open door, just in time to catch
a momentary glimpse of the deserter as he
vanished into a back room. Rodney's heart
sank. He had had all his work and worry for
nothing. Of course his unwelcome visitors,
who were Federal cavalrymen, would take the
deserter to Baton Rouge when they went and
ship him off to a Northern prison. The officer
in command of the squad, which was a much
larger one than Rodney had ever seen scouting
through the country before, proved to be a
captain whose acquaintance he had formed
during one of his visits to the provost marshal's office, and he walked out on the porch
and faced him as if he had nothing to conceal.

"Good-morning," said he, with a military
salute. "What brought you out here in such
a hurry and so far from your base?"

The captain waved his hand toward the
back-yard as if to say to his men that they
were at liberty to break ranks and quench
their thirst at the well, and then he answered
Rodney's question.

"We came out to pay our respects to the

conscript officer in Mooreville, but he was uncivil enough to light out before we could exchange a word with him," said the captain. "We didn't want to ride all the way out here for nothing, and so we changed our scouting party into a cotton-burning expedition. I don't suppose you would know a bale of cotton if you ran against it, would you?"

The words were spoken in jest, but Rodney knew there was a good deal of truth in them, for he looked over the captain's shoulder and saw a negro standing at the bars under guard. He was one of Mr. Randall's field-hands, who had assisted in hauling his master's cotton into the swamp.

CHAPTER IV.

THE PHANTOM BUSHWHACKERS.

"I AM not exactly on a cotton-burning expedition either," continued the captain, after he had drained the gourd which one of his men brought him, filled with water fresh from the well, "but I am ordered to look around and find it, so that I can tell whether or not it will pay the government to send out wagons to haul it in. But if it is in such a bad place that we can't get it out, of course we shall have to burn it to keep the enemy from profiting by it. I understand that there is a good deal of cotton hidden about here somewhere, but I hope yours is where nobody will find it."

"I haven't a bale to bless myself with," replied Rodney.

"Perhaps not, but your father has; several of them," said the officer with a smile. "But I tell you it will go against the grain for us to touch anything that belongs to you, after what you did for some of our escaped prisoners."

"Then why can't you give us a chance to take it inside your lines and sell it?" inquired Rodney. "If it is the policy of the Federal government to drain the South of cotton, don't you see that every bale we put into your hands will be one bale less for the Confederates?"

"I understand that very well, but you see your rebel record is dead against you. You fought us like fury for more than a year, and now, when you find that you are in a fair way to get soundly whipped, you want to turn around and make money out of us. That plan won't work, Johnny. If you could blot out your war record, or if you knew some solid Union man you could trust to sell your cotton for you, why then——"

"There isn't a man, Union or rebel, in Louisiana that I would trust to do work of that kind," declared Rodney with emphasis. "I don't say whether my father has any cotton or not; but if he has he would tell you Yanks to burn it and welcome before he would give any friend of his a chance to cheat him out of it. Who buys cotton in the city—the government?"

"No; speculators. The government grabs it without so much as saying 'by your leave.'"

"Do you give those speculators military protection?"

"Not yet. They take their own chances, and protect themselves if they go outside the pickets. But they are working for protection, and some day they'll get it."

"Do they pay in gold?"

"Not as anybody has ever heard of," replied the captain with a laugh. "Confederate scrip for one thing, and——"

"I wouldn't look at it," exclaimed Rodney. "I wouldn't give a bale of good cotton for a cart-load of Confederate scrip."

"A fine loyal grayback you are to talk that way about your country's shinplasters," said the captain with another hearty laugh. "If all rebel soldiers are like you, I don't see why your armies didn't fall to pieces long ago."

"It is because they are held together by discipline that would drive Union soldiers into mutiny in less than a week," said Rodney bitterly. "I'll take to the woods with the rest of the outlaws before they shall ever have an opportunity to try it on me again, and I know hundreds of others who feel the same way. But I wish you would tell a sorry rebel how to change cotton into money. If you will, I may become a trader myself."

"If by *money* you mean something besides Confederate rags, I must tell you that it is what you will not see until every rebel has laid down his arms and quit fighting the government, because all cotton brought within our lines has to be purchased on contracts for payment at the close of the war——"

"Then go ahead with your burning expedition," said Rodney, who thought he had never heard anything quite so preposterous. "You'll get mighty little cotton about here on those terms."

"——at the close of the war," continued the captain, paying no heed to the interruption, "because, if paid for in coin or greenbacks, the money would be sure, sooner or later, to find its way into the rebel treasury.

Your authorities will not steal their own money, for they know how worthless it is; but they'll steal ours, and use it too, every chance they get. I suppose that darky out there at the bars can show me where the cotton is concealed?"

"He knows where every bale of it is," answered Rodney. "He helped hide it."

"He declares he don't want to go to Baton Rouge with us, but if he acts as my guide I shall have to take him along, or you fellows who lose cotton will kill him."

"And no doubt you will kill him if he refuses to act as your guide, so he is bound to be killed any way you fix it," said Rodney in disgust. "He'll not be harmed if he stays at home after you leave, and nobody knows it better than he does. Ask him and see."

"Prepare to mount!" shouted the captain, thinking his men had wasted time enough at the well. "By the way," he added, in a lower tone, "who's your company, and why did he dig out in such haste when I rode up to the door? He's a reb, I know it by the cut of his jib."

"He's a conscript I know, but he's a deserter as well, and as good a Union man as you are. He was in pretty bad shape when I found him running from the hounds, but he is able to travel now, and if you will leave him here a few days longer he will be glad to take refuge inside your lines," whispered Rodney, believing that the surest way for his patient to escape trouble was to give the captain opportunity to parole him then and there. "He hasn't done any fighting, and never means to if he can help it."

"Then he can stay and welcome, for all I care," replied the captain. "I never run a man in as a prisoner unless I have reason to think he is dangerous."

"Where did you find Mr. Randall's black man, and how did you come to pick him up for a guide?" inquired Rodney.

"I don't know that I ought to tell you, but didn't one of your neighbors lose some cotton a while ago? His name is Randolph, and he wants us to look out for a worthless fellow named Lambert, who, he thinks, burned the cotton for him. He told me to go quietly up to Randall's and ask for Mose, and I would find in him a good guide; but I was in no case to speak Randolph's name in anybody's hearing, and you see what pains I have taken not to do it. But I don't care. It's spite work on Randolph's part."

"Of course it is," answered Rodney, who was so discouraged that he had half a mind to say that he would return to the army, and stay there until one side or the other was whipped into submission. "Mr. Randolph will work against everyone in the settlement now."

"Very likely. Misery loves company, you know; and perhaps there are more men working against you than you think for. Do you know this Lambert, and has he any cause to be down on you?"

"I do know him, but he hasn't the shadow of an excuse to be at enmity with me or any of my family," said Rodney in surprise. And then it was on the end of his tongue to add that Lambert was working for him—standing guard over his cotton to see that no one troubled it, but he afterward had reason to be glad that he did not say it.

"Then he is jealous, or I should say envious, of you, because you are rich and he is poor," said the captain, reining his horse about in readiness to follow his men, who were now riding toward the bars. "If he and his friends can sell your cotton so that they can pocket the money they'll do it——"

"But they can't. He shan't," exclaimed Rodney, who was utterly confounded. "He hasn't brains enough to carry out such a bare-faced cheat, nor the power, either; though no doubt his will is good enough."

"Randolph says it is; and he says further, that when Lambert finds that he can't make anything out of that cotton, he'll burn it. But I must be riding along. I'll be back before dark, and if this deserter of yours would be glad of my escort, I'll take him to Baton Rouge with me. What would your Home Guards do to you if they should jump down on you and find him here under your roof?"

"It's a matter I don't like to think of," answered Rodney, "and I shall feel safer if you take him away. Good-by; but I can't wish you good luck. I wish I had never seen you," he added under his breath, "for you have robbed me of all my peace of mind. So Lambert is a traitor, is he? and my plan for gaining his good will hasn't amounted to shucks. I'll tell father about it the first thing in the morning, and would do it to-day if I didn't want to see that captain when he returns."

The deserter came out of his hiding-place when summoned, and eagerly promised to be on hand to accompany the Federal soldiers to Baton Rouge. He didn't know what he would do for a living when he got there, he said, but it would be a great comfort to know that he would not be forced into the army to fight against the old flag. Rodney was too down-hearted to say anything encouraging, but he gave him a short note to Mr. Martin, who would see that he did not suffer while he was looking for employment. Then he walked out on the porch, for he wanted to be alone, and at that moment Ned Griffin rode into the yard.

"O Rodney!" he exclaimed. "Did that cotton-burning expedition stop here, and do

you know that there's the very mischief to
pay? That nigger of Randall's will never
show them where his master's cotton is hidden,
but he'll take them as straight as he can to
yours and Walker's. I tell you that cotton is
gone up unless we do something."

"Have you any suggestions to make?"
asked Rodney.

"Let's engage all the teams we can rake
and scrape and haul it somewhere else," said
Ned at a venture.

"What good will that do? It's in as fine a
hiding-place now as there is in the country,
and where are the wagons to come from? And
the harness? It is all I can do to find gears
for eight plough-mules."

Ned rode away to turn his horse into the
stable-yard, spent a long time in taking a
drink at the well, and finally came back and
sat down on the porch.

"What do you think of that scoundrel
Lambert, anyway?" he inquired.

"That my plan for getting on his blind side
did not work as well as we thought it was going
to. He has got even with Tom Randolph for

drawing a sword on him, and now he intends to get square with my father for threatening him with a nigger's punishment."

"I was with the mob that night," said the young overseer angrily, "heard every word that was said, and know that your father never threatened Lambert with anything. He defended him and Tom as well, and sent me to warn them that they had better clear out while the way was open to them. And the last time I saw Lambert he pretended to be grateful to Mr. Gray for what he said and did that night. Oh, the villain!"

But it did no good to rail at Lambert for his perfidy, nor yet to discuss the situation, for the one was safely out of their reach, and talking and planning only served to show them how very gloomy and perplexing the other was. It was simply exasperating to know that they were utterly helpless, but that was the conclusion at which they finally arrived. Time might make all things right, or it might reduce Mr. Gray to poverty; and all they could do was to wait and see what it had in store for them.

Ned Griffin had been in Rodney's company about two hours when one of the hounds suddenly gave tongue, and the whole pack went racing down to the bars. There was no one in sight, but after listening a moment the boys heard the tramping of a multitude of hoofs up the road in the direction in which the Federal soldiers had disappeared with Mr. Randall's field-hand for a guide. As the boys arose to their feet the leading fours of the column came into view.

"Sure's you live that's them," whispered Ned. "But what brought them back so soon?"

Rodney hadn't the least idea, but suggested that possibly the negro guide had missed his way.

"If he did he missed it on purpose; but that's a thing he could not be hired to do for fear the Yankees would shoot him," replied Ned. "He may have given them the slip."

"Never in this world," answered Rodney emphatically. "When that darky left my bars he was riding double with one of the troopers, and there was a guard on each side

7

of him. If he tried to run, he is dead enough now."

The boys ran to the bars to wait for the captain, who rode at the head of the column, to approach within speaking distance, and when he did the words he addressed to them almost knocked them over. He appeared to be as pleasant and good-natured as usual, but some of the men behind him looked ugly.

"Why didn't you tell me that that cotton down there in the swamp is guarded by a battalion of phantom bushwhackers?" said he.

"A battalion of what?" exclaimed Rodney, as soon as he could speak.

"Bushwhackers. Sharpshooters," replied the captain.

"Home Guards?" inquired Ned.

"I don't know about that, but I judge that they have your cotton under their protection, for all they tried to do was to kill the darky so that he couldn't show us where it was. The men who rode in the rear of the line never heard the whistle of a bullet, although they sung around me and the nig pretty lively; and when the nig dropped .they ceased firing on the instant. We charged the woods in every direction, but never saw one of them, nor did they make the least attempt to ambush us, as they could have done if they had felt like it."

Rodney Gray had seldom been so aston-ished. He looked hard at the captain and did not know what to say. The whole thing was a mystery he could not explain on the spur of the moment. The captain sat on his horse in front of the bars while he talked, but the line passed on until the rear fours came up and halted. Then the boys saw that there was a rude litter slung between two of the horses, and that the form of Mr. Randall's unfortu-nate field-hand was stretched upon it. Rod-ney walked up to the litter at once, but Ned timidly held back. There was a crimson stain on the bandage the negro wore about his head, and Ned could not endure the sight of blood.

"Oh, he isn't dead," said the captain, "but he's too badly hurt to go any farther just now. Besides, we can't move as rapidly as we would like as long as we have him with us, and I would take it as a favor if you will care for him until his master can be sent for."

"Throw down those bars, Ned," said Rodney, looking back over his shoulder as he started on a run for the house. "Bring him along and I will have a place fixed for him. Phantom bushwhackers!" he said to himself. "Now who do you suppose they were? Not Lambert and his gang certainly, for they haven't the pluck to do such a thing; but I can think of no others who would be likely to turn bushwhackers. Now's your chance for freedom and safety," he added, pausing long enough to shake hands with the deserter and help him down from the porch. "Be ready to mount behind one of those Yanks when you get the word, and good luck to you."

Rodney's first care was to see that the wounded guide was made as comfortable as circumstances would permit, and his second to send one of his own field-hands to bring Mr. Randall and a doctor. After that, when he had answered a farewell signal from the deserter, and the last of the Federal column had disappeared down the road, he and Ned went back to the porch, and sat down to talk the matter over.

"I am as frightened now as I ever was in the army," said Rodney honestly. "I never could stand a mystery."

"There's no mystery about this business," replied Ned. "The Yanks lost their guide, and had sense enough to give up the search and come back. That's all there is of it."

"But who shot him?"

"Lambert and his crowd, and nobody else," answered Ned positively. "If they were Home Guards, why were they so careful that their bullets should miss everyone except the darky? They didn't want to hurt the soldiers; they only wanted to send them back, and they took the only method they could to do it."

"Well, if it was Lambert, and he is determined to protect that cotton for his own profit, how am I going to haul it from the swamp myself if I ever have a chance to move it?" demanded Rodney. "Will he not be likely to bushwhack me too?"

"By gracious!" gasped Ned, sinking back

in his chair, "this is a very pretty mess, I must say. I never once thought of such a thing; but if that's his game, he'll bushwhack you or anybody else who tries to move that cotton. However," he added a moment later, his face brightening as a cheering thought passed through his mind, "what's the odds? We are not ready to move the cotton yet, and until we are let's take comfort in the thought that no one who wants to steal it, be he Union or rebel, will dare venture near it. Perhaps by the time you are ready to sell it, Lambert will have been bushwhacked himself. How do you intend to treat him from this time on?"

"As an enemy with whom I cannot afford to be at outs," replied Rodney. "If he does any work for me I shall pay him for it; and although I shall not try to put any soldiers on his trail, I'll go into the woods myself and hunt him down like a wild hog the minute I become satisfied that he is trying to play me false. I came to this plantation on purpose to watch father's cotton, and I really wonder if Lambert imagines he can spirit it away without my knowing anything about it."

"It's the greatest scheme I ever heard of," said Ned. "But it cannot be carried out. We've got to go to work in earnest now to put up the bacon and beef your father promised to give as the price of my exemption, and while we are doing it, it will be no trouble for us to keep an eye on that cotton."

Rodney Gray afterward declared that work and plenty of it was all that kept him alive during the next three months, and it is a fact that as the year drew to a close, with anything but encouraging prospects for the ultimate success of the Union forces in the field, Rodney's spirits fell to zero. Although he never confessed it to Ned Griffin, the latter knew, as well as he knew anything, that all Rodney's hopes and his father's were centred on the speedy putting down of the rebellion, but just now it looked as though that was going to be a hard, if not an impossible, thing to do. "Burnside's repulse at Fredericksburg in the East had its Western counterpart in Sherman's defeat on the Yazoo, and indeed the whole year presented no grand results in favor of the national armies except the capture of

New Orleans." But if Rodney had only
known it, some things, many of which took
place hundreds of miles away and on deep
water, were slowly but surely working together
for his good. He knew that General Banks
had relieved General Butler in command of
the Department of the Gulf; that he had an
army of thirty thousand men and a fleet of
fifty-one vessels under his command; that his
object in coming was to "regulate the civil
government of Louisiana, to direct the military movements against the rebellion in that
State and in Texas, and to co-operate in the
opening of the Mississippi by the reduction of
Port Hudson," which was on the east bank of
the river twenty-five miles above Baton Rouge.
As he straightway made the latter place his
base of operations, and gradually brought
there an army of twenty-five thousand men,
Mooreville and all the surrounding country
came within his grasp. Major Morgan and
his fifty veterans took a hasty leave, Camp
Pinckney was abandoned, and Confederate
scouting parties were seldom seen at Rodney's
plantation and Ned's, although it was an every-

day occurrence for companies of blue-coats to stop at one place or the other and make inquiries about the "Johnnies" that were supposed to be lurking in the neighborhood. They never said "cotton" once, and this led Ned Griffin to remark that perhaps the new general had driven the speculators away from Baton Rouge and did not intend to allow any trading in his department.

"Don't say that out loud, or you will give me the blues again!" exclaimed Rodney. "If it gets to Lambert's ears, good-by cotton."

"I didn't think of that," answered Ned, frightened at the bare suggestion of such a misfortune. "It will be much more to our interest to make Lambert believe, if we can, that traders will be thicker than dewberries the minute Port Hudson and Vicksburg are taken. That will make him hold his hand if anything will."

As to Lambert, he "showed up" as often as he stood in need of any supplies, and sometimes loitered about for half a day, as if waiting for the boys to question him concerning a matter that, for reasons of his own, he did not

care to touch upon himself. He would have
given something to know what they thought
of the "phantom bushwhackers" and their
methods, but Rodney and Ned never said a
word to him about it. The negro guide, who
was more frightened than hurt, quickly recovered from his injuries, and within a day or
two after he was taken to his master's house
ran away to the freedom he knew was awaiting him in Baton Rouge, and that made one
less to tell where the cotton was concealed.

"I suppose the next bushwhacker will be a
fellow about my size," was what Rodney often
said to himself. "I have half a mind to
pounce on Lambert the next time he comes
here and take him to Baton Rouge, but I
don't know whether that would be the best
thing to do or not, and my father can't advise
me." Then he would recall the Iron Duke's
famous ejaculation, and adapt it to his own
circumstances by adding, "Oh, that a Union
man or the end would come!"

Since he was so positive that a Union man
was the friend he needed, it would seem that
Rodney ought not to have been at a loss to

find him right there in the settlement. If there were any faith to be put in what he saw and heard every time he went to Mooreville and Baton Rouge, there were no other sort of men in the country—not one who had ever been a Confederate or expressed the least sympathy for those who openly advocated secession. According to their own story, scraps of which came to Rodney's ears now and then, Mr. Randolph and Tom had done little but talk down secession and stand up for the Union ever since Fort Sumter was fired upon, and Mr. Biglin, the red-hot rebel who put the bloodhounds on the trail of the escaped prisoners Rodney was guiding to the river, declared that his well-known love for the old flag had nearly cost him his life. He was glad to see Banks' army in Baton Rouge, he said, for now he could speak his honest sentiments without having his sleep disturbed by the fear that his rebel neighbors would break into his house before morning and hang him to the plates of his own gallery. The country was full of cowardly, hypocritical men like these, and what troubled Rodney

and Ned more than anything else was the fact
that they seemed to have more influence and
be on closer terms with the Federals than did
the honest rebels who had ceased to fight
because they knew they were whipped. Rodney's friend, Mr. Martin, who lived in Baton
Rouge and kept a sharp eye on these "converted rebels," whose hatred for the Union
and everybody who believed in it was as
intense and bitter as it had ever been, told
him that Mr. Biglin and others like him were
using every means in their power and making
all sorts of false affidavits to secure trade permits, and seemed in a fair way to get them
too. Indeed, so certain were they that they
would succeed in their efforts, that they were
going out some day to look at the cotton in
the Mooreville district, and see what the prospects were for hauling it out. They were even
engaging teams to do the work. They were
not to have military protection, Mr. Martin
said, but that was scarcely necessary, for the
Union cavalry had swept the country of Home
Guards and conscript soldiers for a hundred
miles around.

"But the Union cavalry hasn't cleared the country of the bushwhackers who shot Mr. Randall's nigger," said Ned Griffin, who always had a cheering word to say when Rodney was the most disheartened. "If Mr. Martin's story is true, I hope Biglin will come himself and give them a fair chance at him."

And Mr. Biglin did come himself, although Rodney thought he was too much of a coward to venture so far into the country. He and half a dozen other civilians rode into the yard one day and asked Rodney for a drink of water, but that was only done to give them a chance to draw from him a little information about cotton. Rodney greeted them in as friendly a manner as he thought the occasion called for, and conducted them around the house to the well.

"I tell you it seems good to get out in the fresh air once more, and to know that while here I am in no danger of being gobbled up by a conscript officer and hustled away to fight under a flag I have always despised," said Mr. Biglin, putting his hands into his pockets and walking up and down in front of the well.

"So you have turned overseer, have you, Rodney?"

"I believe that was what I told you on the day I saw you in Mr. Turnbull's front yard," was the answer. "I mean just before that darky of yours came up——"

"Yes, yes; I remember all about it now," said Mr. Biglin hastily. And then he tried to turn the conversation into another channel, for fear that Rodney would go on to tell that the information that darky brought was what caused Mr. Biglin to put the hounds on the trail of the escaped Union prisoners. "Fine place you have here. A little rough, of course, but it's new yet. And I presume it suits you, for, if I remember rightly, you always were fond of shooting and riding to the hounds. Have you any cotton?"

"Not a bale. Not a pound."

Mr. Biglin looked surprised, and so did his companions. The former looked hard at the boy for a moment, and then changed the form of his inquiry.

"Oh, ah!" said he. "Has your father got any?"

"Perhaps you had better go and ask him," replied Rodney.

"That's just what we did not more than an hour ago, but he wouldn't give us any satisfaction."

"Then you have good cheek to come here expecting me to give you any," said the young overseer, growing angry. "My father is quite competent to attend to his own business."

"I suppose he is. Why, yes; of course; but what's the use of cutting off your nose to spite your face? We know you have cotton and plenty of it; and since you can't sell it yourselves——"

"Why can't we?" interposed Rodney.

Mr. Biglin acted as though he had no patience with one who could ask so foolish a question.

"Because of your secession record," said he. "You were in the Southern army, and your father is a rebel."

"So are you," said Rodney bluntly.

"I may have appeared to be at times in order to save my life, but I never was a secessionist at heart," said Mr. Biglin loftily. "I don't care who hears me say it, I am for the Union now and forever, one and—and undivided. And General Banks' provost marshal, or whatever you call him, knows it."

"If he believes it, he is the biggest dunderhead in the world and isn't fit for the position he holds," exclaimed Rodney. " I know you to be a vindictive, red-hot rebel, and since things have turned out as they have, I am sorry I did not tell the —th Michigan's boys that you put the hounds on——"

"I never did it in this wide world," protested Mr. Biglin, trying to look astonished, but turning white instead.

"Never did what?" inquired Rodney.

"Put hounds on anybody's trail. You had better be careful what you say."

"You don't show your usual good sense in talking that way," said one of the civilians. "Our friend has influence enough to make you suffer for it if he feels so inclined."

"And I had influence enough to make his house a heap of ashes long ago if I had felt like it," retorted Rodney. "I can prove every word I say any day and shall be glad of the chance." And then he wondered what he would do if his visitors should take him at his word. He knew that he could not prove his assertions without mentioning the name of Mrs. Turnbull, and that was something he could not be made to do until he had her full and free consent.

"You are quite at liberty to tell what you know about me and my record during this war," observed Mr. Biglin, as he swung himself upon his horse and turned the animal's head toward the bars, "and you may *have* to tell it, whether you want to or not."

With this parting shot, which he hoped would leave Rodney in a very uncomfortable frame of mind, Mr. Biglin rode away, followed by his friends, and passing through the bars turned up the road leading toward the swamp in which Mr. Gray's cotton was concealed. No sooner had they disappeared than Ned Griffin, who was always on the watch and knew when Rodney had visitors he did not want to see, threw down the bars and rode into the yard.

8

CHAPTER V.

THE COTTON THIEVES.

"WHO are those men, and what did they want?" inquired Ned, as he got off his horse at the foot of the steps. "Are they cotton traders?"

"I wish I hadn't gone at them quite so rough," replied Rodney. "You know what a red-hot rebel Biglin has always been, don't you?"

"I should say so. If he could have his way he'd hang every Union man in the country."

"Well, he had the impudence to declare in my presence, not more than five minutes ago, that he'd always been strong for the Union and dead against secession, and it made me so indignant that I said things which drove him away before he had time to make his business known. But he told me he had questioned my father about cotton and got no satisfaction."

"And did he think you would give it to him when your father would not?" demanded Ned.

"He and his friends seemed to think so, but I gave them to understand—Great Scott!"

"Hallo! What's come over you all on a sudden?" exclaimed Ned, as Rodney jumped to his feet and gazed anxiously up the road in the direction in which Mr. Biglin and his party had just disappeared.

"Who knows but I have let them go to their death?" answered Rodney. "They don't know that one party who tried to find that cotton was fired upon in the woods, and I was so provoked at Biglin that I forgot to tell them."

"W-h-e-w!" whistled Ned. "I never thought of it either. Well, let them go on and find it out for themselves. They wouldn't have believed you if you had told them. They would have said right away that you were trying to keep them out of the woods, and that would have made them all the more determined to go in. I should be sorry to see any of them shot, but now that I am here I'm going to stay with you and see the thing out."

Nothing could have suited Rodney Gray better. He was lonely and depressed and felt the need of cheerful company, so he went with Ned when the latter turned his horse into the stable-yard, and repeated to him every word of the conversation that took place while Mr. Biglin and his friends were at the well.

"There's just one thing about it," said Ned, when he had heard the story. "If Biglin hasn't already got a permit to trade he is certain as he can be that he's going to have it, and that's what brought him out here. But I can't imagine what he meant when he said you might be obliged to tell what you know about him and his record."

"No more can I, but I should be glad to do it if it were not for bringing Mrs. Turnbull's name into the muss. Has Biglin got any money, do you think, or does he intend to pay for his cotton in promises? If I were in father's place I would not take his note for a picayune, for there's no telling where Biglin will be at the close of the war."

"That's so," assented Ned. "But we'll not worry about money until we see some in prospect, will we? We haven't lost the cotton yet."

And they didn't lose it that day and neither did Mr. Biglin and his party find it, for the very thing happened that Rodney was afraid of. He and Ned sat on the porch for an hour or more, conversing in low tones and waiting for and dreading something, they could scarcely have told what, when the clatter of hoofs up the road set the hounds' tongues in motion and took them out to the bars in a body. It took Rodney and Ned out there too, and when they gained the middle of the road they saw three horses bearing down upon them with their bridles and stirrups flying loose in the wind and their saddles empty. A little farther up the highway were a couple of mounted men, who were bending low over the pommels of their saddles, plying their whips as rapidly as they could make their arms move up and down, and a few rods behind them were two more riderless horses. Both men and animals appeared to be frightened out of their senses. The leading horses would not stop, but dashed frantically into the bushes by the roadside rather than permit the two boys to capture them, and the men, as well as the horses that brought up the rear, went by like the wind, and without in the least slackening their head-long flight.

"Well, I do think in my soul! What's up?" whispered Ned, who had dodged nimbly out of the road to escape being run down.

"There were seven in the party, and only two have returned," murmured Rodney.

"They must have seen something dreadful in there," faltered Ned.

"Beyond a doubt they have been fired upon, but I don't believe they saw anything," answered Rodney. "They heard the whistle of bullets and buckshot, most likely, and it scared them half to death. Come on. Let's hurry."

"Where are you going?" demanded Ned, as Rodney turned about and ran toward the house.

"After my horse. There are five men missing, and it may be that some of them were shot. And even if they were unhorsed and not hurt at all, they need help if they are as badly frightened as the two that just went by."

Not being a soldier, Ned Griffin was in no haste to ride into a dark swamp to brave an invisible bushwhacker, who might be as ready to shoot him as anybody else, but when Rodney broke into a run and started for the stable-yard, he kept close at his heels. The two saddled their horses with all haste, and with the eager and excited hounds for a body-guard, rode through the bars just in time to meet the two survivors of Mr. Biglin's party, who had at last found courage enough to stop their frantic steeds and come back.

"O Rodney; this is an awful day for us!" cried one of the frightened men. "I wish we had never heard of that cotton."

"The cotton is all right if you will keep your thievish hands off from it," replied Rodney. "What's the matter with you, and where are Mr. Biglin and the rest?"

"Dead or prisoners, the last one of them. There's a whole regiment in there, and they opened on us before we had left the road half a mile behind."

" A whole regiment of what?"

" Indians, judging by the way they yelled, though I suppose they were Yankee soldiers out on a scout."

" Not much!" exclaimed Rodney.

" How do you know what they were? You didn't see them."

" Did you?"

" Well, no; but I heard them yell, and I heard their bullets singing, too. The swamp is full of them."

" If they were Federal scouts you would have seen them," said Rodney. "They would have closed around you before you had a chance to draw the revolver I see sticking out of your coat pocket."

"It's empty," said the man, producing the weapon. "I never was in a fight before and never want to be again ; but I tried to give them as good as they sent."

" If you did not see any of the attacking party, what did you shoot at?"

"I fired in the direction from which the yells sounded, and so did all of us. As for the bullets, you couldn't tell which way they came from, for they clipped the trees on all sides. Where are you and Griffin going?"

"Into the swamp to see if we can be of use to anybody."

"I really wish you would, for I wouldn't dare go back there myself. If they were not Yankees, who were they?"

"Didn't you just tell me that I wasn't there?" asked Rodney.

"But all the same you have a pretty good idea who they were, and you don't want to bring yourself into trouble by shielding them."

"I am not trying to shield anybody," answered Rodney.

"Do you think they were citizens who tried to kill us because they didn't want us to find their cotton?" inquired the second man, who had not spoken before.

"If you had a fortune hidden out there in the woods, would you let anybody steal it from you if you could help it?" asked Rodney in reply. "I don't think you would."

"But we expect every day to get a permit to trade in cotton," said the first speaker,

"and that will give us license to take it wherever we can find it."

"I reckon not," said the boy hotly. "General Banks has a right to order his soldiers to
take cotton or anything else for the benefit of
his government or to cripple the Confederacy,
but he has no shadow of a right to license
stealing by civilians, and I don't think he will
do it. If he does, there will be some of the
liveliest fighting around here he ever heard
of."

"If I thought those villains in there were
citizens I'd——"

"You'd what?" said Rodney, when the
man paused and looked at his companion.
"Do you want to kick up another civil war
right here in your own neighborhood? Both
of you own property, and if you desire to save
it you will take care what you do. If you
will go into the house and sit down for an hour
or two we may be back with news of your
friends."

"I'll not do it," replied the man, who had
not yet recovered from his fright, "for there's
no telling how soon those ruffians may come

this way. I will ride into Baton Rouge and send some soldiers out here."

So saying he and his companion wheeled their horses and galloped away, and the two boys rode on toward the swamp.

"Now look at you!" said Ned, when they were once more alone. "You have paved the way for the neatest kind of a fuss. Did you notice what Mr. Louden said about sending soldiers out here?"

"I did; but when he tries it I think he'll find he has not been hired to take the command of the Department of the Gulf out of the hands of General Banks. If Banks is anything like the generals I have served under he'll not take suggestions from anybody, much less a civilian. I told the truth when I hinted that that cotton might have been protected by citizens, for that is what Lambert and his gang are."

"But Louden thought you meant planters," urged Ned.

"I can't help what he thought; and I noticed, too, that he suspected me of shielding the bushwhackers, because I would not tell who they were. Oh, I know we shall see fun before we hear the last of that cotton, but we'll hold fast to it as long as we can."

The boys rode rapidly while they talked, and in a few minutes turned off the road and plunged into the tangled recesses of as gloomy a piece of timber as could have been found anywhere—just the finest place in the world for an ambuscade, as Rodney remarked when he led the way into it. They could not see ten feet in any direction, but they heard something before they had gone a mile into the swamp.. The hounds gave tongue savagely and dashed away in a body, a wild shriek of terror arose from a thicket close in front of Rodney's horse, and in the next instant up bobbed Mr. Biglin. But he didn't show any of the courage of which he had boasted. His face was very white, and his empty hands were held high above his head. He had as fair a view of Rodney's face as he ever had in his life, but was so badly frightened that he did not recognize him.

"Don't you see that I surrender?" he yelled. "Call off your bloodhounds."

"All right," said the boy, who rather enjoyed the spectacle. "The dogs won't hurt you. Come out of the bushes and tell us all about it."

"O Rodney, is that you?" exclaimed Mr. Biglin, but he wasn't quite sure of it, and didn't think it safe to lower his uplifted hands. "Where are they? They have been beating the woods in every direction to find me."

"They? Who?"

"I am sure I don't know, but there's a regiment of them. They shot down every horse in the party before we knew there was danger near, and then set out to hunt us at their leisure. Have you seen them? Where are they now?"

"Come out and tell us where the other four are," said Rodney, who had by this time satisfied himself that Mr. Biglin had escaped uninjured. "Your horses are all right, and so are Miles and Louden. Ned and I had a short talk with them not more than an hour ago."

"I am surprised to hear it," said Mr. Biglin, with a long-drawn sigh of relief. "I was sure they had all been killed." He put down his hands and came out of his concealment as he spoke, but he stepped cautiously as if afraid of making a noise, and cast timid glances on all sides of him. "It's just awful to be shot at in that cold-blooded way, isn't it? I don't see how you stood it so long in the army."

"Do you imagine that I stayed there and let the Yanks pop at me because I thought it was funny?" demanded Rodney. "I stayed so long for the reason that I couldn't help myself. Miles and Louden have gone on to the city, and I reckon your horses must be there by this time if they kept on running."

"And did the horses escape also?" said Mr. Biglin, who looked as though he didn't know whether to believe it or not. "It's really wonderful how any of us came out alive."

Instead of replying Rodney threw back his head and shouted "Hey-youp!" so loudly that the woods rang with the sound.

"What made you do that?" said Mr. Biglin in a frightened whisper, at the same time backing toward the thicket from which he had just emerged. "Do you want to show the enemy where we are?"

"No; but I want to let your four friends know where we are."

He raised his war-whoop a second time, following it up by calling out the names of the missing men and telling them to come on, for there was nothing to be afraid of. There was a long silence—so long that Rodney began to fear the party had become widely separated during the hurried stampede of its members; but after a while a faint answering shout came to his ears, then another and another, and finally he could hear the missing men making their way through the bushes in his direction. When they came up it was found that not one of them had been injured by the shower of bullets which had whistled about their ears thicker than any hailstones *they* ever saw, but they were all pale and nervous, and begged Rodney and Ned to take them out of the woods by the shortest and easiest route. Seeing that two of them were almost ready to drop with fear or exhaustion, the boys gave them their horses and led the way on foot. Not a word was said until they found themselves safe in the road, and then Mr. Biglin recovered his courage and the use of his tongue.

"Quite a thrilling experience for men who do not claim to be fighters," said he, taking off his hat and wiping away the sweat which stood on his forehead in big drops. "And a most wonderful escape for all of us. If I'd had the least suspicion that such a thing was going to happen, you wouldn't have caught me going into that swamp. But the men who fired on us, whoever they are, must be punished for their audacity. They couldn't have been Union troops, for as soon as we recovered from the astonishment and panic into which we were thrown by their first volley, we shouted to them that we had a permit from General Banks, but it didn't do any good."

"It did harm, though," remarked one of his companions, "for I am positive that their yells grew louder and that the bullets came much thicker than before. Have you boys any idea who they were?"

This was a question that neither of them intended to answer if he could help it. If they said what they thought, Mr. Biglin would carry their story straight to the Federal provost marshal, or to someone else in authority in Baton Rouge, and it might lead to something that would end in bloodshed. Lambert's actions said as plainly as words that if he couldn't profit by the sale of that cotton himself, nobody else should lay hands upon it, and having driven away two parties who had tried to discover its hiding-place, it was barely possible that he might have gained courage enough to resist soldiers, if any were sent into the swamp to drive him out. Lambert was showing himself a good friend just now, however disagreeable and dangerous he might prove to be by and by, and Rodney did not want General Banks to send troopers after him. When the Union man he was waiting for "turned up," the general might rid the settlement of Lambert's presence as soon as he pleased.

"If I didn't know that Tom Randolph's company of Home Guards was broken up, I

9

should blame them for this day's work," said one of Mr. Biglin's companions.

"How do you know the company was broken up?" inquired Rodney.

"Why, I heard they were all conscripted long ago."

"That may be ; but they didn't all go to Camp Pinckney. Some of them took to the woods."

"But even if they would fire upon their old friends and neighbors, which isn't probable, they have no interest in protecting the cotton in the swamp, for they don't own a dollar's worth of it."

"I don't care who they are," said Mr. Biglin. "They will find that the arm of our government is long enough to reach them wherever they hide themselves."

"*Our* government!" repeated Rodney. "Which one do you mean?"

"There is but one, young man, and you rebels can't break it up, try as hard as you will."

It made Rodney angry to hear Mr. Biglin talk in this strain, but before he could frame a suitable rejoinder the planter switched him off on another track by inquiring :

"Now, how are we to get to the city?"

"I am sure I don't know unless you walk," answered Rodney.

"Can't you raise five saddle nags on your place?"

"No, sir. And if I could, I wouldn't let them go inside the Yankee lines. I'd never see them again."

"I give you my word that I will take the best of care of them."

"You couldn't take any sort of care of them. In less than five minutes after you reached the city my horses would be gone, and when you found them again, if you ever did, they would have some company's brand on them. I know what I am talking about, for I have been a cavalryman myself. I have known regiments in the same brigade to steal from one another."

"In that case wouldn't the brand show where the horse belonged?"

"It might if it was let alone, but it is easy to change it. I stole a horse from company *I* once, and when he was found in my possession

a week or two afterward, there was my company letter *D* on his flank as plain as the nose
on your face."

"And didn't you have to give him up to his
rightful owner?"

"Course not. I said if he wasn't my horse,
how came that letter *D* branded on him, and
that settled it. Won't you go in and rest a
few minutes?"

As Rodney said this he waved his hand toward the house, whose front door stood invit-
ingly open, but Mr. Biglin replied that he did
not care to sit down until he was out of sight
of the swamp, and beyond the reach of the terrible Home Guards who made their hiding-
place there. So he and his companions walked
on, and Rodney and Ned turned into the yard.

" *Our* government!" Rodney said over and
over again while they were at the well watering
their horses. "He'd give everything he's got
if he could see it broken up this minute."

"Of course he would, but he and his kind
stand higher with the Federals than you do,"
replied Ned. "Now, all we can do is to pos-
sess our souls in patience and wait for the

next act on the programme. Let's see if Mr.
Biglin's government will send soldiers to protect him in his cotton-stealing."

It was very easy for Ned to talk of waiting
patiently, but it was a hard thing to do. He
and Rodney looked anxiously for the appearance of the cavalry that Mr. Biglin and one of
his friends had threatened to send against the
men who had driven them from the swamp,
but they never came. They saw and talked
with a good many troopers, who drank all
the milk they could find and asked about the
Johnnies that were supposed to be "snooping
around" in that part of the country, but to
the boys' great relief they did not say a word
about cotton or Home Guards, and Rodney
hoped he had seen the last of Mr. Biglin. He
was ready to make terms with a genuine Yankee who would offer him sixty cents a pound
for his father's cotton, but he wanted nothing
to do with converted rebels. He and Ned
made several trips to the city, bringing out
each time some things that were not contraband of war, and some others that would have
caused the prompt confiscation of his whole

wagon load if they had been discovered, but
his friend Mr. Martin, on whom he relied for
information of every sort, could not give him
any advice on the subject that was nearest to
his heart.

"The city is full of men who are working
their level best to get permits," said he, "but
I am told it takes lots of influence and a clean
record to get them."

"Then Biglin will never have the handling
of my father's cotton," said Rodney with a
sigh of satisfaction. "His record is as bad as
mine."

"Much worse," answered Mr. Martin, "for
you never went back on your friends and became a spy and informer. That is just what
that man Biglin has done, but I have reason
to think he isn't making much at it. Someone has been telling true stories about him,
and the provost marshal knows his history
like a book. O Rodney, why didn't you
keep out of the rebel army and proclaim yourself a Union man at the start, no matter
whether you were or not. You would have
plain sailing now."

Rodney laughed and said it was too late to think of that; and besides, why didn't Mr. Martin proclaim himself a Union man at the start? Perhaps he wouldn't have been so closely watched.

Rodney saw and talked with Lambert about three times a week, but the ex-Home Guard did not volunteer any information regarding his doings in the swamp, and the boy took care not to ask him for any. He never inquired how or where the man lived, how many companions he had, whether or not they ever held communication with their friends in Mooreville—in fact, Lambert more than once complained to Ned Griffin that Rodney did not seem to care any more for the conscripts· who were watching night and day to protect his father's cotton than he did for the wild hogs he was shooting for his winter's supply of bacon. When Rodney first began hunting these hogs it was with the expectation that every pound of meat he secured would have to be turned over to the agents of the Confederate government as the price of Ned Griffin's exemption; but when General Banks began

massing his army at Baton Rouge with a view
of operating against Port Hudson, and the
country roundabout had been cleared of rebel
soldiers and conscript officers, Rodney hadn't
troubled himself much about the exemption
bacon. He was glad to believe he would not
be called on to pay it.

Affairs went on in a very unsatisfactory way
until the middle of February before any event
that was either exciting or interesting occurred
to break the monotony, if we except one single
thing—the Emancipation Proclamation. Of
course the news that the slaves had been freed
created something of an excitement at first,
especially among such men as Lambert and
his outlaws who never had the price of a pick-
aninny in their pockets, but it had little effect
upon Rodney Gray and his father, because
they had been looking for it for six months.
In September President Lincoln told the
Southern people very plainly that if they did
not lay down their arms and return to their
allegiance he would declare their slaves free,
and now he had kept his promise. Rodney
remembered how he had laughed at his cousin

Marcy, and how angry he was at him when the latter declared that if the South tried to break up the government she would lose all her negroes, but now he saw that Marcy was right. More than that, he knew that the North had the power and the will to enforce the proclamation. Mr. Martin gave him a copy of it and he took it home with him, intending to read it to his negroes; but the news reached the plantation before he did, and he found the field-hands gathered about the kitchen waiting for him.

"Is Moster Linkum done sot we black ones all free?" they demanded in chorus, as Rodney rode among them.

"Who told you anything about it?" he asked, in reply.

"De cutes' little catbird you ebber see done sot hisself up dar on de ridge-pole, an' sung it to we black ones," answered the driver; and then they all shouted and laughed at the top of their voices. "Is we free sure 'nough?" added the driver.

"That depends upon whether you are or not," answered Rodney, taking the proclama-

tion from his pocket and holding it aloft so
that all could see it. "In the first place, who
owns this part of Louisiana right around here?
In whose possession is it?"

"De Yankees, bress the Lawd," said the
negroes, with one voice.

"Then you are not free, and Mr. Lincoln
says so."

"Why, Moss Rodney, please sar, how come
dat?" stammered the driver, and all the black
faces around him took on a look of deep disappointment and sorrow.

"I have Mr. Lincoln's own words for it,"
replied Rodney. "This paper says, in effect,
that the slaves are free in all States in rebellion, *except* in such parts as are held by the
armies of the United States. Do the Yankees
around here belong to the armies of the United
States, and are they holding this country—
this part of the State? Then you will not be
free until the rebels come in and drive them
out."

"O Lawd! O Lawd!" moaned the driver.
"Den we uns won't nebber be free. Dem
rebels won't luf us go."

"That's what I think, so you had better dig out while you have the chance. You are bound to have your freedom some day, and you might as well take it now. Don't go off like thieves in the night, but come up here boldly and shake hands with me as you would if you were going back to the home plantation. And when you get sick of the Yankees and their ways, come back, and I will treat you as well as I ever did. Bob, you had better go for one. You don't earn your salt here."

This was all Rodney had to say regarding the Emancipation Proclamation, but it was more than his darkies bargained for. While they were glad to know that they were free men and women, they were not glad to see Rodney so perfectly willing to let them go. He didn't care a snap whether they went or stayed, and that made them all the more anxious to stay where they were sure of getting plenty to eat and clothes to wear. Bob and one other worthless negro took Rodney at his word, and left the plantation that very afternoon, but they did not go to the house to bid him good-by.   They packed their bundles in secret, and slipped away "like thieves in the night"; but, before they had been gone two hours, Lambert marched them back to the bars at the muzzle of his rifle.

CHAPTER VI.

THE MAN HE WANTED TO SEE.

"WHAT in the world did you bring those useless fellows back here for?" was the way in which Rodney Gray welcomed Lambert when he marched the two negroes up to the porch where he was sitting. "I was in hopes I had seen the last of them."

"Why, dog-gone it, they're yourn, an' I jest want to see if what they have been tellin' me is the truth," said Lambert in a surprised tone. "I found 'em pikin' along the highway with them packs onto their backs an' no passes into their pockets——"

"Don't need no passes no mo'," interrupted Bob in a surly voice. "I am jes as free as you be, Mistah Lambert."

"Jest listen at the nigger's imperdence!" cried Lambert, astonished and angry because Rodney did not at once take Bob to task for his freedom of speech. "This is what comes of havin' so many Yankees prowlin' about the country."

"That's about the size of it. Bob is as free as you or I, and here is the paper that says so," declared Rodney, taking a printed copy of the proclamation from his pocket.

" Who writ that there paper, an' where did you get it ? "

"The city is flooded with copies of it, and the first scouting party that rides through here will scatter it right and left among the negroes. President Lincoln wrote it."

" What right's he got to do anything of the sort ? The niggers don't belong to him."

" Well, he's done it, any way, and you and your friends will have to come out of the swamp and go to work if you hope to get anything to eat. My father says we can't help ourselves, and that's why I talked to Bob and the rest the way I did a while ago."

"But I aint agreein' to no such arrangement," replied Lambert, who could scarcely have felt more aggrieved and insulted if he had been the largest slaveholder in the State.

" Nobody asked my father if he would agree

to it, either; but he'll have to take war as it comes, and so will you and all of us. The blacks are lost to us and you will have to go to work; I don't see any way out of it. You might as well turn your prisoners loose and let them go among the Yanks if they want to."

The ignorant Lambert could not yet understand the situation, for it took him a long time to get new things through his head, and this was the first he had heard of the Emancipation Proclamation. He looked hard at Rodney to see if he was in earnest, then swung his clubbed rifle in the air and shouted "Git!" at the top of his voice; whereupon the frightened darkies took to their heels and disappeared in an instant. But they did not retreat in the direction of the road. They made the best of their way to their cabins in the quarter and hid themselves there. When they were out of sight Lambert put his rifle under his arm and pulled out his cob pipe.

"I'm more of a secessioner now nor I ever was before," said he. "We uns have just got to whop in this war, kase if we don't our niggers will be gone, an' where'll I get a job of overseein' ?''

"You'll never be an overseer again," answered Rodney. "You will have to go into the field and hoe cotton and cane yourself."

"Not by no means I won't," said Lambert fiercely. "That there is nigger's work, an' I can't seem to stoop to it. It don't make no sort of difference to rich folks like you how the war ends, kase you've got cotton, an' cotton is money these times. I aint got nary thing."

Lambert watched Rodney out of the corners of his eyes while he was applying a lighted match to the tobacco with which he had filled his pipe, but the boy had nothing to say. He thought there was a threat hidden under Lambert's last words.

"There's one thing about it," the latter continued after a little pause, " if we get whopped I won't be the only poor man there is in Louisiany, tell your folks."

With this parting shot he turned his mule about and rode out of the yard. And Rodney, angry as he was, let him go. He knew now just what he had to expect from the ex-

Home Guard, and made the mental resolution that, if his father would consent, he would be prepared to make a prisoner of Lambert the next time he met him.

"Something of the sort must be done, and before long, too," thought Rodney when he went to bed that night, "or the first thing we know our cotton will go the way Mr. Randolph's did. If the cotton was mine I would promise to hand Lambert a few hundred dollars as soon as it was sold, but then he is so treacherous I couldn't put any faith in his promises. I wish he had kept away from here to-day. His visit worried me more than Lincoln's proclamation."

Rodney intended to go home and lay the matter before his father as soon as he had seen the hands fairly at work in the morning ; but just as he arose from his breakfast Mr. Gray rode into the yard, accompanied by a stranger whose appearance and actions attracted Rodney's attention at once and amused him not a little. He sat on a bare-back mule (Mr. Gray's fine horses and saddles had disappeared with Breckenridge's men), with his shoulders

10

humped up, his head drawn down between them, his arms stiffened and his hands braced firmly against the mule's withers, and his broad back bent in the form of an arch. He wore a blue flannel suit, a black slouch hat, a flowing neck-handkerchief tied low on his breast, and finer shoes and stockings than Rodney himself had been in the habit of wearing of late. He had a sharp blue eye, a bronzed face, a heavy blond mustache, and gazed about him with the air of one who might know a thing or two, even if he didn't know how to ride a mule bare-back. Rodney hastened down the steps to welcome his father, and then looked inquiringly at the young man in blue, who placed his clenched hands on his hips and stared hard at Rodney.

> " De oberseer he gib us trouble,
>   An' he dribe us round a spell ;
>   We'll lock him up in de smokehouse cellar,
>   Wid de key frown in de well.
>   De whip is los', de hand-cuff broken,
>   An' ole moster'll have his pay ;
>   He's ole 'nough, big 'nough, an' oughter knowed
>   better
>   Dan to went an' run away,"

sang the stranger in a melodious tenor voice. "Hallo, Johnny!"

"Hallo, yourself," replied Rodney. He was so astonished at this strange greeting that he did not know what else to say. He gazed earnestly at the singer, but there was no smile of recognition under the blond mustache, though the blue eyes twinkled merrily. Then he looked toward his father for an explanation, but that gentleman, who had by this time dismounted, stood with his folded arms resting on his mule's back, and had not a word of explanation to offer.

"You are a very nice-looking rebel, I must say," were the visitor's next words.

"I am aware of it," returned Rodney; "but they are the best I've got to my back."

"I was speaking of you and not of your clothes," said the stranger hastily. "My good mother away up in North Carolina long ago taught me——"

"Jack! O Jack!" shouted Rodney joyfully. With one jump he reached his cousin's side, and seizing his outstretched hand in both his own, fairly dragged him to the ground.

"Easy, easy!" cautioned Mr. Gray. "That's Jack, but he isn't quite as sound as he was the last time you met him."

"I am overjoyed to see you after so long a separation," said Rodney, in some degree moderating the energy of his hand-shaking. "How did you leave Marcy and his mother? and has Marcy always been true to his colors, as he so often declared he would be, no matter what happened? How came you here when nobody dreamed of seeing you, and where have you been to get hurt?"

"I have been offsetting your work," replied Jack, rolling alongside Rodney, sailor fashion, as the latter slipped an arm through his own and led him to the porch. "You worked fifteen months to make this unholy rebellion successful, and I worked sixteen months and more to put it down; so you might as well have stayed at home with your mother."

"Then you have been at sea?" exclaimed Rodney.

"Correct. There's where I belong, you know. And I heard in a roundabout way that Marcy has had a brief experience, also. He was pilot on one of our gunboats during the fights at Roanoke Island, but where he is now I haven't the least idea. It is a long time since I got a word from home," said the sailor sadly. "I am on my way there now, and figuring to make some money by the trip. I am dead broke."

"Haven't you a discharge?"

"A sort of one, but nary cent of cash."

"How does that come? Why didn't your paymaster settle with you when he handed over your discharge?"

"Well, the first one couldn't very handily, because he was captured, together with his money and accounts; and the second one couldn't do it either, for he was captured too, and his money and books went to the bottom of the Gulf of Mexico, or into the hands of that pirate Semmes, which amounts to the same thing."

"Why, Jack, what do you mean? You must have been in a fight."

"That was what I thought when I found myself stranded on the deck of a strange ship without a bag or hammock to bless myself with, and no mess number," said Jack, with a laugh. "My first vessel, the *Harriet Lane*, was captured at Galveston on New Year's Day, and my second, the *Hatteras*, was sunk on the night of the 11th by the *Alabama*. Yes, I have been in two or three fights."

"Of course we heard about the two you mention, but never once thought of your being there," said Rodney. "Were you shot?"

"Oh, no. I was struck on the shoulder by something, don't know what, when the gunboat *Westfield* was blown up by her crew to keep her from falling into the hands of the rebels. If I hadn't been a good swimmer I should now be rusticating at Tyler, Texas, or some other Southern watering-place."

"Well, now, take this big chair—you have grown to be a pretty good-sized fellow since I last saw you—and settle back at your ease and tell us all about it," said Rodney. "What do you mean when you say you are figuring on making some money this trip? And if you are dead broke, where did you get that blue suit? They don't issue that style of clothes to the foremast hands in the navy, do they ? Or are you an officer ?"

"One at a time," replied Jack. "One at a time, and your questions will last a heap longer. I am a trader."

"O Jack," exclaimed Rodney, who was all excitement in a moment. "Then you are just the man we are looking for. Have you a permit ?"

"Well, I—you see—that is to say, no ; I haven't."

"Then you are not the man we want to see at all," said Rodney in a disappointed tone. "You can't trade without it."

"I am painfully aware of the fact. And perhaps you wonder how I am going to buy cotton when I am dead broke, don't you ? I have influential friends ; and thereby hangs a tale as long as a yardarm."

"Suppose you leave off bothering your cousin now and go home with us," suggested Mr. Gray, when he saw that Rodney was settling himself to listen to a lengthy story. "We haven't seen you at the house very often of late, and you are almost as much of a stranger to your mother as you would be if you lived in Vicksburg. We haven't heard all Jack's war history yet, and perhaps he will give it to us to-night after supper."

Rodney was glad to agree to the proposition, and at his request Ned Griffin was invited to make one of the party, for he was sure to be one of the most interested listeners. In fact the Grays had come to look upon Ned as one of the family. Jack's story was not a long one, and you ought to hear it, in order to know how he happened to "turn up" there in Mooreville when, as Rodney said, no one dreamed of seeing him, and we will tell it in our own way, leaving out a good deal of what Jack called "sailor lingo."

The last time we saw Jack Gray was so long ago that you have perhaps forgotten that we ever mentioned his name. Instead of following in the footsteps of his father and becoming a planter, Jack had sailed the blue water from his earliest boyhood, and was the elder brother of our Union hero, Marcy Gray, who was taken from his home at dead of night by a party of blue-jackets to serve as pilot on

Captain Benton's gunboat during the fight at Roanoke Island. Jack was Union all over, and, even when it was dangerous for him to do so, could hardly refrain from expressing his contempt for those who were trying to break up the government. When we first brought him to your notice he had already had some thrilling experience with the enemies of the flag under which he had sailed all over the world, his vessel, the brig *Sabine*, having been one of the first to fall into the power of the Confederate cruiser *Sumter*.

If you have read "Marcy, the Blockade-Runner," you will remember that the *Sabine* was under the command of men who did not intend to remain prisoners a minute longer than they were obliged to ; that the rebel banner had no sooner been hoisted at the peak in the place of their own flag, than they began laying plans to haul it down again, and that the captured brig was in the hands of the prize crew not more than twelve hours. Captain Semmes could not burn her as he would have been glad to .do, for it so happened that she had a neutral cargo on board. The sugar

and molasses with which her hold was filled
were consigned to an English port in the island
of Jamaica, and if he had destroyed it by
applying the torch to the *Sabine*, the rebel
commander would surely have brought his
government into trouble with England. That
was something he could not afford to do, so he
determined to take his prize into the nearest
Cuban port, in the hope that the Spanish authorities would permit him to land the cargo and
sell the brig for the benefit of the Confederate
government. There is every reason to believe
that he would have been disappointed, for
Spain was too friendly to the United States to
give aid and comfort to her enemies; but
before the matter could be put to the test the
Sabine's men, with Jack Gray at their head,
quietly overpowered the rebel prize crew that
had been put aboard of her and filled away
for Key West, which was the nearest Federal
naval station. When they arrived there they
turned their five prisoners over to the commandant and set sail for Boston, taking with
them the valuable cargo that ought to have
gone to Jamaica. When off the coast of North

Carolina they had a short but rather exciting race with Captain Beardsley's privateer
Osprey, on which Marcy Gray, Sailor Jack's
brother, was serving as pilot ; but the *Sabine*
was too swift to be overhauled, and her skipper
too wide-awake to be deceived by the sight
of the friendly flag which their pursuers
gave to the breeze in the hope of alluring the
defenceless merchantman to her destruction.

How the brig's owners accounted for the
cargo of molasses and sugar they so unexpectedly found on their hands Jack Gray
neither knew nor cared, for his first and only
thought was to reach home and see how his
mother and Marcy were getting on. In this
the master of the *Sabine* stood his friend by
securing for him a berth as second officer on
board the fleet schooner *West Wind*, which,
while claiming to be an honest coaster, was
really engaged in a contraband trade that
would have made her a lawful prize to the
first Federal blockader that happened to over-
haul and search her. Jack knew all about it
and understood the risk he was taking ; but
he accepted the position when it was offered,

because he could not see that there was any
other way for him to get home. Although the
schooner's cargo was consigned to a well-known
American firm in Havana, the owners did not
mean that it should go there at all. They intended that it should be run through the
blockade and sold at Newbern. Captain Frazier explained all this to Jack, and though the
latter did not believe in giving aid and comfort
to the enemies of the Old Flag, he not only
accepted the position of second mate and pilot
of the *West Wind*, but also invested two-thirds
of his hard-earned wages in quinine, calomel,
and other medicines of which the Confederacy
stood much in need, and sold them in Newbern
so as to clear about twelve hundred dollars.
But it wasn't money that Jack Gray cared for
just then. He wanted to see his mother and
Marcy.

The enterprise was successful. Captain
Frazier ran down the coast without falling in
with any of the blockaders, Sailor Jack took
the schooner through Oregon Inlet without
the least trouble, the Confederates were ready
to pay gold for her cargo, and then Captain

Frazier loaded with cotton for Bermuda, while
his pilot, with one of the *West Wind's* foremast hands for company, set out for home on
foot. We have told how he came like a thief
in the night and aroused his brother by toss-
ing pebbles against his bedroom window, and
what he did during the short time he remained
under his mother's roof. We have also described some of the exciting incidents that
happened when Marcy took him out to the
blockading fleet in the *Fairy Belle*—how they
ran foul of Captain Beardsley's schooner as
they were passing through Crooked Inlet, and
were afterward hailed by a steam launch, whose
commanding officer would have given everything he possessed if he could have brought
that same schooner within range of his howitzer for about two minutes—but they found
one of the cruisers, the *Harriet Lane*, without
much trouble and Sailor Jack remained aboard
of her, while Marcy filled away for home.
And we may add that the latter never heard
from his brother again until he read in the
papers that his vessel had been captured at
Galveston.

Bright and early the next morning, after a short interview with Captain Wainwright, the commander of the *Harriet Lane*, Jack Gray was shipped with due formality and rated as "seaman" on the books of the paymaster, who ordered his steward to serve him two suits of clothes and the necessary small stores. Ten minutes afterward, having rigged himself out in blue and tossed his citizen's suit through one of the ports into the sea, Jack was working with the crew as handily as though he had been attached to that particular vessel all his life. Of course he had never been drilled with small-arms or in handling big guns; but being quick to learn, his mates never had reason to call him a lubber, nor was he ever sent to the mast for awkwardness or neglect of duty.

The *Harriet Lane* had been built for the revenue service, and was considered to be the finest vessel in it. She was small, not more than five hundred tons burden, but she was swift; and if a suspicious craft appeared in the offing, the *Lane*, oftener than any other steamer, was sent out to see who she was and

what business she had there. Consequently
the life Jack led aboard of her was as full of
excitement and active duty as he could have
wished it to be. Much to Marcy's regret she
took no part in the fight at Roanoke Island.
Not being intended for so heavy work, she
remained outside to watch for blockade runners, and so Marcy never had a chance to see
how his brother looked in a blue uniform.

Not long after that they were still farther
separated. For weeks there had been rumors
that the government intended to make an
effort to recapture some of the ports on the
Gulf of Mexico that had been seized by the
Confederates ; but whether New Orleans, Galveston, or Mobile was to be taken first, or
whether the *Lane* was to have a hand in it,
nobody knew. The last question was answered when all the vessels that could be
spared from the Atlantic blockading fleet,
Jack's among the number, were ordered to
report to Flag-officer Farragut at Ship Island
in the Gulf of Mexico. On the way they
picked up a large fleet of mortar schooners
which had been ordered to rendezvous at Key

West, and reached their destination six weeks in advance of the army of General Butler, which was to co-operate with them in the capture of New Orleans. But the time was not passed in idleness. They ran down to the mouths of the Mississippi, and worked a full month to get their vessels over the bar into the river. They found but fifteen feet of water there, while many of the fleet drew from three to seven feet more, so that, when they had been lightened almost to the bare hull, the tugs had to pull them through a foot or more of mud. It was tiresome and discouraging work, but the same patience, determination, and skill that carried Flag-officer Goldsborough safely through the gale at Hatteras enabled Farragut to overcome the obstructions at the mouths of the Mississippi, and on the 8th of April five powerful steam sloops, two large sailing vessels, seventeen gunboats, and twenty-one mortar schooners were fairly over the bar and ready for business. But three more weary weeks passed before active operations were begun, during which Farragut and Butler met at Ship Island and decided upon a plan of operations, and the river up to the forts was carefully surveyed, so that the Union commanders, by simply looking at the compasses in their binnacles, could tell how far off and in what direction each fort and battery lay, and how they ought to elevate and train their guns in order to reach them. Of course the rebels were not idle while these surveys were being made, and protested against them with every cannon they could bring to bear upon the boats and men engaged in the work; but "in spite of all dangers and difficulties the surveys were accomplished and maps prepared showing the bearing and distance from every point on the river to the flagstaffs in the forts."

On the morning of the 17th the rebels began the fight in earnest by sending down a fire-raft that had been saturated with tar and turpentine; but a boat which put off from the *Iroquois* towed the raft ashore, where it burned itself out, doing no harm to anybody. Then the mortar schooners took a hand and pounded Fort Jackson with their thirteen-inch shells until they set it on fire and destroyed all the

11

clothing and commissary stores it contained.
Then the barrier which extended straight
across the river from Fort Jackson, and was
formed of dismantled vessels securely anchored
and bound together with heavy chains, was
cut, and Farragut was ready to perform the
feat that made him famous the world over and
placed him where he rightfully belonged—at
the head of our navy. He ran by the forts
with the loss of but a single vessel, the *Varuna*,
which was the swiftest and weakest in the
squadron. Having been built for a merchantman she was not intended for such work as
Farragut put upon her, but she won the honors
of the fight before she went down, having
helped sink or disable six of the rebel fleet,
any one of which was fairly her match.

The *Lane* took no part in this fight, but
remained behind to guard Porter's mortar
schooners, which dropped down the river as
soon as Farragut's boats had passed the forts
and closed with the Confederate fleet which
came gallantly down the river to meet them.

"But our position was one of great danger,
and we knew it," said Sailor Jack at this point

in his narrative. "There were at least fifteen vessels in the rebel fleet, two of which, the *Louisiana* and *Manassas*, the former mounting sixteen heavy guns, were the main reliance of the enemy, and supposed to be able to deal with us as the *Merrimac* dealt with the *Cumberland* in Hampton Roads. But we never saw the *Louisiana* until the thing was over, although we afterward learned that she had been assigned an important position in the fight. The other iron-clad was on hand, and began operations by shoving a fire-raft against the flagship, which ran aground in trying to escape from her. But instead of coming on down the river and destroying our mortar fleet, as she could have done very easily, for such wooden boats as the *Lane* could not have stood against her five minutes, she rounded to and went back after Farragut, who ordered the *Mississippi* to sink her. She didn't succeed in doing that, but she riddled the *Manassas* with a couple of broadsides, set her on fire, and let her float down the river with the current. I tell you I was frightened when I saw that ugly-looking thing bearing down on us. We opened fire on her, and in a few minutes she blew up and went down out of sight."

Shortly after this, Jack went on to relate, one of the most important and impressive incidents of the seven days' fight took place on board the *Harriet Lane*. When Porter received a note from Flag-officer Farragut stating that he had passed the forts in safety, destroying the Confederate flotilla on the way, and was on the point of starting for New Orleans, and suggesting that possibly the forts might surrender if summoned to do so, Porter sent a boat ashore to see what the rebels thought about it; and the answer was that they didn't acknowledge that they had been whipped yet. Although the forts had been battered out of shape by the shower of heavy shells that had been rained into them, the garrisons could still find shelter in the bomb-proofs, and if it was all the same to Porter they would hold out a while longer. But the men who had to fight the guns did not look at it that way. They were ready to give up, for they knew they would have to do it sooner or later; and when

Porter began another bombardment, which he did without loss of time, the men began deserting by scores, and the next day the rebel commander hauled down his flag.

"These battles were all won by the navy," said Jack proudly, "and everything on and along the river was destroyed by or surrendered to the navy, for the soldiers didn't come up till the trouble was all over. We went up with our little fleet and anchored abreast of Fort Jackson. A boat was sent ashore, and when it came back it brought General Duncan and two or three other high-up rebel officers, who did not act at all like badly beaten men, and they were received aboard the *Lane* and taken into the cabin, where the terms of capitulation were to be drawn up and signed. They hadn't been gone more than five minutes when some of the crew happened to look up the river, and there was that big iron-clad, the *Louisiana*, bearing down on us, a mass of flames. Then I was frightened again, I tell you. Mounting, as she did, sixteen heavy guns, she must have had all of twenty thousand pounds of powder in her magazine, and what would become of us if she blew up in the midst of our fleet? There wouldn't be many of us left to tell the story. It was an act of treachery on the part of the rebel naval officers which Farragut was prompt to punish by sending them North as close prisoners, while the army officers were given their freedom under parole."

"Did she do any damage when she blew up?" asked Rodney, who was deeply interested in the story.

"Not any to speak of," replied Jack, "because the explosion took place before she got among us. Of course word was sent below as soon as we caught sight of her, and the order was promptly signalled to every vessel in sight to play out her cable to the bitter end, and stand by to sheer as wide as possible from the blazing iron-clad as she drifted down; but we had hardly set to work to obey the order when there was a wave in the air, which I felt as plainly as I ever felt a wave of water pass over my head; the *Lane* heeled over two streaks, everything loose on deck was jostled about, and then there was a rumbling sound, not half as loud as you would think it ought to be, and the danger was over. The *Louisiana* blew up before she got to us, and that was a lucky thing for the *Harriet Lane.*"

And Jack might have added that it was a lucky thing for the whole country, for the commander, Porter, who was in the *Lane's* cabin with the rebel officers, was afterward the fighting Admiral Porter, who commanded the Mississippi squadron. His death at that crisis would have beeen a national loss.

CHAPTER VII.

SAILOR JACK IN ACTION.

THE city of New Orleans surrendered to
Flag-officer Farragut, who held it under
his guns until General Butler came up with
his soldiers to take it off his hands; and then
he kept on up the river with a portion of his
victorious fleet to effect a junction with the
Mississippi squadron at Vicksburg, while the
remainder of his vessels, one of which was the
Harriet Lane, sailed away to hoist the flag of
the Union over the port of Galveston, and
break up the blockade running that was going
on there. This force appeared before Galveston in May, but no earnest efforts were made
to compel a surrender until October; and even
then no serious attempt was made to take and
hold the city. The commanding naval officer
was content to establish a close blockade of the
port, and nothing could have suited Jack
Gray better. Galveston was a noted place for

blockade runners, and it was seldom indeed
that one escaped when the *Lane* sighted and
started in pursuit of her. Every capture
meant prize money.

"We made the most of the money that was
made off that port last summer, but of course
we didn't get it all ourselves," explained Jack.
"If you are cruising by yourself and make a
capture while another ship is within signalling
distance of you, the law says you must divide
with that ship, although she may not have
done a thing to help you take the prize ; but
if you belong to a squadron, every vessel in it
has a share in every prize you make. Fortunately for us there were but four ships in
our squadron off Galveston, and every time we
took a prize. somebody would sing :

" 'Here's enough for four of us ;
Thank Heaven there's no more of us—
God save the king.' "

Things went on in this satisfactory way
until General Banks took command at New
Orleans in December, and sent a regiment to
assist the naval forces at Galveston, it being
a part of his duty to "direct the military

movements against the rebellion in the State of Texas." Not more than a third of the regiment had arrived, the rest being on its way, when the rebel general Magruder, who had just been appointed to the chief command in Texas, formed a bold plan for the recapture of the city, and carried it out successfully on New Year's morning. He had six thousand men and several cotton-clad vessels to help him, and of course the battle could end in but one way.

Galveston stands upon a long, narrow island in the bay, and is connected with the mainland by a bridge two miles in length, built upon piles. This bridge ought to have been destroyed, but it wasn't, and when Magruder charged across it with his six regiments, he confidently expected to sweep away like so many cobwebs the little handful of Federals standing at the other end; but he didn't. Aided by a hot fire from the *Harriet Lane* and *Westfield*, they repulsed every charge he made, and no doubt would have continued to do so if two of his best vessels, the *Neptune* and *Bayou City*, protected by cotton bales piled twenty feet high upon their low decks, so that at a distance they looked like common cotton transports, and manned by a regiment of sharpshooters, had not hastened to his aid.

"We had our own way with the troops on the bridge until those two boats came dashing down at us, and then things began to look squally," said Jack. "We steamed up to meet them, but it wasn't long before we wished we hadn't done it. We didn't disable them with our bow-guns as we hoped to do, and, indeed, it was as much as a man's life was worth to handle the guns at all, for the sharpshooters behind the cotton bales sent their bullets over our deck like hailstones. One time I grabbed hold of a train tackle with four other men to help run out the No. 2 gun, and the next I knew I was standing there alone. The four had been shot dead, but I wasn't touched. All this while the rebel boats were coming at us full speed, and the next thing I knew they struck us with terrible force, bow on, one on each side. But," added Jack, with a chuckle of satisfaction, "one of them got hurt worse than we did. The *Nep-*

tune was disabled by the shock, and grounded in shoal water; but the men on her were game to the last. They fought to win and shot to kill; for, no matter which way I looked, 1 saw somebody drop every minute."

"And what became of the other boat?" inquired Rodney.

"The *Bayou City?* Oh, she drifted away, but rounded-to and came at us again, hitting us pretty near in the same place; but the second time she didn't drift away. She made fast to and boarded us. When I saw those graybacks swarming over the hammock nettings, and heard that Captain Wainwright and most of the other officers had been killed, I knew I had to do something or go to prison; so I just took a header overboard through the nearest port and struck out for the *Westfield*, which was a mile or so astern, and trying to come to our aid."

Jack was not quite correct when he said he "struck out," after taking a header through the port. He turned on his back and floated, for he was afraid that if he showed any signs of life he would be discovered and picked off by some sharpshooter. He permitted the current to whirl him around now and then, so that he could keep his bearings and hold a straight course for the *Westfield*, but before he had floated half a mile, he discovered that he was making straight for as hot a place as that from which he had just escaped. The flagship *Westfield* had run hard and fast aground within easy range of a battery which the rebels had planted on the shore, and although two other gunboats came up and tried to drag her into deep water, she was being literally cut to pieces before Jack Gray's eyes; and more than that, her commander was making preparations to abandon her to her fate.

"Then I began to look wild again, and took a sheer off to give the flagship plenty of room to blow up in," said Jack. "Captain Renshaw, her commandant, was a regular, and I knew well enough that he would not leave his vessel in such shape that the rebels could fix her up and use her against us, though I was not prepared for what happened a few minutes later. While I was moving along with the current, not daring to swim lest I should attract the notice of some wide-awake sharp-shooter, I saw Renshaw send off his men by the boat-load until at last there were but two boats left alongside the *Westfield*. One of these put off loaded to the water's edge, but the other remained, and I knew it was waiting for Renshaw to fire the train he had laid to the magazine; and that made me sheer off a little farther, although I began swimming the best I knew how in the hope that one of the boats would wait for me to catch on behind. In a minute or two more Captain Renshaw came out, and that was the first and last I ever saw of him. He stepped into his boat, but before it had moved twenty feet away the flagship blew up, smashing the two small boats into kindling-wood and sending every man in them to kingdom come."

No one else who was as close to the *Westfield* as Jack Gray was at that moment escaped with his life, and he did not come off unscathed. While he was gazing around him in a dazed sort of way, gasping for breath and utterly unable to realize what had happened, a piece of the *Westfield's* wreck which had been blown high in air descended with frightful velocity, and barely missing his head struck him a glancing blow on the shoulder and shot down into the water out of sight.   And it was but one of a score of such dangerous missiles which rained upon him during the next few seconds.   They plunged into the water perilously near to him and splashed it in his face from all directions. The most of them were no bigger than the head they threatened to break, while others were as large as a barn door.   At first Jack thought the safest place would be nearer the bottom of the river ; but when he saw how some of the heaviest pieces of the wreck dove out of sight when they struck the water, he decided that he could not go deep enough to escape them, and that the best plan would be to look upward and try to dodge them when he saw that they were coming too close ; but by the time he came to this conclusion and turned upon his back, the storm was over and the air above him was clear.   It was the narrowest escape he had ever had, and Jack Gray had been in some tight places.

Having satisfied himself that he was no

longer in danger of being knocked senseless
by falling wreckage, Jack turned upon his
face and struck out for the nearest gunboat, or
rather tried to ; for his right arm was almost
useless. He could thrust it through the water
in front of him, but when he endeavored to
swim with it, it dropped to his side like a piece
of lead.

"And that's the way it felt for three or four
days, although I was under good care all the
time," continued Jack. "I was picked up after
I had floated and swum with one hand a distance
of three miles, reported the loss of my vessel,
and told what little I knew about the blowing
up of the *Westfield*, and then I was glad to
go into the hands of the doctor, for I found
that I was worse hurt than I thought I was.
But you may be sure I didn't say so. If
there is anything that is despised aboard ship
it is a sojer, which is the name we give to men
who can work and won't, and so I kept on
doing duty when I ought by rights to have
been in my hammock. I pulled twenty miles
on the night of the 11th of January to escape
capture, and of course the exertion gave me a

big set-back; but I haven't got to that part of my story yet."

Jack Gray watched and waited anxiously to hear from some of his shipmates, but not a word did he get from anybody; and this led him to believe that he was the only one of the *Harriet Lane's* crew who escaped death or capture. The direct results of the fight were that the rebels, with very small loss to themselves, captured the *Lane*, caused the destruction of the flagship of the squadron, secured possession of two coal barges that were lying at the wharf and nearly four hundred prisoners; but "the indirect results were still more important." The whole State of Texas came back under their flag, and blockade running went on as though it had never been interfered with at all. It was done principally by small schooners like Captain Beardsley's *Hattie*, which took out cotton and brought back medicines, guns, ammunition, and cloth that was afterward made into uniforms for the Confederate soldiers. And the worst of it was that it was kept up to the end of the war. Of course word was sent to New Orleans at once,

12

and Commodore Bell came down with a small fleet to shut up the port ; but he brought no soldiers with him to hold the city, for General Banks couldn't spare a single regiment. He had made up his mind to capture Port Hudson, and needed all the men he could get.

Among the vessels that came down with Commodore Bell was the *Hatteras*, the slowest old tub in the fleet, and much to his disgust Jack Gray was ordered aboard of her. The badge he wore on his arm showed that he had been a quartermaster on board the *Lane*, but he was transferred without any rating at all, it being optional with Captain Blake, the commander of the *Hatteras*, whether he would continue him as a quartermaster or put him before the mast. Jack had already served four months beyond the year for which he enlisted, but he made no complaint, although he had firmly resisted all efforts on the part of the *Lane's* officers to induce him to re-enlist for three years or during the war.

" I might have had a commission as well as not," said Jack, "for there wasn't a watch officer aboard the *Lane* who could have passed

a better examination than I could. Indeed, I
hadn't been aboard of her twenty-four hours
before I found that I knew more about a ship
than most of the men who commanded me.
But as often as I thought of staying in the
service, something told me I had better get
out ; and that was the reason why I refused to
re-enlist or accept a commission.''

The fact was that, so long as the speedy
Lane was capturing a valuable blockade runner or two every week, and money was coming
into his pockets faster than he could have
earned it in any other business, Jack Gray was
quite willing to remain a quartermaster, and
so he said nothing to Captain Wainwright concerning the honorable discharge that rightfully belonged to him ; but now the case was
different, and Jack wanted to go home and see
how his mother and Marcy were getting on.
He had been ordered aboard a vessel that
couldn't catch a mud-turtle in a stern chase,
and consequently there was no more excitement or prize money for him. The paymaster
who ought to have paid him off and given him
his discharge had been captured with all his

money and books, and Jack knew that his accounts would have to be settled in Washington; and there was so much red tape in Washington that there was no telling whether or not they would ever be settled. After thinking the matter over, Jack wrote a letter to Commodore Bell, telling him how the matter stood and asking for his discharge, and gave it into the hands of the captain of the *Hatteras* to be forwarded. The first result was about what he thought it would be. He had to pull off his petty officer's badge and go before the mast. He was also assigned to an oar in the first cutter, and that was one of the best things that ever happened to Jack Gray.

Nowhere else in the world is life such a burden as aboard a vessel lying on a station with nothing but routine work to do. Jack found it so and chafed and fretted under it, but not for long. One day, about an hour after the dinner pennant had been hauled down, the lounging, lazy crew of the *Hatteras* were startled by the cry of "Sail ho!" from the lookout. Signal was at once made to the *Brooklyn*, Commodore Bell's flagship, and the answer that came back was an order for the *Hatteras* to run out and see who and what the visitor was. Of course the crew were glad to be afloat once more, and some of them began talking about prize money; but others declared that if the stranger had any speed at all and desired to keep out of the way, the *Hatteras* would never get nearer to her than she was at that moment. But the sequel proved that the stranger did not want to keep out of the way, although at first she acted like it. She rounded to and turned her head out to sea as if she were fleeing from pursuit; but all the while the war ship came nearer and nearer to her, until the officer at the masthead made out that the chase was a large steamer under sail. This fact was duly communicated to the flagship by signal, and then the old *Hatteras* seemed to wake up and try to show a little speed; but Captain Blake became suspicious and ordered his ship cleared for action, with everything in readiness for a determined attack or a vigorous defense.

The pursuit continued for twenty miles, and finally night set in with no moon but plenty of starlight. Jack Gray, who had stood at one of the broadside guns until he was tired, had just given utterance to the hope that the chase would improve the opportunity to run out of sight or else come about and give them battle, just as she pleased, when an officer at the masthead sent down the startling information that the stranger had rounded-to and was coming back. Beyond a doubt that meant that something was going to happen. She hove in sight almost immediately, and in less time than it takes to tell it stopped her engines within a hundred yards, the captain of the blockader ringing his stopping bell at the same instant.

"What ship is that?" shouted the Union commander, from his place on the bridge.

"Her Britannic Majesty's steamer *Vixen!*" was the reply. "What ship is that?"

"This is the United States ship *Hatteras*," answered Captain Blake. "I will send a boat aboard of you."

"When we heard this conversation," said Jack, "we made up our minds that we had been chasing an English ship. Mind you, I don't say a friendly ship, for England never was and never will be friendly to the United States. She would be glad to see us broken up to-morrow, and is doing all she dares to help the rebels along. Of course it was our captain's duty to find out whether or not the other captain had told him the truth, and the only way he could do it was by sending an officer off to examine his papers. He had the first cutter called away, and, as that was the boat to which I belonged, I lost no time in takoff my side-arms and tumbling into her. And that was all that saved me from falling into Semmes' power a second time."

Jack then went on to say that, as soon as the officer had taken his place in the stern-sheets, the cutter was shoved off from the *Hatteras* and pulled around her stern; but just as she began swinging around with her bow toward the supposed English ship a most exciting and unexpected thing happened. A voice came from the latter's deck, so clear and strong that the cutter's crew could hear every word:

"This is the Confederate steamer *Ala-bama!*" And before the astonished blue-jack-

ets had time to realize that they had been
trapped the roar of a broadside rent the air,
and shells and solid shot went crashing into
the wooden walls of the doomed *Hatteras*.
Semmes afterward took great credit to himself
because he did not strike the Federal ship in
disguise, but gave her "fair warning." How
long was it after he gave warning that he fired
his broadside into her? Not two seconds. He
took all the advantage he could, and yet there
was no one who protested louder or had more
to say about trickery and cowardice when the
Federal officers took advantage of him. He
made a great fuss because Captain Winslow
protected the machinery and boilers of the
Kearsarge with chains, as Admiral Farragut
protected *his* vessels when he ran past the
forts at New Orleans.

The roar of the Confederate steamer's guns
had scarcely ceased before an answering broadside came from the Union war ship. Without
the loss of a moment both vessels were put under steam and the action became a running fight,
the blue-jackets standing bravely to their guns
and giving their powerful antagonist as good

as she sent. The cutter's crew tried in vain to return to their vessel. They rowed hard, but every turn of her huge paddle-wheels left them farther behind, and finally they gave up in despair and laid on their oars and watched the conflict. It was desperate but short. In just thirteen minutes from the time it began the *Hatteras* hoisted a white light at her mast-head and fired an off-gun to show that she had been beaten.

"Fortune of war," sighed the officer who was sitting in the cutter's stern-sheets beside the coxswain. "But I tell you, men, I hate to see our old ship surrendered to that pirate. Back, port; give way, starboard! We haven't surrendered, and we want to get away from here before they catch sight of us."

No cutter's crew ever pulled harder than Jack Gray and his shipmates pulled in obedience to this order. Jack forgot that he had a crippled arm, and when the cutter came about and pointed her head toward the shore more than twenty miles away, he rowed as strong an oar as he ever did in his life. He listened anxiously for the hail that would tell him the

cutter had been discovered, but heard none ;
but he saw and reported something that sent
an exultant thrill through the heart of every
one of his companions.

"Mr. Porter," said he, in tones which intense excitement rendered husky. "Our old
tub has been surrendered, but she'll never do
the rebels any good. She's sinking, sir."

"Thank Heaven!" murmured the officer,
whirling around as if he had been shot.

He couldn't see anything through the darkness except the white light that the blockader
had hoisted at her masthead in token of surrender, and which was swaying about in a
way that would have been unaccountable to a
landsman ; but the blue-jackets knew she was
going to the bottom. She went rapidly, too,
for Captain Blake afterward reported that in
two minutes from the time he left her the
Hatteras disappeared, bow first. Then Jack
thought that Mr. Porter would order the
cutter back to assist in picking up the crew,
but he didn't do it. They would have reached
the sinking vessel too late to be of any service,
and besides Mr. Porter thought it his duty to

report to the Flag-officer at once, believing
that if the *Brooklyn* were promptly warned
she could capture or sink the *Alabama* before
she had time to get very far away.   But the
fleet had already been warned by the sound of
the guns that the *Hatteras* had encountered
an armed enemy of some description, and
several steamers were hastening to the rescue;
scattering widely in the pursuit, to cover as
much space as possible and increase their
chances of falling in with the enemy.   The
cutter passed these vessels at so great a distance that she could not attract the attention
of any of them, and it was not until they had
pulled all the way to Galveston, and boarded
one of the blockading fleet which remained
behind, that the particulars of the fight
became known.   None   of   the   pursuing
steamers ever saw the *Alabama*, which sailed
away for the coast of Yucatan; but as one of
them was returning to her anchorage the next
morning, baffled and beaten in the chase, she
fell in with the sunken *Hatteras*, whose royal
masts were just above water.   The night pennant floating from one of them told the melan-

choly story; but if Jack Gray and his shipmates had not escaped just as they did, it
might have been a long time before Commodore Bell would have known that the
dreaded *Alabama* had been in his immediate
vicinity. But her day was coming. The first
time she met a Union war ship that was anywhere near her match she was sent to the
bottom.

Once more Jack was without a vessel, and
had no clothes "to bless himself with" except
those he stood in; but that didn't trouble him
half as much as did the discharge he was
anxious to get. He and the rest of the
cutter's men were sent aboard the flagship
when she returned to her anchorage, and that
suited him, for it gave him a fair chance to
gain the commodore's ear—a task he set himself to accomplish as soon as the excitement
had somewhat died away. But the Flag-
officer was a regular, and like all regulars he
moved in ruts of opinion so deep that a yoke
of oxen could not have pulled him out. He
couldn't give Jack a discharge, he said,
because he didn't know when or where he

enlisted, for how long, or anything about it. He couldn't give him any money, either, for his name was not borne on the paymaster's books. He could give him a paper stating that he had done service in the Union navy and let him go home, and that was all he could do for him.

"And that's the kind of a discharge I got," said Jack with a laugh. "But it proved to be good enough and strong enough to take me through the provost guards in New Orleans and get me a pass to come up here. I have not drawn a cent from Uncle Sam, so he owes me a year's wages and better, as well as a lot of prize money. The commodore dispatched a vessel to New Orleans with his report of the loss of the *Hatteras*, and I was permitted to take passage on her."

"How did you feel when you found yourself in a strange city with no money in your pocket and no friends to go to?" inquired Ned Griffin.

"I didn't think much about it, because I never let a little thing like that worry me," said Jack with another laugh. "I did not by any means intend to go hungry, or sleep on the Levee, if my pockets were empty. There were several of our vessels in the river, and I knew I could ship whenever I felt like it ; but I had made up my mind that I would not go afloat again until I had said ' hello ! ' to my relatives up here in Mooreville."

The first boat that left the dispatch steamer took Jack ashore and landed him on the Levee among some river craft that belonged to the quartermaster's department of Banks' army. Being a deep-water man he did not bestow more than a passing glance upon them, but turned his face toward the docks above at which a large fleet of sea-going vessels was moored ; and as he walked he kept a bright lookout for two things—a sailorman who could tell him what had happened in the world since he left it (being on the blockade Jack thought was almost as bad as being out of the world), and a soldier who could direct him to the office of the provost marshal. As he stepped from the Levee to the nearest dock his gaze became riveted upon a rakish looking fore-and-aft schooner that lay there discharging a miscellaneous cargo. She looked familiar to him. She was painted white with a green stripe at her water-line, and bore the name "*Hyperion,* Portland," on her stern ; but Jack Gray was positive that he had known and sailed on her when she was painted black with a red stripe at the water-line, and went by a very different name. He dodged up the after gang-plank to the deck and took another look. He had had charge of that deck more than once. Everything on and about it was familiar to him, not excepting the face of the lank Yankee skipper, whose head and shoulders at that moment emerged from the companion-way. Jack turned about and approached him with a comical smile on his countenance.

"Want a pilot this trip, Captain Frazier ?" said he.

"No, I don't," was the surly reply. He looked searchingly into Jack's face, but could not remember that he had ever seen him before.

"No offence, I hope," continued the latter. "But I served you so well before that I think you might give me a lift when you see me stranded here without a shot in the locker. I took the *West Wind* through Oregon Inlet when——"

"Mr. Gray—Jack!" said the captain, in an excited whisper. "Sh! Not another word out of you; not a whimper. Come below with me."

Shaking all over with suppressed merriment Jack Gray followed the skipper down the stairs and into the cabin, the door of which was quickly but softly closed and locked.

"Sit down," continued the captain. "And if you care a cent for me don't speak above your breath. Where have you been? That uniform says you belong to the navy."

"I did, but I don't belong now," replied Jack. "Shortly after I made that trip with you I shipped for a year, but have been kept over my time. I have been on the blockade, and have helped capture many a fine craft like this one."

"Sh! Don't speak so loud," whispered Captain Frazier, for it was he. "But you couldn't do harm to this craft now, for she is engaged in honest business."

"No private ventures stowed away among her cargo?" said Jack.

"Nary venture. There's no need of it, for I make money hand over fist in an honest way. I am a cotton trader. Got a permit and everything all square. And cotton will be worth a dollar a pound by the time I get back to New York."

"What do you pay for it here?"

"That depends on the man I am dealing with. If he is a Union man I give him from seven to ten cents in greenbacks, which will buy eighty per cent. more stuff than Confederate scrip. If he is a good rebel, or if he is surrounded by rebel neighbors who are keeping an eye on his movements, I give him ten cents in rebel money."

"Where do you get rebel money?" asked Jack.

"Anywhere—everywhere. I can get all I want for thirty cents on a dollar, and have bought some as low as twenty. It will be lower than that in less than a month. But, mind you, no one around here knows that I have been a blockade runner. And I am not

13

at the head of this business. My Boston owners are doing it all and I am simply their agent. But are you really aground?"

"I never told a straighter story in my life," answered Jack, who went on to describe how he happened to be in that condition. When his hasty narrative was finished Captain Frazier said:

"There's always room aboard my schooner for such a sailorman as I know you to be, and if you want to sign with me as my chief officer I shall be glad to have you. And you must let me advance you money enough to provide for your immediate wants."

When Jack reached this part of his story Rodney knew where that blue suit came from.

CHAPTER VIII.

SAILOR JACK and his old commander spent two hours locked in the *Hyperion's* cabin, and if a stranger could have seen how very cordial and friendly they were, or had heard the peals of laughter that arose when one or the other described some amusing scene through which he had passed since they last met, he never would have dreamed that one had risked life and liberty in doing what he could to put down the rebellion, while the other had run an equal risk in bringing aid and comfort to it.

Captain Frazier had been a daring and successful blockade runner as long as his Boston owners could make money by it, and there were not many cruisers on the Atlantic coast that had not, at one time or another, sighted and given chase to the fleet *West Wind*, nor were there very many officers and sailormen who could not recognize her as far as they could see her. When light swift steamers were added to the blockading fleet the business became too uncertain and dangerous to be longer followed, and Captain Frazier was honest enough to say that he was glad to stop it, for, being a Yankee, he had never had any heart for it any way.

When the Mississippi was cleared as far as Port Hudson, and all that immense cotton country on both sides the river was thrown open to traffic, Captain Frazier's owners saw an opportunity to do business in an honest way and were prompt to improve it. Armed with a pocketful of credentials one of the firm hastened to New Orleans to obtain a permit to trade in cotton, and the *West Wind* was ordered to a neutral port "for repairs." When she again appeared on the high seas she did not look at all like herself, and even her name had been changed. She went to Portland, Me., and stayed there long enough to get a charter, and then sailed to Boston and loaded up with commissary stores for Banks' army. On the way down she was boarded by more than one officer who had chased her when she was a blockade runner, and now she was in New Orleans (safe, too, although surrounded by Federal war ships) and making ready to take a cargo of cotton to New York.

"I grew ten years older during the twelve months I was engaged in running the blockade," said Captain Frazier, in concluding his story, "but I had lots of fun and saw no end of excitement. And now to come back to business. Didn't I hear you say, while you were serving as pilot and second mate of the *West Wind*, that you have relatives here in Louisiana and that they raise cotton? I thought so. Well, now, have they got any that they want to sell?"

"I don't know; but I can find out. I did not intend to leave this country without seeing them. How far is Baton Rouge above here?"

"Not far; a hundred and fifty miles, I should say."

"Well, if I can get there and obtain a pass that will take me through the lines as far as Mooreville, I can easily find them."

"You can get there, and I'll see that you have a bushel of passes if you need them. If they've got any cotton I want it."

"You can't have it, captain, for any such price as you have been paying others. I'll not stand by and see my uncle gouged in any such way as that. And I shall hold out for greenbacks, too."

"Certainly; of course. That's all right; but as for the price, I guess you will take what I please to——"

Captain Frazier stopped and looked hard at Jack, who gazed fixedly at him in return. Each knew what the other was thinking of.

"I don't know that my uncle Rodney has any cotton," continued Jack. "But if he has, you can afford to give him at least twenty-five cents a pound, greenback money, for it. He is bound to lose his niggers, and, if he is robbed of his cotton, what will he have to start on when the war is over?"

"Judging by the way you look out for the pennies you're as much of a Yankee as I am," said Captain Frazier with a laugh. "You'll swamp my owners at this rate ; but seeing it's you, I' suppose I shall have to submit to be robbed myself. Now listen while I tell you something. General Banks came here on purpose to take Port Hudson, Grant is coming down to capture Vicksburg, and when the Mississippi is open from Memphis to the sea there'll be a fortune for the first man who is lucky enough to get a permit to trade in cotton on the river. My agent, who has an office ashore and to whom I will introduce you this afternoon, has heard enough to satisfy him that there are half a million bales concealed in the woods and swamps along the river, and that the owners, both Union and rebel, are eager to sell before the Confederate government has a chance to destroy it ; and they would rather sell it for a small sum in good money than for ten times the amount in such money as they grind out at Richmond. Now, my idea is to charter a river steamer—a light-draught one—so that she can run up any small tributary, and put a man with a business head on board of her with instructions to buy every pound of cotton he can hear of between this port and Memphis. How would you like the berth ?"

"That depends on whether or not I can be of any service to my uncle and his friends," replied Jack. " What is there in it ?"

" A big commission or a salary, just as you please."

The matter wasn't settled either one way or the other at this interview. Jack took dinner with Captain Frazier and went ashore with him in the afternoon to be introduced to the "agent," who wasn't an agent at all, but the head of a branch house which the enterprising Boston firm had established in New Orleans. He might properly have been called a cotton factor. When the captain told him who and what Jack was, and what he had done to make the firm's first venture in contraband goods successful, adding that he was going up to Baton Rouge to see whether or not there was any cotton to be had at or near that place, the agent became interested, and promised to assist Jack by every means in his power.

"1 didn't see how a civilian could help me along with the military authorities," said

Jack, in concluding his interesting narrative, "but I wasn't long in finding out. The agent, as I shall always speak of him, gave me a letter to the provost marshal in New Orleans and another to the officer holding the same position in Baton Rouge, and those letters made things smooth for me. I supposed, of course, that I should have to foot it from the city to Mooreville, but the marshal kindly furnished me with a horse to ride, the only condition imposed being that I should send it back the first good chance I got. Captain Frazier advanced me money to buy a citizen's outfit and pay travelling expenses, and here I am."

"And right glad I am to see you," said Rodney, as Jack settled back in his chair with an air which seemed to say that he had finished his story at last. "But you are a slick one."

"No more so than some other folks," retorted Jack. "It's a wonder you have not brought yourself into serious trouble by your smuggling and giving aid to escaped prisoners."

"But, Jack, I assure you that we were in sore need of the things I have smuggled through the lines," said Rodney earnestly.

"We couldn't possibly get along without them."

"And neither can I get along without making this war refund to my mother every dollar she is likely to lose by it," answered his cousin. "The whole South is going to be impoverished before this thing is over. My folks had no hand in bringing these troubles upon us, and I don't mean that they shall suffer through the folly of a few fanatics, if I can help it."

"But, Jack, you will take up with the agent's offer and put a trading boat on the river, will you not?" said Rodney.

"Port Hudson and Vicksburg have not been captured yet," suggested Mrs. Gray.

"No, but they're going to be," said Jack confidently. "And until that happens I might better be at home than anywhere else, for I can't do anything here. If I find that mother and Marcy are getting on all right, you have my promise that I will return and do my best to get your four hundred bales to market."

"Bully for you," exclaimed Rodney joyfully. "You *are* just the man we wanted to see after all. I wish you could take the cotton to-night, don't you, father?"

"I'll tell you what I'll do. I will speak to the agent and Captain Frazier about it, and see if I can induce them to send a boat after your cotton, so that the *Hyperion* can take it out on her next trip. I might have made some such arrangement before I left New Orleans, but I didn't know whether or not you had any cotton. What's become of those bushwhackers of whom Uncle Rodney has given me an interesting account?"

"Do you mean Lambert and his men? I suppose they are still hiding in the swamp."

"Protecting your cotton?" added Jack. "Well, they'll have to be 'neutralized,' as McClellan said of the *Merrimac*. As I understand it, those bushwhackers don't mean that you or anybody else shall touch that cotton unless they can make something by it. It's a little the queerest thing I ever heard of, but so far they seem to have been your best friends."

"I have been studying about that a good deal," answered Rodney. "And the conclusion I have come to is that when we get ready take charge of our property, and not before, we'll have to get rid of Lambert in some manner. He is the leader, and if he were out of the way I think his men would scatter. I'll make a prisoner of him if father will consent."

"O Rodney, you must not attempt it," exclaimed his mother. "Lambert has the reputation of being a dangerous man."

"I don't know where or how he came by that reputation," said the boy with a smile. "I know he is treacherous, and if I should make the attempt and fail, I should have to look out for him. He'd as soon bushwhack me as anybody else. But I don't intend to fail."

Sailor Jack's time was so short, and there were so many other things to be talked about, that this matter was presently dropped, to be taken up again and settled at some future day. When Jack started for Baton Rouge the next morning, with his uncle and cousin for company, the only conclusion they had been able to reach was that Mr. Gray should hold fast to his cotton, if he could, until he heard from Jack, who would forward his letter under cover to the provost marshal in Baton Rouge so that it would be sure to reach its destination.   If it were sent to the care of Rodney's Confederate friend, Mr. Martin, the Federal authorities might not take the trouble to deliver it.

The next step was to obtain the provost marshal's consent to the arrangement, and that was easily done.   He knew that Jack had risked his life for the Union, and that his cousin lent a helping hand to escaped prisoners as often as the opportunity was presented ; so he readily promised to take charge of all the letters that came from the North addressed to Rodney Gray, and hand them over without reading them.   He gave Jack a pass authorizing him to leave the city on business, and a note to the quartermaster which brought him a permit to take passage for New Orleans on one of the steamers attached to the quartermaster's department.   Rodney and his father saw him off and then turned their faces toward the hospitable home of Mr. Martin, where they were to remain until morning.

"It was just no visit at all," said Rodney in a discouraged tone.   "When Jack said he was a trader and that he had influential friends,

I wouldn't have taken anything I can think of now for our chances of getting that cotton off our hands. As the matter stands, every-thing depends on 'ifs.' *If* Marcy and his mother are getting on all right, and *if* Jack decides to come back and take up with Captain Frazier's offer, we shall have a show; other-wise not."

This state of affairs was galling to Rodney Gray, who could not bear to be kept in sus-pense; but exciting events were transpiring up the river every day, and in trying to keep track of them Rodney lost sight of his troubles for a brief season. General Grant, who had taken command of the army that was operat-ing against Vicksburg, had gone to work as if he were thoroughly in earnest, and there wasn't a soldier under him who was more anxious for his complete triumph than was this ex-Con-federate hero of ours. Rodney was soldier enough to know that neither Vicksburg nor Port Hudson could be taken by assault, and that they could not be starved into surrender so long as supplies of every sort could be run into them from the Red River country. They must be surrounded on the river side as well as on the land side, and Rodney was impatient to learn what General Grant was going to do about it. Fortunately the latter had an able assistant in David D. Porter, who had commanded Farragut's mortar schooners at New Orleans. He was now an acting rear admiral and commanded the Mississippi squadron, and most loyally did he second General Grant in his efforts to capture the rebel stronghold.

The very first move Porter made excited Rodney's unbounded admiration and made his heart beat high with hope. He ordered the ram *Queen of the West* to run the batteries and destroy the transports that were engaged in bringing supplies to Vicksburg. Owing to some trouble with her steering gear it was broad daylight when the ram started on her dangerous mission, and she was a fair target for the hundred heavy guns which the rebels had mounted on the bluffs. But she went through, stopping on the way long enough to make a desperate attempt to sink the steamer *Vicksburg*, which the rebels, after General Sherman's defeat at Chickasaw Bayou, had brought down from the Yazoo to be made into a gunboat. She failed in that, but ran by the batteries without receiving much injury, and began operations by capturing a steamer which she kept with her as tender, and burning three others that were loaded with provisions.

"If she keeps that up Vicksburg is a goner," said Rodney to his friend Ned Griffin.

"One would think you are glad of it," said the latter. "That's a pretty way for a rebel soldier to talk."

"Rebel soldier no longer," replied Rodney. "I know when I have had enough. I'm whipped, and now I want the war to end. It's bound to come some of these days, and I wish it might come this minute."

But unfortunately the *Queen* did not "keep it up" as Rodney hoped she would. As long as her commander obeyed orders and devoted his attention to transports, he was successful; but when he got it into his head that he could whip a fort with his single wooden vessel, he ruined himself just as Semmes did when he thought he could beat a war ship in a fair fight, because he had sunk one weak block-ader and burned sixty-five defenceless mer-chantmen. Colonel Ellet, who commanded the *Queen*, ran up Red River, where he captured the *New Era* with a squad of Texas soldiers, twenty-eight thousand dollars in Confederate money, and five thousand bushels of corn; and flushed with victory ran up twenty miles farther to the fort—and lost his vessel. He escaped with a few of his men, but the ram fell into the hands of the enemy, who repaired her in time to assist the *Webb* in sinking the *Indianola*—a fine new iron-clad that had run the Vicksburg batteries without receiving a scratch. Then all the rebels in Rodney's vicinity were jubilant, and Rodney himself was correspondingly depressed. On the day the unwelcome news came Lambert rode into the yard on his way home from Mooreville. He wasn't afraid to go there now that there was no conscript officer to trouble him.

"I heered about it," he said, in answer to an inquiry from the anxious Rodney. "We allow to raise that there fine iron-clad, an'

14

show the Yanks what sort of fighting she can do when she's in the hands of men. That'll make three good ships we'll have, an' with them we can easy clean out the Yankee fleet at Vicksburg."

That was just what Rodney knew the rebels would try to do, and their exploit with the *Arkansas* proved that they were at all times ready to take desperate chances. Lambert never would have thought of such a thing him-self, so he must have been talking with some-one who was pretty well informed.

"What do you mean by *we?*" asked Rodney.

"I heered Tom Randolph an' others among 'em discussin' the projec' down to the store," replied Lambert.

"Tom Randolph! He's a pretty fellow to talk of cleaning anybody out."

"That's what I thought. He never had no pluck 'ceptin' on the day he drawed his sword on me. An' he never would 'a' done it if his maw hadn't been right there to his elbow. I aint likely to disremember him for that."

"But you took an ample revenge by burning

his father's cotton, did you not? Lambert, that was a cowardly thing for you to do."

Rodney's tone was so positive that the ex-Home Guard did not attempt to deny the accusation. "Who's been a-carryin' tales on me?" he demanded. "I want you to understand that nobody can't draw a sword on me an' shake it in my face too, like Tom Randolph done. I just dropped in to see if you could let me have a side of bacon this evenin'."

Without making any reply Rodney arose from his chair and led the way toward the smoke-house. While he was taking down the bacon Lambert kept up an incessant talking to prevent him from saying more about Mr. Randolph's cotton, and when Rodney handed the meat out of the door he wheeled his mule and rode quickly away; but he had said enough to make the boy very uneasy. How long would it be before he would avenge some fancied insult by touching a match to Mr. Gray's cotton?

During the next few days Rodney did not do much overseer's work on his plantation, and neither did Ned Griffin. To quote from the latter they became first-class all-around loafers ; and so anxious were they to miss no item of news which might have come down from Vicksburg that they visited every man in the neighborhood who was known to have made a recent trip to Baton Rouge or have a late paper in his possession, and the information they picked up during their rides was far from encouraging. There was a heavy force of men at work upon the sunken iron-clad, as well as upon the *Webb*, which had been seriously injured during her fight with the *Indianola*, and when the latter was raised and the other fully repaired, the control of the river below Vicksburg would be fairly within the grasp of the Confederates. If Porter sent a few more boats below the batteries to be captured, the rebels would soon have a powerful and almost irresistible fleet; but in this hope they were destined to be disappointed, as they had been in many others.

It so happened that the next boat to pass under the iron hail of Vicksburg's guns was very different from the *Indianola*. The papers described her as a " turreted monster—

the most formidable thing in the shape of an iron-clad that had ever been seen in the Western waters." It was just daylight when the Confederate gunners discovered her moving slowly down with the current, and the fire that was poured upon her by almost eighteen miles of batteries ought, by rights, to have sunk anything in the form of a gunboat that ever floated; but the monster, with the heavy black smoke rolling from her chimneys, passed safely on through the whole of it without firing a single gun in reply, and disappeared from view. Then there was excitement in Vicksburg and in Richmond too, for the news went to the capital as quickly as the telegraph could take it. The *Queen of the West*, which now floated the Confederate flag and had come up to Warrenton to see how her friends were getting on, turned and took to her heels, and orders were sent down the river to have the *Indianola* blown up without delay, so that she might not be recaptured by this new enemy. The order was obeyed, and the powerful iron-clad which might have given a better account of herself in rebel hands than she did while in possession of her lawful owners, was once more sent to the bottom.

Meanwhile the turreted monster held silently on her way, moving as rapidly as a five-mile current could take her, and at last grounded on a sand-bar. Not till then did the rebels awake to the fact that they had been deceived. When they found courage enough to go aboard of her they saw, to their amazement and chagrin, that she was not a gunboat at all, but a coal-barge that had been fitted up to represent one. She had been set afloat for the purpose of bringing out the whole fire of the batteries, so that Admiral Porter and General Grant, who had decided to effect a lodgement below the city, might know just how severe would be the cannonade that their vessels would be subjected to. Of course the Confederates were angry over the loss of the *Indianola*, but the soldiers of Grant's army, who had thronged the bank on the Louisiana side and shouted and laughed to see the fun, looked upon the whole affair as the best kind of a joke. In speaking of it in his report Admiral Porter said: "An old coal-barge picked up in the river was the foundation we had to build on. The casemates were made of old boards in twelve hours, with empty pork-barrels on top of each other for smoke-stacks and two old canoes for quarter-boats. Her furnaces were built of mud, and were only intended to make black smoke instead of steam." This was the contrivance which frightened the rebels into destroying the finest gunboat that ever fell into their hands, and which is known to history as "Porter's dummy." The enemy's chances for getting control of the river were farther off than before, and Rodney said he would surely see the day when his cousin's trading boat would be making regular trips up and down the Mississippi.

"But do you suppose the rebels will throw no obstacles in your way?" demanded Ned Griffin. "Do you imagine that they will let you run off cotton at your pleasure? When Vicksburg and Port Hudson fall the river will be lined with guerillas, and some day they will burn your trading boat."

Taken in connection with what happened

afterward these words of Ned's seemed almost prophetic.

Having become satisfied that the rebels were not going to build up a navy in the river as they fondly hoped to do, Rodney began to think more about his absent cousin and the letters he had promised to write. The first one that came through the hands of the provost marshal was mailed at New Orleans and did not contain a word that was encouraging. Captain Frazier's agent could not put a boat on the river just now for three reasons: He couldn't get a permit, it wouldn't be a safe venture at this stage of the game, and he had as much cotton on hand already as he could attend to.

"That hope is knocked in the head," said Rodney.

"It is no more than I expected," replied Mr. Gray, after he had read the letter. "Saving that cotton is going to be the hardest task you ever set for yourself. Others have been ruined by this terrible and utterly useless war, and why should we think to escape? Let us keep our many blessings constantly in mind, and spend less time in worrying over the troubles that may come upon us in the future. None of our family have been killed or sent to prison, and isn't that something to be thankful for?"

And Mr. Gray might have added that another thing to be grateful for was the fact that the family had not become bitter enemies, as was the case with some whose members had fought under the opposing flags. Jack and Marcy were strong for the Union, and Rodney had been the hottest kind of a rebel; but that made no sort of change in the affectionate regard they had always cherished for one another. Some Union men bushwhacked their rebel neighbors, and some Confederate guerillas relentlessly persecuted their Union relatives; but there was no such feeling in the family whose boys have been the heroes of this series of books. Consequently, when the next letter came from Jack, written at his home in far-away North Carolina, and containing the startling intelligence that Marcy Gray had been forced into the rebel army in spite of all his efforts to keep out of it, Rod-

ney was as angry a boy as you ever saw, while
his father and mother could hardly have
expressed more sorrow if they had heard that
Marcy had been killed. The paragraph in
Jack's letter which contained the bad news
read as follows:

"I almost wish I hadn't been so anxious to
see home and friends once more, for no news
at all is better than the crushing words mother
said to me as soon as I got into the house. I
wished I had stayed in the service; and if I
ever go back you may rest assured that I shall
fight harder than I did before to put down
this rebellion. Poor Marcy wasn't here to
welcome me. He was surprised and captured
in mother's presence, thrust into the common
jail at Williamston, and finally shipped south
with a lot of other conscripts, to act as guard
at that horrible prison-pen at Millen, Ga.
For months Marcy had been a refugee, living
in the swamp with a few other Union men and
boys who hid there to escape being forced into
the army, and until a few weeks ago he beat
Beardsley, Shelby, Dillon, and the rest at

every job they tried to put up on him; but he was caught napping at last, and I never expect to see or hear of him again. Mother is almost broken-hearted, but being a woman she bears up under it better than I do. But hasn't there been a time here since Marcy was dragged away! The work was done by strange soldiers, but Marcy's friends knew who was to blame for it, and took vengeance immediately. The three men whose names I have mentioned were burned out so completely that they didn't have even a nigger cabin to go into, and two pestiferous little snipes, Tom Allison and Mark Goodwin by name, whose tongues have kept the settlement in a constant turmoil, were bushwhacked.

"I will write you fuller particulars after a while, but just now I am rather 'shuck up.' Of course this upsets all my plans; my place is at home with mother. I inclose Captain Frazier's card, to which I have appended his New Orleans address. I told him all about your cotton, and he and the agent will be only too glad to help you get it to market as soon as they think it safe to make the attempt.

You can trust them, but be sure and hold out for twenty-five cents, greenback money. Captain Frazier promised me he would give it."

The rest of the page was filled with loving messages from Marcy's sorrowing mother, and at the bottom was a hasty scrawl that stood for Sailor Jack's name.

Mr. Gray brought this letter from Baton Rouge, and finding Rodney at home with his mother, gave it to him to read aloud. The boy's voice became husky before he read half a dozen lines, and Mrs. Gray's eyes were filled with tears. When it was finished Rodney handed it back to his father with the remark:

"I am a good deal of Jack's opinion that we shall never see or hear of Marcy again. I know by experience that the petty tyrants we call officers make the service so hard that a volunteer can scarcely stand it, and how much mercy do you think they will have on a conscript? They would as soon kill him as to look at him. No better fellow than Marcy ever lived, and to think that I—I deserve killing myself."

Rodney arose hastily from his chair, staggered up to the room he still called his own,
threw himself upon the bed and buried his
tear-stained face in his hands. He had not
forgotten, he never would forget, that episode
at the Barrington Military Academy in which
Bud Goble and his minute-men bore prominent parts. Marcy had freely forgiven him
for what he did to bring it about, but it was
always fresh in Rodney's mind. How terribly
the memory of it tortured him now !

CHAPTER IX.

RODNEY GRAY had promised himself no end of pleasurable excitement when his sailor cousin returned to take command of a trading boat on the river, for he had made up his mind that he would accompany Jack wherever he went. He was as well satisfied as Ned Griffin was that the fall of Vicksburg and Port Hudson would be the signal for instant and increased activity among the guerillas who infested the country as far up as New Madrid, and that picking up cotton along the river with an unarmed boat would be a hazardous undertaking.

The Mississippi is the most tortuous of rivers, and there is none in the world better adapted to guerilla warfare. Frequently the distance a steamer has to traverse in going around a bend is from twelve to thirty times greater than it is in a direct line across the

country. The great bend at Napoleon is a
notable example. A steamboat has to run
fifteen miles to get around it, while the neck
of land that makes the bend is but a mile
wide. This was a famous guerilla station
during the war until Commander Selfridge
cut a ditch across the neck and turned the
Mississippi into a new channel. A band of
guerillas, with a howitzer or two mounted in
wagons, would fire into a transport at the
upper end of the bend (they seldom troubled
armed steamers), and failing to sink or disable
her there, would travel leisurely across the
country and be ready to try it again when the
steamboat arrived at the lower end. What
made this sort of warfare particularly exasperating was the fact that the guerillas did
not live along the river, but came from remote
points, fifty or a hundred miles back in the
country. If a gunboat hove in sight they
would take to their heels ; and if the gunboat
landed a company or two of small-arm men
and burned the nearest dwellings, as all gunboats were ordered to do in cases like the one
we are supposing, the chances were that they

punished people who were no more to blame
for what the guerillas did than you or your
chum.

The majority of the men who carried on this
style of fighting were worthless fellows, like
Lambert and Moseley, who had everything to
make and nothing to lose by it; and we may
anticipate events a little by saying that they
came to look upon trading boats as their legiti-
mate prey. If there was a fortune for the man
who was lucky enough to get a permit to trade
in cotton, there was also plenty of danger for
him. Rodney would have entered upon this
adventurous life with the same enthusiasm he
exhibited when he set out for the North to aid
in "driving the Yankees out of Missouri,"
but there was little prospect that he would
ever see any of it now that Jack had decided
to remain at home with his mother. To do
him justice he did not mourn over his disappointment, or the possible loss of his father's
cotton, as he did over the dire misfortune that
had befallen his cousin Marcy.

"I wish I stood in his shoes this minute,
and that he stood in mine," Rodney said to

his mother more than once. "I could stand the hard knocks he is likely to receive, but Marcy can't."

Remembering that Jack had promised to send "fuller particulars" when he felt more in the humor for writing, Rodney spent more time in riding to and from the provost marshal's office than he did in managing his plantation, but that official had received no letters for him. In the meantime the situation at Vicksburg grew more encouraging every day. Severe battles had been fought and the soldiers of the Union, always victorious, had gained a footing below Vicksburg where there was no water to interfere with their movements, as there was in the inundated Yazoo country, and Colonel Grierson, at the head of seventeen hundred cavalry, was raiding through the State in the direction of Baton Rouge, stealing nothing but fresh horses and food for his men, but thrashing the rebels whenever he met them (except on one occasion when he lost seven hundred men in a single engagement), cutting railroads and telegraph lines in every direction, and destroying commissary trains

15

and depots by the score. It was this famous raid which first "demonstrated that the Confederacy was but a shell, strong on the outside by reason of its organized armies, but hollow within and destitute of resources to sustain, or of strength to recruit these armies."

"They say he's coming sure enough," remarked Ned Griffin one day, "although in some places he has had to ride over wide stretches of country where the water stood six feet deep on a level. That's pluck. What are you going to do with our exemption bacon?"

"And our horses," added Rodney. "If the Yanks are hungry when they reach this plantation, they can take the exemption bacon and welcome. I'd much rather they should have it than it should go to feed rebels. But our horses they can't have; or at least they'll have to hunt for them before they get them. Where is Grierson now?"

"They've got the report in Mooreville that he was last heard from up about Port Hudson," replied Ned.

"Then we've no time to lose," said Rodney. "His scouts, of course, are a long way ahead of him, and may be here any hour. Let's take care of the horses the first thing we do. There's nothing else on your place or mine worth stealing, unless it is the bacon."

The boys were none too soon in looking out for their riding nags, for the expected scouts arrived the next morning about breakfast time, and although Rodney had seen some dusty, dirty, and ragged soldiers in his day, he told himself that these rough-riding Yankees, who threw down his bars and rode into the yard as though they had a perfect right there, would bear off the palm. They were a jovial, good-natured lot, however, and well they might be ; for their long raid from La Grange, Tenn., was nearly finished. Another night would see them safely quartered among their friends in Baton Rouge.

"Hallo, Johnny," was the way in which the foremost soldier greeted Rodney, who advanced to meet the raiders. "Where's your well or spring or whatever it is you get drinking water from ? Any graybacks around here ? Trot out your guns and things of that sort, and save us the trouble of looking for them."

"The well is around there," replied Rodney, jerking his thumb over his shoulder. "And there's nothing in the house more dangerous than a case-knife. If you don't believe it, look and see."

This invitation was quite superfluous, for some of the raiders, who had ridden around to the well and dismounted, were in the house almost before Rodney ceased speaking. He heard their heavy footsteps in the hall in which his black housekeeper had just finished laying the breakfast, and when he turned about they had cleared the table of the victuals they found on it, and one was in the act of draining the coffee-pot.

"Where are all your horses, Johnny?" asked the latter, as he put down his empty cup. "Mine's played out, and I must have another."

"You'll not find him on this plantation," was the reply. "General Breckenridge's men passed through here not long ago, and that means that there are few horses in the country. If yours has given out you will have to take a mule or walk."

"How does it come that you are not in the army?" inquired another, with his mouth full of bacon and corn pone.

"I've been there, but you Yanks whipped me so bad I was glad to get home."

By this time the lieutenant in command of the troopers had made himself known, and to him Rodney presented his papers, which included his discharge, standing pass from the provost marshal, and his permit to trade within the Union lines. As he handed the papers to the officer his attention was drawn to two persons near him, who were by far the most dilapidated specimens of humanity Rodney had ever seen. Every line of their faces was indicative of exposure and suffering, and their clothing, what little they wore, looked as though it might fall in pieces at any moment. They were plainly fit candidates for the hospital, and it was a mystery to Rodney how they managed to keep the heavy infantry muskets which rested across their saddles from slipping out of their grasp. By the time he made these observations the lieutenant had read the first line of the pass, which happened to be the first paper he opened, and when he saw the name it bore he looked at one of the dilapidated specimens of whom we have spoken and said, with a grin :

"If you have been telling a straight story, Johnny, how does it come that you don't recognize your cousin when you see him standing before your face and eyes?"

Rodney Gray was utterly confounded. He looked at the officer and then at the person to whom the words were addressed, but he could not speak until he heard the reply given in a familiar voice :

"I have told you nothing but the truth, sir, and if that is Rodney Gray he will bear me out in everything I have said."

The sick and exhausted stranger reeled about on his mule for an instant, his musket fell to the ground, and he would have followed headlong if Rodney had not sprung forward and received him in his arms. He eased him tenderly to the ground, supported his head on one knee, and looked up at the lieutenant.

"Who is it?" he asked in a husky voice.

"He says his name is Marcy Gray, that he lives in North Carolina, and is an escaped conscript," was the answer. "That's all I know about him. Captain Forbes picked him and his partner up somewhere about Enterprise, and they've been with us ever since."

Rodney took one more glance at the white face on his knee, and then raised the limp, almost lifeless form in his arms, carried it into the house, and laid it on his own bed.

"I said you could never stand the hard knocks that would be given to a conscript, and I reckon you've found it out, haven't you?" were the first words he spoke.

But Marcy—Rodney began to believe now that it was really his cousin Marcy who had come to him in this strange way, though he never would have suspected it if the officer had not told him so—did not even whisper a reply. He never moved a finger, but lay motionless where Rodney had placed him. He was so still, his face was so white, and his faint breath came at so long intervals that Rodney feared he was already past such help as he could give him ; and it was not until half a bucket of water had been dashed into his face, a cupful at a time, that he began showing any signs of life. Then he put his arms around his cousin's neck and drew the latter's tanned face close to his own white one; but it was very little strength he could put into the embrace.

"O Rodney, I am so tired," he said, in a scarcely audible whisper.

"It's a wonder you are not dead," replied his cousin in a choking voice. "I never thought to see you again, but you are all right now. Every Yank in this country is my friend."

"Then look out for Charley, and don't let them hurt him," whispered Marcy, for he was too weak to talk. "They haven't been very civil to us, for they think we are spies sent out to draw them into ambush."

"You look like it, I must say," exclaimed Rodney. "But who is Charley?"

"Charley Bowen, my partner; the man who escaped when I did, and who has stuck to me like a brother through it all. He knows the country, and if it hadn't been for him I wouldn't have got ten miles from the stockade.

Give me a big drink of water, and then go out and say a good word for him. Bring him in if they will let you."

After Marcy had drained the cup that was held to his lips Rodney hastened out to see what he could do for Charley, and to secure his papers, which were worth more than their weight in gold to him. He found them on the gallery where the lieutenant had left them, and the lieutenant himself was in the back yard looking on while one of the soldiers shifted his saddle from his broken-down beast to the back of one of Rodney's plough-mules, all of which had been brought in from the field.

"A fair exchange is no robbery, Johnny," said the officer, as Rodney approached him. "And besides, you get the butt end of this trade. My mule is bigger than yours, and will be better and stronger after he has had a rest and a chance to fill out."

"What are you going to do with those conscripts?" inquired Rodney.

"I haven't orders to do anything with them," answered the lieutenant. "But of course I am expected to take them to Baton

Rouge and turn them over to the provost marshal."

"Why can't you leave them here with me? I will look out for them."

"And you a discharged rebel? You're a cool one, Johnny."

"But that boy in the house is my cousin, and as strong for the Union as you or any man in your squad. Besides, he is ill and can't go any farther, and he wants his partner to stay with him. If the provost marshal doesn't tell you that I am all right with the authorities in Baton Rouge, you can come back here and get him."

"You are very kind; but we are not making any excursions into the country just for the fun of the thing. We have ridden far enough already. What's the matter out there, Allen?"

"Big dust up the road, sir," replied the soldier who had been left at the bars. "Coming fast too, sir."

"Boots and saddles!" exclaimed the lieutenant, throwing himself on the back of Rodney's plough-mule. "Sergeant, form skirmish-line among the trees to the right of the house."

"You're taking trouble for nothing," said Rodney. "There are no rebs about here. That's a Yankee scouting party from Baton Rouge."

The lieutenant didn't know whether it was or not, and so, like a good soldier, he made ready to fight, and to send word to his superior in the rear if he found himself confronted by a force of the enemy too strong for him to withstand. He kept his eye on the sentry, who had faced his horse toward the bars in readiness to dash through them and join his comrades if the rapidly approaching squad proved to be rebels, but he did not retreat, nor did he discharge his carbine, which he held at "arms port." He stuck to his post until the foremost of the squad rode into view around a turn in the road and then called out:

"Who comes there?"

Rodney did not hear the reply, and the challenged parties were concealed from his sight by trees and bushes; but he knew they were

Federal troopers when he heard the sentry continue :

"Halt! Dismount! Advance one friend and give an account of yourself." Then he waved his hand toward the house as a signal for some officer to come out and receive the report.

The lieutenant answered the signal and Rodney went with him; and when he reached the bars whom should he see standing in the road talking to the sentry but the corporal of the —th Michigan cavalry, who seemed to have a way of turning up most opportunely. He shook hands with Rodney, and told the lieutenant that he had been sent out with a few men to see if he could learn anything about Colonel Grierson, who ought to have been safe in Baton Rouge two or three days ago.

"Judging by their looks, and the way they eat and trade mules, these are some of Grierson's men," said Rodney.

The lieutenant corroborated the statement, and said that the reason they had been so long delayed was because they were obliged to pass through miles of bottom land where the water was almost swimming deep. The colonel was but a short distance in the rear, and might be expected to come along any moment. Then he plied the corporal with questions as to what Grant and Porter were doing at Vicksburg, and it was not until his patience was well-nigh exhausted that Rodney saw opportunity to say a word for himself. The instant there was a pause in the conversation he broke in with :

"Now, corporal, be kind enough to tell the lieutenant how I stand with the provost marshal."

"All right in every spot and place," replied the soldier quickly. "What's the matter? Have these raiders been stealing something?"

"Oh, I don't mind the little grub they ate, or the mules they took in exchange for their crow-baits," answered Rodney. "They're welcome to everything on the place if they will only leave my cousin with me. Is my word good when I say that I will be responsible for his safe keeping?"

"Your word is always good," said the corporal, who was much astonished. "But how came your cousin back here? I thought he went to New Orleans to ship on a cotton boat."

"But this is another one—his brother Marcy, who came here with these Yanks. They'll kill him if they try to take him any farther, and I want him left here with me. His partner, too."

"Well, if this isn't a little ahead of anything I ever heard of I wouldn't say so," exclaimed the corporal. "Where did you pick him up, lieutenant?"

The latter explained briefly, as we shall do presently, adding that he didn't think he had any right to grant Rodney's request.

"I didn't really suppose you had, sir," said the corporal. "But I was going to make a suggestion. I will ride on until I meet the colonel—that is what my orders oblige me to do—and when I see a chance I'll say—have you got any grub in the house?"

"Plenty of it, such as it is," answered Rodney.

"It's good enough for a hungry soldier, I'll be bound. Tell your housekeeper to dish up enough for the colonel and three or four of his staff, and I'll ride on and ask him if he's hungry. He can't well help it after such a raid as he has made, and then I'll tell him that I know where he can get a good breakfast and bring him right here to your house. After he has eaten his fill he'll be goodnatured, and then you and I will talk to him about your cousin."

The lieutenant laughed heartily as he listened to this programme. "It's a very ingenious arrangement, corporal," said he, as the non-commissioned officer beckoned to his men, who were still waiting at the place where they had been halted by the sentry. "And I think it ought to succeed. But as I can't wait for the colonel without disobeying my orders, which are to scout on ahead, what shall I do with the conscripts?"

"Leave a guard with them," suggested Rodney.

"I suppose I might do that, and since the colonel is a volunteer like myself, I'll risk it. If he were a regular I wouldn't think of it for a moment."

"Another cousin!" muttered the corporal, as he swung himself into his saddle. "How many more of your family are going to fall down on you out of the clouds? It's the strangest thing I ever heard of."

"And you'll never hear the like again," answered Rodney. "But I do not look for any more. Two cousins are all I have."

The corporal laughed and rode on up the road to meet the expected raiders, and the lieutenant told his sergeant to call in the men who were still holding their positions on the skirmish-line which had been formed when that warning dust was seen rising above the tree-tops. He told Charley Bowen that he could remain behind to receive orders from Colonel Grierson when he arrived, and detailed two troopers to keep watch on him and Marcy Gray.

"This isn't at all regular; I ought to take those conscripts to Baton Rouge, and I am soldier enough to know it," said the lieutenant, addressing himself to Rodney. "But you seem to be all right with that corporal, and if you and he can make it all right with

Colonel Grierson I shall be glad of it. I have heard your cousin's story and should be glad to listen to the additions I know you can make to it, but haven't time just now."

"It confirms one's faith in human nature to meet a kind-hearted soldier now and then," said Rodney, who knew that the lieutenant could have compelled the conscripts to go on with him if he had been so disposed. "I am very grateful to you, and will do you a good turn if I get half a chance. Whenever you scout through this country drop in and have a bowl of milk. I can't offer you any to-day, for your men have made away with all I had. Good-by. This is what I get by befriending escaped prisoners," he added mentally, as he started on a run for the house. "If I hadn't taken so much trouble to help that corporal where would Marcy be now?"

As it was, he was lying at his ease on Rodney's bed instead of riding along the dusty road toward Baton Rouge, reeling in his seat from very weakness. Charley Bowen sat close by holding his hand, and the two troopers who had been detailed to guard them

16

were lounging on the gallery just outside the window. The hand that rested in Bowen's palm was not white like its owner's face, but very much swollen and discolored, and Rodney noticed it at once.

"What's the matter?" he inquired. "How did you get hurt?"

"He was triced up by the thumbs till he fainted," replied Bowen, speaking for his comrade.

Rodney's face turned all sorts of colors.

"General Lee himself couldn't make me believe that the punishment was deserved," said he through his teeth. "That boy drilled alongside of me for almost four years at the Barrington Military Academy, and a better soldier never shouldered a musket. He knows more than the man who triced him up. What was it done for?"

"Because Marcy didn't shoot a Yankee prisoner whose hand was inside the dead-line," replied Bowen.

"And his hand wasn't inside the dead-line," said Marcy in a faint voice. "It was under the rail which marked the line, and the poor fellow was trying to get hold of an old tin cup that someone had thrown there, so that he could dig a hole in the ground to pro-tect him from the weather. If I had been a volunteer and had shot that man, I would have received a month's leave of absence."

Rodney sat down on the edge of the bed and looked at the two troopers who were lean-ing half-way through the window, listening. His face showed that he could hardly believe the story even if his cousin did tell it.

"There's a man in our company who escaped from Andersonville, and he declares that such things really happened," said one of the soldiers. "Besides being starved to death our fellows are shot without any provocation at all."

"And because you wouldn't murder that Yankee' somebody triced you up by the thumbs," said Rodney in a voice that was choked with anger. "Who reported you?"

"The sentry in the next box, who saw it all," replied Marcy. "He tried to get a shot at the man himself, but the prisoner's friends closed around him and hustled him out of sight; and that made the sentry so angry that he reported me before we were relieved from post."

"How can the rebels hope to win in this war when they torture their own men for not committing murder?" exclaimed Rodney hotly.

"Why, I thought you were a rebel," said one of the soldiers at the window.

"So I was," answered Rodney honestly. "But, as I have said a hundred times before, I know when I have had enough. When I was whipped I quit."

Both the troopers extended their hands, and after Rodney had shaken them cordially he walked over and shook hands with Charley Bowen, and tried to thank him for what he had done for Marcy; but his voice grew husky and finally broke, and so he gave it up as a task beyond his powers.

"I am a Georgia cracker," said Bowen, "and the boys used to call me 'goober-grabbler'; but I know a good fellow when I see him, and I don't want any thanks for doing for your cousin what I am sure he would have done for me if he had known the country as well as I do. He assured me that we could find friends if I would guide him to Baton Rouge, and I was doing the best I could at it when we fell in with Captain Forbes."

"I know I should never have seen Marcy again if it hadn't been for you, because he told me so, and you are more than welcome to a share in everything the war has left us. Now I must tear myself away for a few minutes, for I have work to do. Don't let Marcy talk; he is too weak."

So saying Rodney hastened from the room to order Colonel Grierson's breakfast, and to write a short note to his mother, requesting that the only doctor in the country for miles around who had been able to keep out of the army might be sent to his plantation as soon as he could be found, to prescribe for Marcy Gray, who had come to him in a most remarkable manner. He didn't stop to explain how, for he hadn't time; but he made his mother understand that Marcy was in need of prompt medical attention. Rodney knew that his father would at once answer the note in person, and when he arrived he could tell him as much of his cousin's story as he knew himself.

The note was sent off by one of the negroes, who was quickly summoned from the field to take it; and after Rodney had satisfied himself that the colonel's breakfast was coming on as well as he could desire, and had given instructions regarding a second meal that was to be made ready for the conscripts and their guards, he went back to Marcy.

CHAPTER X.

MATTERS could not have worked more to Rodney Gray's satisfaction if he had had the planning of them himself. The hasty note he wrote to his mother brought Mr. Gray to the plantation within an hour, and with him came the doctor, who, for a wonder, was found at home by the messenger whom Mrs. Gray had despatched to bring him. He lanced Marcy's hands, which had not received the least medical attention since the day they were wounded by the cruel cord that held him suspended in the air so that his toes barely touched the ground, bandaged them in good shape, and gave him some medicine ; and all the time Mr. Gray stood in an adjoining room listening, while his eyes grew moist, to Rodney's hurried description of the events of the morning. Before he had time to ask many questions the bars rattled again, and the hounds gave tongue as Colonel Grierson and two or three of his officers rode into the yard. His weary, travel-stained soldiers were close behind, but the most of them kept on down the road, while only a small body-guard remained to watch over the safety of the commanding officer. Rodney's friend the corporal came into the yard with the colonel, and winked and nodded in a way that was very encouraging. Rodney stood on the veranda and saluted, while the two troopers seized their carbines and presented arms.

"Come right in, sir," said the boy. "I have been waiting for you."

"Thank you. The corporal promised us a breakfast if we would stop here, and so we thought it advisable to stop. I hope you'll not object if we sit down just as we are," said the colonel, who was as dirty and ragged as any of his men, "for we have scant time to stand on ceremony. Are these the guards that were left with the conscripts? Forbes, step in and see if they are the ones you picked up at Enterprise."

Forbes was the captain who had been sent with a squad of thirty-five men to perform the perilous duty of cutting the telegraph-wires north of Macon, and the gallant and daring exploit by which he saved his small force from falling into the clutches of three thousand rebels we have yet to describe. He recognized Marcy and his friend Bowen as the conscripts who had surrendered themselves to him at Enterprise, shook hands with one, patted the other on the head and said he guessed it was all right, and that they could remain with Rodney as long as they pleased.

"There," said the doctor. "Those words will do the patient more good than all the medicine I could give him. Homesickness is what troubles him more than anything else, but now that he is safe among his relatives he will soon get over that."

Captain Forbes replied that he hoped so, and went out to join the colonel at the table, while Rodney made haste to serve up the breakfast that had been prepared for the two conscripts and their guards. Of course the corporal was not forgotten, and he said he had been living

on army bacon and hard-tack just long enough
to give him a sharp appetite for the chicken
and corn bread with which his plate was filled.
When Rodney went into the hall to see if his
other guests were well served, Captain Forbes
cheered his heart by remarking that, as the
conscripts were not prisoners, they were at
liberty to do as they pleased about going or
staying.

In twenty minutes more the colonel had
galloped away with his body-guard, the plantation house was quiet, Marcy was sleeping
the sleep of exhaustion, and Charley Bowen
was sitting on the porch with Mr. Gray and
Rodney, who listened with deep interest while
he told of the adventures that had befallen
him and his partner since they took leave of
the stockade at Millen, which was as much of
a prison to the conscript guards as it was to the
unhappy Union soldiers who were confined on
the inside. Their food was of rather better
quality, and they had more of it; but that was
about all the difference there was between
them. Bowen's short narrative prepared them
to hear something interesting when Marcy

awoke; but that did not happen for eighteen hours, and during that time the doctor made a second visit and Mr. Gray went home and brought his wife, who shed tears abundantly when she saw the thin, wan face on the pillow. But his long refreshing sleep and the knowledge that he was among friends, and that the dreaded stockade with all its harrowing associations was miles away, never to come before him again except in his dreams, did wonders for Marcy Gray. When he awoke his eye was as bright as ever, and the strong voice in which he called out: "If there is a good Samaritan in this house I wish he would bring me a drink of water," was delightful to hear. Rodney, who had just arisen from the lounge on which he had passed the night in an adjoining room, lost no time in bringing the water, and his cousin's hearty greeting reminded him of the good old days at Barrington before the war came with its attendant horrors, and set the boys of the family to fighting under different flags.

"The only thing I have had enough of since I left home is water," said Marcy; and Rod-

ney was glad to see that he was strong enough
to sit up in bed and hold the cup with his own
hand. "This isn't all a dream, is it? If it is,
I hope I shall never wake up."

"It is not a dream," Rodney assured him.
"Look at your hands. Do you dream that it
hurts you to move them? And do you dream
that you see your aunt?" he added, making
way for Mrs. Gray, who at that moment came
into the room and bent over the couch.

Another good sign was that Marcy awoke
hungry. He did not say so, for it was too early
in the morning for breakfast and Marcy never
made trouble if he could help it; but Rodney
suspected it, and in a few minutes the banging
of stove-lids bore testimony that he was busy
in the kitchen, where he was soon joined by
Charley Bowen, who said he was the best cook
in Georgia. The latter had been given a room
to himself, but finding the shuck mattress too
soft and warm for comfort, he went out on the
gallery during the night and slept there, with
Rodney's hounds for company. While these
two worked in the kitchen, Mrs. Gray sat by
Marcy's bedside and told him of Sailor Jack's

visit, and of the letters that had since been received from him, so he could understand that, although his sudden appearance was a great surprise to his friends, it was not quite as bewildering as it would have been had they not been aware that he was doing guard duty at Millen. She was going on to tell of Jack's plans, which had been upset by Marcy's arrest, when Rodney, who stood in the door listening, broke in with :

"What will you put up against my roll of Confederate scrip that we don't see Jack in this country again in less than a month? I wrote him yesterday, and it was a letter that will bring him as quickly as he can come ; that is, if he thinks it safe to leave his mother. And, Marcy, you'll have to stay, for you can't go back among those rebels without running the risk of being dragged off again ; and I know what I am talking about when I say that in our army desertion means death."

"What sort of a fellow are you to talk about 'rebels' and 'our army' in the same breath?" demanded Marcy.

"I am as strong for the Union as General

Grant, and wish I could do as much for it as he is doing to-day," replied Rodney earnestly. "You never expected to hear me utter such sentiments, did you? Well, I am honest. I want peace, and so does everybody except Jeff Davis and a few others high in authority. I'll bring Jack here if I can, and then we'll become traders, all of us. We want to save what we can from the wreck."

By the time breakfast was served and eaten, and the conscripts had exchanged their rags for whole suits of clothing, Mr. Gray and Ned Griffin came to swell their number, and to hear Marcy tell how he and his comrade managed to escape from Millen and to elude their pursuers afterward. Marcy protested that he wasn't going to lie abed when there was no need of it, so he was propped up with pillows in the biggest rocking-chair the house afforded, and pulled out to the porch, where the family assembled to listen to his story, which ran about as follows:

When we took leave of Marcy Gray to resume the history of his cousin Rodney's adventures and exploits, he was a refugee from home and living in the woods in company with a small party of men and boys who had fled there to avoid the enrolling officers, as well as to escape persecution at the hands of their rebel neighbors. By a bold piece of strategy Marcy had relieved his mother of the presence of her overseer, Hanson by name, who had managed to keep her in constant trouble and anxiety ever since the first gun was fired from Sumter. Hanson made it his business to keep informed on all matters that related to the private life of the occupants of the great house; in fact it was suspected that Beardsley, Shelby, and some other wealthy rebels paid him to do it. It was rumored that Mrs. Gray had a large sum of money hidden somewhere about her premises, and if that was a fact, these enemies, who were all the while working against her in secret, desired above all things to know it. They wanted the money themselves if it could be found, and even went so far as to bring four ruffians from a distant point to break into the house at night and steal it. If they failed to line their own pockets, it was their intention to induce the

Richmond authorities to interest themselves in the matter. A law enacted by the Confederate Congress at the breaking out of the war provided that all debts owing to Northern men should be repudiated, and the amount of those debts turned into the Confederate treasury. Marcy often declared that his mother did not owe anybody a red cent; but it would have been easy for such men as Beardsley and Shelby to swear that she did, and that, instead of complying with the law, she was hoarding the money for her own use. If this could be proved against her, Mrs. Gray would have to surrender her gold or go to jail; but somehow Marcy was always in the way whenever her secret enemies tried to collect evidence against her. Being always on his guard he never could be made to acknowledge that there was a dollar in or around the great house, and Beardsley undertook to remove him so that he and his fellow-conspirators could have a clear field for their operations; and he did it by taking Marcy to sea with him as pilot on his privateer and blockade runner.

But for a long time nothing worked to Beardsley's satisfaction. His fine dwelling was burned while he was at sea, and the Federal cruisers drove his blockade runner into port and kept her there until Marcy set fire to her as she lay at her moorings. This he did on the night he left home to join the refugees in the swamp. He had a narrow escape that night, and would certainly have been packed off to Williamston jail before morning if it had not been for the black boy Julius, who loyally risked his own life to give Marcy warning. Beardsley and Shelby were finally "gobbled up" by Union cavalry and taken to Plymouth, which had been captured by some of Goldsborough's gunboats and garrisoned by the army; but, unfortunately for Marcy, they did not remain prisoners for any length of time. If Beardsley had any luck at all it showed itself in the easy way he had of slipping through the hands of the Yankees. He was captured by Captain Benton, who commanded the vessel on which Marcy did duty as pilot during the battles of Roanoke Island, and in the end was turned

17

over to General Burnside, who made the mistake of parolling him with the captured garrison. That was the plea that Beardsley set up when he and his companions, of whom there were about a dozen, were taken into the presence of the Federal commander at Plymouth.

"I've been parolled," said he, "me and all the fellers you see with me. We promised, honor bright, that we wouldn't never take up arms agin the United States, and we've kept that promise. So what makes you snatch us away from our peaceful homes and firesides, and bring us here to shut us up, when we aint never done the least thing?"

"But all the same you belong to the Home Guards who were organized for the purpose of persecuting Union people," said the colonel.

"Never heered of no Home Guards," replied Beardsley, looking astonished. "There aint no such things in our country, is there, boys?"

Of course Beardsley's companions bore willing testimony to the truth of the statement, and when he and Shelby boldly declared that they would prove their sincerity by taking the oath then and there, if the colonel would ad-

minister it to them, it settled the matter so far
as they were concerned. Their companions
were willing to follow their example rather
than suffer themselves to be sent to a Northern
prison, and the result was that in less than
forty-eight hours after Marcy Gray received
the gratifying intelligence that he had seen
the last of Beardsley and Shelby, for a while
at least, they were at home again and eager to
take vengeance on the boy whom they blamed
more than anyone else for their short cap-
tivity.

"How did the Yankees get onto our trail so
easy, and know all about that Home Guard
business, if Marcy Gray didn't tell 'em?" said
Beardsley, when he and his friends found themselves safe outside the trenches at Plymouth
and well on their way homeward. "When
Marcy made a pris'ner of his mother's overseer and took him among the Yankees he give
'em our names, told 'em where we lived and
all about it; and I say he shan't stay in the
settlement no longer. I'll land him in Williamston jail before I am two days older; and
when he gets there he won't come back in

a hurry. I'll see if I can't have him sent to
some regiment down on the Gulf coast; then,
if he runs away, as he is likely to do the first
chance he sees, he can't get home."

"Be you goin' to keep that oath, cap'n?"
inquired one of Beardsley's companions.

"Listen at the fule! Course I'm going to
keep it. I didn't promise nothin' but that I
wouldn't never bear arms agin the Yankee
government, nor lend aid and comfort to its
enemies, without any mental observation, did
I? What do you reckon that means, Shelby?"

"Mental reservation," corrected Colonel
Shelby, who did not like to be addressed with
so much familiarity. "It means that you did
not swear to one thing while you were thinking about another."

"Then I took the oath honest, 'cause I
wasn't thinkin' about Marcy Gray at all while
the colonel was readin' it to me; but I am
thinkin' of him now. I didn't promise that I
wouldn't square yards with him for settin' the
Yanks onto me, and I'll perceed to do it before
I sleep sound."

Beardsley was as good as his word, or tried

to be; but it took him longer than two days
to land Marcy Gray in Williamston jail. He
laid a good many plans to capture him, but
somehow they were put into operation just too
late to be successful. And what exasperated
Beardsley and Shelby almost beyond endurance, and drove Tom Allison and Mark Goodwin almost frantic, was the fact that Marcy
did not keep himself in hiding as closely as he
used to do. He rode to Nashville whenever
he felt like it, and went in and out of the post-
office as boldly as he ever did; but he was
always accompanied by Ben Hawkins and
three or four other parolled rebels, and no one
dared lay a hand on him. Ben Hawkins, you
will remember, was the man who created something of a sensation by making a defiant
speech in the post-office shortly after he had
been released on parole by General Burnside.
He declared that he had had all the fighting
he wanted and did not intend to go back to
the army; and when that blatant young rebel
Tom Allison, who had never shouldered a
musket and did not mean to, so far forgot his
prudence as to call Hawkins a coward, the

latter flew into a rage and threatened to "twist" Tom's neck for him.

"Did Hawkins and his parolled comrades know that you served on a Union gunboat during the fight at Roanoke Island?" asked Rodney, when his cousin reached this point in his narrative.

"Of course they knew it; and they knew, too, that Jack was serving on one of the blockading fleet, but it didn't seem to make the least difference in their friendship for me. Hawkins was the man who helped me get that treacherous overseer out of mother's way, and he and the other parolled prisoners who found a home in our refugee camp had relatives in the settlement; and those relatives found means to warn us whenever a cavalry raid was expected out from Williamston."

"You must have led an exciting life," observed Rodney.

Marcy replied that he found some excitement in dodging the rebel cavalry and in listening to the sounds of the skirmishes that frequently took place between them and the Union troopers that scouted through the coun-

try from Plymouth ; but there wasn't a bit to
be seen during the weary days he passed on
the island, afraid to show his head above the
brush wind-break lest some lurking Confederate should send a bullet into it. Nor was
there any pleasure in the lonely night trips he
made to and from his mother's house whenever it came his turn to forage for his companions. Keeping the camp supplied with
provisions was a dangerous duty, and he had
to do his share of it. It was always performed under cover of the darkness, for if any
of their number had been seen carrying supplies away from a house during the daytime,
it would have been reported to the first squad
of rebel cavalry that rode through the settlement, and that house would have been burned
to the ground. To make matters worse the
refugees learned, to their great consternation
and anger, that there was an enemy among
them ; that one who ate salt with them every
day and slept under the same trees at night,
who took part in their councils, heard all the
reports, good and bad, that were brought in,
and knew the camp routine so well that he

could tell beforehand what particular refugee
would go foraging on a certain night, and
name the houses he would visit during his
absence—someone who knew all these things
was holding regular communication with enemies in the settlement, who made such good
use of the information given them by this
treacherous refugee that they brought untold
suffering to Marcy Gray and his mother, and
severe and well-merited punishment upon
themselves. In order that you may understand how it was brought about we must
describe some things that Marcy did not
include in his narrative, for the very good
reason that he knew nothing of them.

We have said that Tom Allison and his
friend and crony Mark Goodwin were angry
when they saw Marcy Gray and his body-
guard riding about the country, holding their
heads high as though they had never done
anything to be ashamed of. Tom and Mark
were together all the time, and their principal
business in life was to bring trouble to some
good Union family as often as they saw opportunity to do so without danger to themselves.

The burning of Beardsley's fine schooner had opened their eyes to the fact that Marcy and his fellow-refugees could not be trifled with, that there was a limit to their patience, and that it was the height of folly to crowd them too far.

"There's somebody in this neighborhood who ought to be driven out of it," declared Mark Goodwin, while he and Tom Allison were riding toward Nashville one morning, trying to make up their minds how and where to pass the long day before them. "Don't it beat you how Marcy and his body-guard dodge in and out of the woods when there are no Confederate soldiers around, and how close they keep themselves at all other times?"

"Marcy knows what's going on in the settlement as well as he did when he lived here," answered Tom. "He's got friends, and plenty of them."

"Everything goes to prove it," said Mark, "and those friends ought to be driven away from here."

"That's what I say; but who are they? Name a few of them."

"We'll never be able to call any of them by name until we put a spy in the camp of those refugees to keep us posted on all."

"Mark," exclaimed Tom, riding closer to his companion and laying his riding whip lightly on his shoulder, "you've hit it, and I wonder we did not think of it before. Every general sends out spies to bring him information which he could not get in any other way, and although we are not generals we are good and loyal Confederates, and what's the reason we can't do the same? Have you thought of anybody?"

"There's Kelsey, for one."

"Great Scott, man! He won't do. Beardsley, Shelby, and a few others offered Kelsey money to find out whether Marcy and his mother were Union or Confederate, and tried to have him employed on that plantation as overseer after Hanson was spirited away, so that he could find out if there was any money in the house; and Marcy knows all about it."

"There's mighty little goes on that he doesn't know about, and I can't for the life of me see how he keeps so well posted," observed Mark.

"Then Beardsley and Shelby tried to induce Kelsey to burn Mrs. Gray's house, and Marcy knows about that, too," continued Tom. "Wouldn't he be a plum dunce to let such a man as that come into camp to spy on him? Besides, Kelsey is too big a coward to undertake the job."

"And he couldn't make the refugees believe that he had turned his coat and become Union all on a sudden," assented Mark. "No, Kelsey won't do. We ought to make a bargain with somebody who is already in the camp and who is supposed to be Marcy's friend. How does Buffum strike you?"

"Have you any reason to believe that he is not Marcy's friend?"

"No; but I believe that a man who is on the make as he is would do almost anything for gain. He's no more Union than I am. He kept out of the army because he was afraid he would be killed if he went in; and besides, he knew that Beardsley's promise, to look out for the wants of his family while he was gone,

wasn't good for anything.   By taking up with.
the refugees he made sure of getting enough
to eat, but," added Mark, sinking his voice to
a whisper, "he didn't make sure of anything
else—any money, I mean."

"Whew!" whistled Tom.   "Perhaps there
is something in it.   Let's ride over and see
what Beardsley thinks about it.   You are not
afraid to trust him."

No, Mark wasn't afraid to take Captain
Beardsley or any other good Confederate into
his confidence, and showed it by turning his
horse around and putting him into a lope.
They talked earnestly as they rode, and the
conclusion they came to was that Mark had
hit upon a fine plan for punishing a boy who
had never done them the least harm, and that
the lazy, worthless Buffum was just the man
to help them carry it out successfully.   Captain Beardsley thought so too, after the scheme
had been unfolded to him.   They found him
with his coat off and a hoe in his hands working with his negroes ; but he was quite ready
to come to the fence when they intimated that
they had something to say to him in private.

Beardsley's field-hands had disappeared rapidly since the flag which they knew to be the emblem of their freedom had been given to the breeze at Plymouth, and those who remained were the aged and crippled, who were wise enough to know that they could not earn their living among strangers, and the vicious and shiftless (and Beardsley owned more of this sort of help than any other planter in the State), who were afraid that the Yankees would work them too hard. The "invaders" believed that those who wouldn't work couldn't eat, and lived up to their principles by putting some implement of labor into the hands of the contrabands as fast as they came inside the lines.

"They're a sorry lookin' lot," said Captain Beardsley, as he came up to the fence, rested his elbow on the top rail, and glanced back at his negroes, "and I am gettin' tol'able tired of the way things is goin', now I tell you. Sixty thousand dollars' wuth of niggers has slipped through my fingers sence this war was brung on us, dog-gone the luck, and that's what I get for bein' a Confedrit. If I'd been

Union like them Grays, I'd 'a' had most of my hands with me yet.''

"I have a plan for getting even with those Grays, if you've got time to listen to it," said Mark.

" I've got time to listen to anybody who will show me how to square yards with the feller who sneaked up like a thief in the night and set fire to my schooner," replied Beardsley fiercely.

"But when Marcy did that wasn't you trying to make a prisoner of him?" said Tom.

"Course I was. And I had a right to, 'cause aint he Union? If he aint, why didn't he run Captain Benton's ship aground when the fight was goin' on down there to the Island? He had chances enough."

" The Yankees would have hung him if he'd done that."

"S'pos'n they did; aint better men than Marcy Gray been hung durin' this war, I'd like to know? I wish one of our big shells had hit that gunboat 'twixt wind and water and sent her to the bottom with every soul on board;

but it didn't happen so, and Marcy was let come home to burn the only thing I had left in this wide world to make my bread and butter with. Why, boys, everything I've got that schooner made for me on the high seas—niggers, plantation, and all; and now she has been tooken from me, dog-gone the luck. How is it you're thinkin' of gettin' even with him?"

Mark Goodwin had not proceeded very far with his explanation before he became satisfied that he had hit upon something which met the captain's hearty approval, for the latter rested his bearded chin on his breast, wagged his head from side to side as he always did when he was very much pleased and wanted to laugh, and pounded the top rail with his clenched hand. He let Mark explain without interruption, and when the boy ceased speaking he backed away from the fence, rested his hands on his knees, and gave vent to a single shout of merriment.

"It 'll work; I just know it 'll work," said he, as soon as he could speak, "and you couldn't have picked out a better man for the

job than that sneak Buffum. He's beholden
to me and wants money. Go down and tell
him I want to see him directly."

Then Beardsley rested his folded arms on
the fence and fell to shaking his head again.

CHAPTER XI

BEN MAKES A FAILURE.

"BUT, captain," said Tom Allison, who was delighted by this prompt and emphatic indorsement of his friend's plan, "are you sure the thing can be done without bringing suspicion upon any of us? You have a lot of property that will burn, and so has Mark's father's and mine. Remember that. Are you positive that Buffum can be trusted, and has he courage enough to take him through?"

"Nobody aint a-going to get into no trouble if you uns do like I tell you and go and send Buffum up here to me," replied Beardsley. "Am I likely to disremember that I've got a lot of things left that will burn as easy as my dwellin' house did? and do you reckon I'd take a hand in the business if I wasn't sure it would work? Your Uncle Lon has got a little sense left yet. And I'll pertect you uns too, if you will keep still tongues into your heads

18   273

and let me do all the talkin'. You'll find
Buffum down to his house if you go right
now. I seen him pikin' that-a-way acrosst the
fields when I rode up from Nashville not
more'n two hours ago. Tell him I want to see
him directly, and then watch out. Somethin's
goin' to happen this very night."

"Who do you think will be captured first?"
asked Mark.

"Marcy Gray, of course," replied Tom.
"He must be first, or at least one of the first,
for by the time two or three foragers have been
captured on two or three different nights, the
rest of the refugees will become suspicious and
change their way of sending out foragers."

"S'pos'n they do," exclaimed Beardsley.
"Won't Buffum be right there in their camp,
to take notus of every change that is made,
and as often as he comes home can't he slip up
here and post me? Now, you hurry up and
tell Buffum I want to see him directly."

As Beardsley emphasized his words by turning away from the fence and hastening toward
the place where he had dropped his hoe, the
boys did not linger to ask any more questions,

but jumped their horses over the ditch and started in a lope for Buffum's cabin.

"I almost wish we had gone straight to Buffum's in the first place and kept away from Beardsley," said Mark as they galloped along. "It is bound to end in the breaking up of that band of refugees, and when it is done, Beardsley will claim all the honor, and perhaps declare that the plan originated in his own head."

"And he'll have to stand the brunt of it if things don't work as we hope they will," added Tom. "If he lisps it in his daughter's presence it will get all over the State in twenty-four hours, and then there'll be some hot work around here."

Half an hour's riding brought the boys to Buffum's cabin, which stood in the middle of a ten-acre field that had been planted to corn, and so rapidly did they approach it that they caught the owner in the act of dodging out of the door with a heavy shot-gun in his hands. Believing that he had been fairly surprised and was about to fall into the hands of Confederate troopers, the man's cowardly nature showed itself. He leaned his gun against the cabin and raised both hands above his head in token of surrender; but when he had taken a second look and discovered that he had been frightened without good reason, he snatched up his gun again and aimed it at Tom Allison's head.

"Halt!" he shouted. "I'll die before I will be tooken."

"Why didn't you talk that way before you saw who we were?" demanded Tom. "You can't get up a reputation for courage by any such actions. Captain Beardsley wants to see you at his house."

"What do you reckon he wants of me?" inquired the man, letting down the hammers of his gun and seating himself on the door-step. "Aint nary soldier behind you, is they?"

"We haven't seen a soldier for a week," replied Tom. "We haven't come here to get you into trouble——"

"But to put you in the way of making some money," chimed in Mark.

"Well, you couldn't have come to a man

who needs money wuss than I do," said Buffum, becoming interested. "What do you want me to do?"

"We want you to break up that camp of refugees down there in the swamp."

"Then you've come to the wrong pusson," said Buffum, shaking his head in a very decided way. "Don't you know that I'm livin' in that camp, and that I don't never come out 'ceptin' when I know there aint no rebel soldiers scoutin' around?"

"How does it happen that you know when there are no rebel scouts in the settlement?" inquired Mark. "Somebody must keep you posted."

"I've got friends, and good ones, too."

"So I supposed," continued Mark. "And you know on what nights Marcy Gray goes to his mother's house after grub, don't you? I thought so. Well, if you will let us know when he expects to go there again it will be money in your pocket."

"How much money?" asked Buffum; and his tone and manner encouraged the boys to believe that, if sufficient inducement were held

out, he might be depended on to supply the
desired information. He picked up a twig
that lay near him, and broke it in pieces with
fingers that trembled visibly.

"You can set your own price," replied
Mark. "And bear in mind that you will not
run the slightest risk. Who is going to suspect you if you take pains to remain in camp
on the night Marcy is captured? Now will
you go down and talk to Beardsley about
it?"

"You're sure you didn't see nary soldier
while you was comin' up here?" said the
man doubtfully.

"We didn't, and neither did we hear of
any. You don't want to follow the road, for
you will save time and distance by going
through the woods. You will find Beardsley
in the field north of where his house used to
stand. You'll go, won't you?"

Buffum said he would think about it, and
the boys rode away, satisfied that he would
start as soon as they were out of sight.

"So far so good, with one exception," said
Tom, as they rode out of the field into the

road. "We talked too much, and Beardsley told us particularly to keep still."

"I don't care if he did," answered Mark spitefully. "This is my plan, and if it works I want, and mean to have, the honor of it. I hope it will get to Marcy's ears, for when he is in the army I want him to know that I put him there."

"He'll know it," said Tom with a laugh. "Buffum's wife was in the cabin, and heard every word we said."

While Tom and Mark were spending their time in this congenial way, Marcy Gray and his fellow-refugees were finding what little enjoyment they could in acting as camp-keepers, or visiting their friends and relatives in the settlement. Just now there was little scouting done by either side. The Confederates at Williamston had lost about as many men as they could afford to lose in skirmishes with the Federals, who were always strong enough to drive them and to take a few prisoners besides, and had grown weary of searching for a camp of refugees which they began to believe was a myth.

"It's always stillest jest before a storm,"
Ben Hawkins had been heard to say, "and
this here quiet is goin' to make all we uns so
careless that the first thing we know some of
us will turn up missin'."

And on the night following the day during
which Tom Allison and Mark Goodwin paid
their visit to Buffum's cabin, Ben came very
near making his words true by turning up
missing himself. The camp regulations required that every member should report at
sunset, unless he had received permission to
remain away longer, and especially were the
foragers expected to be on hand to make preparations to go out again as soon as night fell.
Ben Hawkins was one of three who went out
on the night of which we write, and he came
back shortly before daylight to report that he
had barely escaped surprise and capture in his
father's house.

"But I've got the grub all the same," said
he, placing a couple of well-filled bags upon
the ground near the tree under which he slept in
good weather. "I was bound I wouldn't come
without it, and that's what made me so late."

"Did you see them?" asked the refugees in concert. "Were they soldiers from Williamston?"

"Naw!" replied Hawkins in a tone of disgust. "They were some of Shelby's pesky Home Guards. Leastwise the two I saw were Home Guards, but I wasn't clost enough to recognize their faces. Now I want you all to listen and ask questions next time you go out, and find, if you can, who all is missin' in the settlement. I had a tol'able fair crack at them two, and I don't reckon they'll never pester any more of we uns."

The man Buffum was there and listening to every word, and he had so little self-control that it was a wonder he did not betray himself. Probably he would if it had not been that all the refugees showed more or less agitation.

"Didn't I say that we uns would get too careless for our own good?" continued Hawkins. "I've got so used to goin' and comin' without bein' pestered that I didn't pay no attention to what I was doin', and 'lowed myself to be fairly ketched in the house. I'd 'a' been took, easy as you please, if I'd 'a' had soldiers to deal with."

"Where are the two foragers who went out with you?" inquired Marcy.

"Aint they got back yet?" exclaimed Hawkins, a shade of anxiety settling on his bronzed features. "I aint seed 'em sence I left 'em up there at the turn of the road, like I always do when we go after grub. They went their ways and I went mine, and I aint seed 'em sence. What will you bet that they aint tooken?"

The refugees talked the matter over while they were eating breakfast and anxiously awaiting the appearance of the missing foragers, and asked one another if Mr. Hawkins would be likely to lose any buildings because Ben had been detected in the act of carrying two bags of provisions from his house. Ben said cheerfully that he did not look for anything else, and that he expected to spend a good many nights in setting bonfires in different parts of the settlement. No one hinted that this sudden activity on the part of the Home Guards might be the result of a con-

spiracy, and, so far as he knew, Marcy Gray
was the only one who suspected it. The
houses toward which the foragers bent their
steps, when they separated at the turn, stood
at least three miles apart and in different
directions, and it seemed strange to Marcy
that those particular houses should have been
watched on that particular night. He thought
the matter would bear investigation, and with
this thought in his mind he set out immediately after breakfast, with the black boy
Julius for company, to see if any of the Home
Guards had paid an unwelcome visit to his
mother since he took leave of her the day
before. On his way he passed through the
field in which the overseer Hanson had been
taken into custody and marched off to Plymouth, and the negroes who were at work
there at once gathered around to tell him the
news. Early as it was, they had had ample
time to learn all about it.

"Did the Home Guards trouble my
mother?" asked Marcy after listening to
their story.

"No, sah; dey didn't. But dey gobble up

two of dem refugees so quick dey couldn't fight, but dey don't git Moster Hawkins kase he too mighty handy wid his gun."

"Do you know whether or not he shot any of them?"

"We's sorry to be 'bleeged to say he didn't," was the reply. "You want to watch out, Marse Mahcy, an' don't luf nobody round hyar know when you comin' home nex' time."

Marcy had already decided to follow this course, but he did not say anything to the talkative darkies about it. If he had decided at the same time that he wouldn't mention it in camp, it would have been better for him.

While Marcy was visiting his mother (and all the while he was in her presence there were four trusty negroes outside, watching the house), Tom Allison and Mark Goodwin were trying to learn what had become of the two refugees who had fallen into the hands of the Home Guards; and when they found that both Beardsley and Shelby were absent from home on business, they thought they knew.

"They have been taken to jail," said Mark, who was delighted over the success of his plan, but angry at Beardsley because the latter did not wait a few nights and make sure of Marcy Gray, instead of capturing two men who were of no consequence one way or the other. "But between you and me, I don't envy the Home Guards the task they have set for themselves. If all the refugees are like Hawkins somebody is going to get hurt."

While Mark talked in this way he and Tom were riding toward Beardsley's plantation, and now they turned through his gate, passed the ruins of his dwelling, and finally drew rein in front of the house in which the overseer lived when Beardsley thought he could afford to hire one, but which was now occupied by his own family. His daughter came to the door, and the boys saw at once that she knew all about it.

"Paw and Shelby has took them two fellers to Williamston," she said in her ordinary tone of voice, as though there was nothing secret in it. "And they're goin' to bring some of our soldiers back with 'em, kase he 'lows, paw does, that it wouldn't be safe for him and Shelby to fool with Mahcy Gray. He's got too many friends, and paw 'lows that he aint got no more houses to lose."

Tom and Mark turned away without making any reply or asking any questions. They did not want to hear any more. Beardsley had cautioned them not to say a word about it, and here he had gone and told it to his daughter, which was the same as though he had written out a full description of Mark's plan and put it on the bulletin-board in the post-office. When Tom looked into his companion's face he was surprised to see how white it was.

"Mark," said he in a low whisper, "we're in the worst scrape of our lives, and if we come safely out of it I'll promise that I will never again try to interfere with Marcy Gray. He can go into the army or stay out of it, just as he pleases. If he ever finds out what we have been up to what will become of us?"

"If he hasn't found it out already it is his own fault," replied Mark, who had never before been so badly frightened. "Everybody in the settlement knows it, and some enemy of ours will be sure to tell him. Tom, I wish we had let him alone."

But Mark's repentance came too late. The mischief had been done, and Marcy Gray was industriously collecting evidence against him and his companion in guilt. He had already heard enough to satisfy him on three points : that the plan for capturing the refugees in detail originated with Tom and Mark, that Captain Beardsley had undertaken to do the work, and that at least one of the refugees was a traitor. But unfortunately he shot wide of the mark when he began casting about for someone on whom to lay the blame. He suspected one of Ben Hawkins' comrades who had been captured and parolled at Roanoke Island. There were seven of them, and one of their number, beyond a doubt, had furnished the information that enabled the Home Guards to capture the two men who had been taken to Williamston. He never once suspected the man Buffum. If he had, he would have dismissed the suspicion with a laugh, for everyone knew that Buffum was too big a coward to take the slightest risk.

When Marcy took leave of his mother he rode straight to Beardsley's, and was not very

much surprised to learn that the captain had
left home early that morning to "'tend to
some business over Williamston way." His
ignorant daughter tried to be very secretive,
and succeeded so well that Marcy would have
been stupid indeed if he hadn't been able to
tell what business it was that took her father
"over Williamston way." Then he changed
the subject and surprised her into giving him
some other information.

"Hawkins made a lively fight for the Home
Guards last night, did he not?" said Marcy.
"How many of them did he kill?"

"Nary one. Didn't hit nary one, nuther,"
answered the girl. "Paw 'lowed that if Ben
had had a gun he'd 'a' hurt somebody; but he
popped away with a little dissolver, and you
can't hit nothin' with a dissolver. Mind you,
I don't know nothin' about it only jest what
the niggers told me."

"Some folks might believe that story, but
I don't," said Marcy to himself, as he wheeled
his horse and rode from the yard. "When the
darkies get hold of any news they don't go to
you with it."

From Beardsley's Marcy went to Nashville, stopping as often as he met anyone willing to talk to him, and going out of his way to visit the homes of the two refugees who had been captured the night before, and everywhere picking up little scraps of evidence against Tom, Mark, and Beardsley; but everyone was so positive that there could not be a traitor in the camp of the refugees, that Marcy himself began to have doubts on that point. Ben Hawkins' father and mother took him into the house and showed him the chair in which Ben was sitting when four masked men rushed into the room, two through each door, and tried to capture him.

"But my Ben, he aint a-skeered of no Home Guards," said Mr. Hawkins proudly. "Before you could say 'Gen'ral Jackson' with your mouth open, he riz, an' when he riz he was shootin'. An' it would 'a' done you good to see the way them masked men humped themselves. They jest nacherly fell over each other in tryin' to get to the doors, an' Ben, he made a grab fur the nighest, thinkin' to pull off the cloth that was over his face, so't we all

19

could see who it was ; but he couldn't get clost
enough.   Then Ben, he run too ; but he come
back after the grub.   He said he had been sent
fur it an' was goin' to have it.   Ben 'lowed
that, if they had been soldiers instead of Home
Guards, we wouldn't never seen him no more.''

"And I am afraid that we shall have to deal
with soldiers from this time on,'' replied Marcy.
"You wait and see if Beardsley doesn't bring
some from Williamston when he comes back.''

"That there man is buildin' a bresh shanty
over his head as fast as he can,'' said Mr.
Hawkins.   "He won't have nary nigger cabin
if this thing can be proved on him.''

"But there is going to be the trouble.   We
can't prove it ; and if some of the Home Guards
could be frightened into making a confession,
Beardsley would have no trouble in proving
by his folks that he wasn't outside of his
house last night.''

It was five o'clock that afternoon when Marcy
returned to camp and made his report.   He
found there several refugees who had spent the
day in the settlement, and the stories they had
to tell differed but little from his own ; but

Marcy noticed that there wasn't one who ventured to hint that there was a spy and informer in the camp. Consequently he said nothing about it himself, but quietly announced that he had concluded to change his night for foraging. He did not hesitate to speak freely, for he noticed that there was not a single parolled prisoner present. But Buffum was there and heard every word.

"It's my turn to skirmish to-morrow night," said he. "But with the consent of all hands I think I will put it off until Monday night."

"You must have some reason for wanting to do that," said Mr. Webster, who you will remember was the man who guided Marcy to the camp on the night Captain Beardsley's schooner was burned.

"I have a very good reason for it," replied Marcy. "The prime movers in this matter— Tom Allison and Mark Goodwin who got up the scheme, and Beardsley who is carrying it out—are enemies of mine, and they would rather see me forced into the army than anybody else." And Marcy might have added

that they were after him and nobody else,
and that when they captured him the rest of
the refugees would be permitted to live in
peace.

"If that is the case, you ought not to go
foraging at all," said Mr. Webster.

"When I cast my lot with you I expected
to share in all your dangers," said Marcy
quietly. "It wouldn't be right, but it would
be cowardly for me to remain safe in camp
eating grub that others foraged at the risk of
being captured or shot, and I'll not do it. I
will do my part as I have always tried to do,
but I claim the right to bother my enemies all
I can by choosing my own time."

"That's nothin' more'n fair," observed
Buffum. "I'll go in your place to-morrer
night an' you can go in mine on Monday."

"All right," said Marcy. "But don't go
near my mother's house to-morrow. It might
be as dangerous for you as for me."

When all the refugees reported at sundown,
as the camp regulations required them to do,
Marcy's plan for escaping capture at the
hands of the Home Guards was explained to

them, and it resulted, as Tom Allison said it
would, in a complete change in the camp
routine. The plan promised to work admira-
bly. The three men composing the new detail
which went foraging that night made their
way to their homes in safety, visited a while
with their families, and returned with a supply
of provisions without having seen any signs of
the enemy; but the old detail would surely
have been captured, for their houses were
watched all night long, not by Home Guards,
but by Confederate veterans who had been
sent from Williamston at Beardsley's suggestion and Shelby's. On the night following
Mrs. Gray's house was not only watched but
searched from cellar to garret; but that was
done simply to throw Marcy off his guard,
and we are sorry to say that it had the desired
effect. The Confederate soldiers knew they
would not find Marcy that night, for Captain
Beardsley told them so; and Beardsley himself had been warned by his faithful spy, Buffum, that Marcy would not go foraging again
until Monday night. By this time all the
refugees became aware that there was some-

one among them who could not be trusted, and the knowledge exasperated them almost beyond the bounds of endurance. The danger was that they might do harm to an innocent man, for they declared that the smallest scrap of evidence against one of their number would be enough to hang him to the nearest tree.

"I can find that spy and will, too, if this thing goes on any longer," said Ben Hawkins, when he and Marcy and Mr. Webster were talking the matter over one day.

"Then why don't you do it?" demanded Marcy. "It has gone on long enough already."

"I'll do it to-morrow night if you two will stand by me," said Ben, and Marcy had never heard him talk so savagely, not even when he threatened to "twist" Tom Allison's neck for calling him a coward.

"We'll stand by you," said Mr. Webster; and although he did not show so much anger, he was just as determined that the man who was trying to betray them into the power of the Confederates should be severely punished. "What are you going to do?"

"I am going to pull that Tom Allison out of his bed by the neck, and say to him that he can take his choice between givin' me the name of that traitor, an' bein' hung up to the plates of his paw's gallery," replied Ben.

"That'll be the way to do it," said Buffum, who happened to come up in time to overhear a portion of this conversation. In fact Buffum was always listening. He showed so great a desire to be everywhere at once, and to know all that was going on, that it was a wonder he was not suspected. But perhaps he took the best course to avoid suspicion. For a man who was known to be lacking in courage, he displayed a good deal of nerve in carrying out the dangerous part of Mark Goodwin's programme that had been assigned to him.

"Will you help?" inquired Hawkins.

"Well, no; I don't know's I want to help, kase you all might run agin some rebels when you're goin' up to Allison's house," replied Buffum. "I'd a heap ruther stay in camp. I never was wuth much at fightin', but I can forage as much grub as the next man."

There was another thing Buffum could do as
well as the next man, but he did not speak of
it.   He could slip away from camp after everybody else was asleep or had gone out foraging,
make his way through the woods to Beardsley's house, remain with him long enough to
give the captain an idea of what had been going on among the refugees during the day, and
return to his blanket in time to have a refreshing nap and get up with the others; he had
done it repeatedly, and no one was the wiser
for it.   He slipped away that night after listening to Ben Hawkins' threat to hang Tom
Allison to the plates of his father's gallery,
and perhaps we shall see what came of it.

Under the new rule it was Ben's turn to go
foraging that night, and he went prepared for
a fight.   He was armed with three revolvers,
Marcy's pair besides his own, and took with
him two soldier comrades who could be depended on in any emergency.   They did not
separate and give the rebels opportunity to
overpower them singly, but kept together,
ready to shoot or run as circumstances might
require.   They were not molested for the

simple reason that the Confederates, as we have said, were watching other houses, knowing nothing of the new regulation that was in force. They returned with an ample supply of food, and reported that Marcy's plan had thrown the enemy off the trail completely.

The next day was Sunday, and Ben devoted a good portion of it to making up for the sleep he had lost the night before, and the rest to selecting and instructing the men that were to accompany him to Mr. Allison's house. There were nine of them, and with the exception of Mr. Webster and Marcy they were all Confederate soldiers. This made it plain to Marcy that Ben did not expect to find the traitor among the men who wore gray jackets. They set out as soon as night fell, marching along the road in military order, trusting to darkness to conceal their movements, and moving at quick step, for Mr. Allison's house was nearly eight miles away. They had covered more than three-fourths of the distance, and Ben was explaining to Marcy how the house was to be surrounded by a right-and-left oblique movement, which was to begin as soon as the little column was fairly inside Mr. Allison's gate, when their steps were arrested by a faint, tremulous hail which came from the bushes by the roadside. In a second more half a dozen cocked revolvers were pointed at the spot from which the voice sounded.

"Out of that!" commanded Ben. "Out you come with a jump."

"Dat you, Moss' Hawkins?" came in husky tones from the bushes.

"It's me; but I don't know who you are, an' you want to be in a hurry about showin' yourself. One—two——"

"Hol'—hol' on, if you please, sah. Ise comin'," answered the voice, and the next minute a badly frightened black man showed himself. "Say, Moss' Hawkins," he continued, "whar's you all gwine?"

"I don't know as that is any of your business," answered Ben.

"Dat I knows mighty well," the darky hastened to say. "Black ones aint got no truck wid white folkses business; but you all don't want to go nigher to Mistah Allison's.

Da's a whole passel rebels up da'. I done see
'em."

"What are they doin' up there?" inquired
Ben, who was very much surprised to hear it.

The black man replied that they were not
doing anything in particular the last time he
saw them, only just loitering about as if they
were waiting for something or somebody.
They hadn't come to the house by the road,
but through the fields and out of the woods;
and the care they showed to keep out of sight
of anyone who might chance to ride along the
highway, taken in connection with the fact
that both Beardsley and Shelby had been
there talking to them, and had afterward left
by the way of a narrow lane that led to a piece
of thick timber at the rear of the plantation—
all these things made the darkies believe that
the rebels were there for no good purpose, and
so some of their number had left the quarter
as soon as it grew dark, to warn any Union
people they might meet to keep away from
Mr. Allison's house.

"Well, boy, you've done us a favor," said
Ben, when the darky ceased speaking, "and

if I had a quarter in good money I would give it to you. But there's a bill of some sort in rebel money. It's too dark to see the size of it, but mebbe it will get you half a plug of tobacco. How many rebs are there in the party?"

"Sarvant, sah. Thank you kindly, sah," said the black boy, as he took the bill. "Da's more'n twenty of 'em in de congregation, an' all ole soldiers. A mighty rough-lookin' set dey is too."

"That's the way all rebs look," said Ben. "I know, for I have been one of 'em. What do you s'pose brought the soldiers there?"

The darky replied that he couldn't make out why they came to the house; but he knew that the officer in command had said some-thing to Tom, in the presence of his father and mother, that threw them all into a state of great agitation. Tom especially was terribly frightened, and wanted to ride over and pass the night with Mark Goodwin; but his father wouldn't let him go for fear something would happen to him on the road.

"Well, Timothy——" began Ben.

"Jake, if you please, sah," corrected the negro.

"Well, Jake, if you keep still about meetin' us nobody will ever hear of it. Off you go, now. The jig's up, boys, an' we might as well strike for camp."

CHAPTER XII.

"I HAVEN'T the least doubt but what the nigger told the truth," continued Ben Hawkins, as Mr. Allison's black boy disappeared in the darkness and his men gathered about him to hear what else he had to say. "Everything goes to prove that we uns talked our plans over in the presence of somebody who went straight to Beardsley an' Shelby with it; an' them two went to work an' brung soldiers enough up to Allison's house to scoop us all in the minute we got there. But we uns aint goin' to be scooped this night, thanks to that nigger. Twenty, or even six veterans is too many fur we uns to tackle, 'specially sence some of us aint never smelled much powder, an' so we're goin' home. Now, who's the traitor, do you reckon?"

There was no answer to this question. If the refugees suspected anybody, they did not speak his name. It was a serious matter to accuse one of their number, none of them were willing to take the responsibility, and so they wisely held their peace.

"We aint got no proof agin anybody," continued Ben, "an' I don't know's I blame you all fur not wantin' to speak out. But mind this: I shall have an eye on everybody in camp—everybody, I said—an' the fust one who crooks his finger will have to tell a tol'able straight story to keep out of trouble. Fall in, and counter-march by file, left. Quick time now, an' keep your guns in your hands, kase when them rebs up to the house find that we uns aint goin' to run into their trap, they may try to head us off."

The return march was made in silence, each member of the squad being engrossed with his own thoughts. Tom Allison and Mark Goodwin were uppermost in their minds, and there was not one of the refugees who did not tell himself that it would be better for the settlement if those two mischief-makers were well out of it. They reached camp without any trouble and reported their failure and talked

about it as freely as though they never suspected that there was somebody in their midst
who was to blame for it.   Acting on the hint
Ben Hawkins gave them the parolled Confederates watched everybody, their comrades
as well as the civilians, and talked incessantly
in the hope that the guilty one might be led to
betray himself by an inadvertent word or ges-
ture ; but they paid the least attention to the
man who could have told them the most about
it.   Ben Hawkins would have suspected himself almost as soon as he would have suspected
Buffum.

Monday evening came all too soon for Marcy
Gray, who, with a feeling of depression he had
never before experienced, made ready to take
his turn at foraging.   He announced that it
was his intention to go to his mother's house
alone, because one person might be able to approach the dwelling unobserved, while three
could not make a successful fight if the enemy
were on the watch.   No one offered objection
to this arrangement, if we except the boy
Julius, who positively refused to be left behind, declaring that if his master would not

take him to the main-land in his boat, he would swim the bayou and follow him anyhow.

When the time came for Marcy to start he shook hands with all the refugees, Buffum included, and pushed off from the island alone. He concealed his canoe when he reached the other shore and was about to plunge into the woods, when a slight splashing in the water and the sound of suppressed conversation came from the bank he had just left. At least two or three persons were shoving off from the island to follow him, and Marcy, believing that he could call them by name, waited for them to come up. The night was so dark and the bushes so thick that his friendly pursuers did not see him until the bow of their boat touched the shore and they began to step out.

"Now, Ben," said Marcy reproachfully, "I shall feel much more at my ease if you will turn around and go back."

"Oh, hursh, honey!" replied Julius. "We uns gwine fight de rebels, too."

"Don't you know that if you and your
20

friends are captured you will be treated as deserters?" continued Marcy, addressing himself to Hawkins and paying no attention to Julius. "You have been ordered to report for duty and haven't done it, and I suppose you know what that means."

"A heap better'n you do at this time, but not better'n you will if you are tooken an' packed off to Williamston," answered Ben. "You'd die in less'n a month if you was forced into the army, kase you aint the right build to stand the hard knocks you'll get. But we uns don't 'low to be took pris'ner or let you be took, either."

"I appreciate your kindness——" began Marcy.

"You needn't say no more, kase we uns has made it up to go with you, an' we aint goin' to turn back," interrupted Ben. "We uns will stay outside the house an' watch, an' you can go in an' get the grub. Pull the boat ashore, boys, an' shove her into the bresh out of sight."

There is no use in saying that Marcy did not feel relieved to know that he would have four friends at his back if he got into trouble, because he did. There were three Confederate veterans, and Julius made the fourth friend ; but Julius counted, for he had already proved that he was worth something in an emergency. Marcy made no further effort to turn them back, but shook them all warmly by the hand and led the way toward his mother's plantation. It took them two hours to reach it, for they kept under cover of the woods as long as they could, and followed blind ditches and brush-lined fences when it became necessary for them to cross open fields, and so cautious were they in their movements that when Ben came to a halt behind a rose-bush in full view of the great house, he gave it as his opinion that an owl would not have seen or heard them, if there had been one on the watch.

"An' although we uns aint seen no rebels, that don't by no means prove that there aint none around," added Ben. "Marcy, you stay here, an' the rest of us will kinder sneak around t'other side the house an' take a look at things. Julius, you come with me, kase

you know the lay of the land an' I don't.
You two boys go that-a-way; an' if you run
onto anything don't stop to ask questions, but
shoot to kill.   It's a matter of life an' death
with all of we uns, except the nigger."

Marcy's friends moved away in different
directions, and, when they were out of sight
and hearing, he walked around the rose-bush
and sat down on the ground so close to the
house that he could recognize the servants
who passed in and out of the open door,
through which a light streamed into the darkness.   He longed to call one of them to his
hiding-place and send a comforting message to
the anxious mother, who he knew was waiting
for him in the sitting room, but he was afraid
to do it.   There wasn't a negro on the place
who could be trusted as far as that.   If he
tried to attract the notice of one of them, the
darky would be sure to shriek out with terror
and seek safety in flight, and Marcy did not
want to frighten his mother.   So he sat still
and waited for Ben Hawkins, who, after half
an hour's absence, returned with the gratifying intelligence that the coast was clear, and

Marcy could go ahead with his foraging as soon as he pleased.

"If there's ary reb in this here garding he must be hid in the ground, or else some of we uns would surely have stepped onto him," said Ben. "Beardsley didn't look fur you to come to-night, an' that's all the proof I want that we uns has got ahead of that traitor of ourn fur once, dog-gone his pictur'."

"Where are the rest of the boys?" whispered Marcy.

"They're gardin' three sides of the house, an' when you go in I'll stay here an' guard the fourth," answered Ben. "Off you go, now. Crawl up."

Marcy lingered a moment to shake Ben's hand, and then arose to his feet and walked toward the house. If Ben's report was correct there was no need of concealment. He stopped on the way to speak to the darkies in the kitchen, and his sudden appearance at the door threw them into the wildest commotion. They made a simultaneous rush for the rear window, intending to crawl through and take to their heels; but the sound of his familiar voice reassured them. Raising his hand to silence their cries of alarm Marcy said impressively :

"Do you black ones want to see me captured by the rebels? Or do you want to frighten my mother to death? If you don't, keep still."

"Moss' Mahcy," protested the cook, who was the first to recover from her fright, "dey aint no rebels round hyar. I aint seed none dis whole blessed——"

"For all that there may be some concealed in the garden and ready to jump on me at any moment," interrupted Marcy. "Now, don't go to prowling about. If you do you will be frightened again, for I have friends out there in the bushes and you might run upon them in the dark."

So saying Marcy turned from the kitchen and went into the house, passing on the way two large baskets which had been filled with food and placed in the hall ready to his hand, so that there would be nothing to detain him in so dangerous a place as his mother's house was known to be. Mrs. Gray came from the sitting room to meet him, for she heard his step the moment he crossed the threshold.

"O Marcy! I am so glad to see you, but I am almost sorry you came," was the way in which she greeted him.

"Seen anything alarming?" inquired the boy.

"No; and that very circumstance excites my suspicion. There are Confederate soldiers in the neighborhood, for Morris saw several of them in Nashville this morning. I shall never become accustomed to this terrible way of living."

"No more shall I, but the only way to put a stop to it is to—what in the world is that?" exclaimed Marcy; for just then a smothered cry of astonishment and alarm, that was suddenly cut short in the middle, sounded in the direction of the kitchen, followed by an indescribable commotion such as might have been made by the shuffling feet of men who were engaged in a hand-to-hand contest. A second afterward pistol-shots—not one or a dozen, but a volley of them rattled around the house, telling Marcy in plain terms that Ben Hawkins and his comrades had been assailed on all sides.

"O Marcy, they've got you!" cried Mrs. Gray; and forgetful of herself, and thinking only of his safety, she flung her arms about his neck and threw herself between him and the open door, protecting his person with her own.

"Not yet," replied the boy between his clenched teeth. "I might as well die here as in the army."

Tightening his grasp on his mother's waist Marcy swung her behind him with one arm, at the same time reaching for the revolver whose heavy butt protruded from the leg of his right boot; but before he could straighten up with the weapon in his hand, two men in Confederate uniform rushed into the room from the hall, and two cocked revolvers were pointed at his head. Resistance would have been madness. The men had him covered, their ready fingers were resting on the triggers, and an effort on Marcy's part to level his own weapon would have been the signal for his death. These things happened in much less time than

MARCY CAPTURED AT LAST.

we have taken to describe them, and all the while a regular fight, a sharp one, too, had been going on outside the house, and with the rattle of carbines and revolvers were mingled the screams of the terrified negroes ; but Marcy Gray and his mother did not know it. Their minds were filled with but one thought, and that was that Beardsley had got the upper hand of them at last.

"If you move an eyelid you are a dead conscript," said the foremost of the two rebels at the door, and whom Marcy afterward knew as Captain Fletcher. As he spoke he came into the room and took the revolver from Marcy's hand.

"Captain, I see the mate to that sticking out of his boot," said the other soldier; and not until the captain had taken possession of that revolver also did his comrade think it safe to put up his weapon.

At this moment the firing outside ceased as suddenly as it had begun. Captain Fletcher noticed it if Marcy did not, and ordered his man to "go out and take a look and come in and report." Then Marcy led his mother to the sofa and sat down beside her, while the captain stood in the middle of the room with his revolver in his hand and looked at him.

"You've got me easy enough," said Marcy, trying to put a bold face on the matter. "And now I should like to know what you intend to do with me."

"My orders are to take you to Williamston," replied the captain, who seemed to be a good fellow at heart. "I am sorry, but you would have saved yourself and me some trouble if you had gone there the minute you were conscripted."

"I never knew before that I had been conscripted," answered Marcy.

"Every man and boy in the Confederacy who is able to do duty must go into the army," said the captain slowly and impressively. "If he will not go willingly he'll be forced in."

"There are so many men and boys in the Confederacy who do not want to go into the service that I should think it would take half your army to hunt them up."

"It's a heap of bother," admitted the captain, "and it takes men we cannot afford to spare from the front just now. Perhaps you had better take a few clothes and a blanket with you ; but I shall have to ask your mother to get them, for I want you where I can keep an eye on you. Captain Beardsley says——"

"Go on," said Marcy, when the captain paused and caught his breath. "You can't tell me anything about Beardsley that I don't know already. He and Shelby are at the bottom of this, and I am well aware of it. I don't see why you don't hang those men. They have taken the oath of allegiance to the United States Government."

"I don't approve of anything like that, but all's fair in war," replied the captain, who seemed to know all about it. "A loyal soldier wouldn't have done it, but Beardsley and Shelby are civilians and the Yanks frightened them into it. However, they are working for our side as hard as they ever did, and that's about all we care for."

When the captain ceased speaking Mrs. Gray arose from the sofa and went to Marcy's room to pack a valise for him. There were no traces of tears on her white, set face, and her

step was as firm as it ever was. She was bearing up bravely, for she had long schooled herself for just such a scene as this. When she
left the room the captain slipped his revolver
into its holster, took possession of an easy-
chair, and leaned back in it with a long-drawn
sigh.

"I'd rather face a dozen Yanks than one
woman," said he. "I hope she'll not break
down when she bids you good-by."

"You need have no fears on that score,"
answered Marcy. "I judge you don't like
the unpleasant work you are engaged in any
too well, and my mother will do nothing to
make it harder for you."

"You're mighty right, I don't like it," said
the captain emphatically. "Any place in the
world but an invalid corps. They have all the
dirty work to do. It suits some cowards, but
I'd rather be at the front, and there I hope to
go next week. Well, corporal?" he added,
turning to the man he had sent out of the
room a few minutes before. "How many of
them were there?"

"A dozen or so, sir, judging by the fight

they made and the work they did," replied the soldier.

"Are you speaking of my friends?" inquired Marcy, who now remembered that there had been something of a commotion outside the house. "Well, there were just three of them, not counting an unarmed negro boy."

"Do you want me to believe that three conscripts could stand off twenty old soldiers?" demanded the corporal.

"Great Scott!" exclaimed Marcy, who was really surprised. "Did you bring twenty men here to capture me? You are a brave lot."

"Braver than you who took to the woods to keep from going into the army," answered the angry corporal. "We can't find hair nor hide of them, sir," he added, turning to his officer. "But they left us four dead men to remember them by, and nary one wounded."

Marcy was horrified. Ben Hawkins had followed his own advice and shot to kill. He was glad to hear the corporal say that his friends had managed to escape in the darkness, but what effect would the gallant fight they made have upon his own prospects? He was glad, too, that there was a commissioned officer among his captors, for he did not like the way the corporal glared at him. And finally, would his capture bring Tom Allison and Mark Goodwin into trouble with the refugees?

"It certainly did bring them into trouble," interrupted Rodney. "They were bushwhacked."

"How do you know?" demanded Marcy, starting up in his chair.

"Jack said so in his last letter. And he said, further, that your good friends Beardsley and Shelby, and one other whose name I have forgotten, were burned out so clean that they didn't have a nigger cabin left to shelter them."

"Were Tom and Mark killed?"

"I suppose they were, but Jack wasn't explicit on that point. You would be sorry to hear it, of course."

"I certainly would, for I used to be good friends with those boys before a few crazy men kicked up this war and set us together by the ears," said Marcy sadly. "But they could blame no one but themselves. I wonder that Beardsley wasn't bushwhacked also."

Then Marcy settled back in his chair and went on with his story. He told how he listened to the conclusion of the corporal's report, during which he learned, what he had all along more than half suspected, that the Confederates had surrounded the house and were lying concealed in the garden when he and his companions arrived. They saw Marcy's friends reconnoiter the premises, but made no effort to capture them for the reason that they had received strict orders not to move until Captain Fletcher gave the signal, which he did as soon as he saw Marcy enter the house. He and the corporal lost no time in following and coming to close quarters with him, for they knew they would find the boy armed, and that it would be dangerous to give him a chance to defend himself. When they left their place of concealment and ran around the kitchen, they encountered Aunt Martha the cook, who saw and recognized their uniforms as they passed her window, and started

at the top of her speed for the house, hoping
to warn her young master so that he could
escape through the cellar, as he had done once
before.   But the corporal seized her, promptly
choked off the warning cry that arose to her
lips, and then began that furious struggle that
had attracted Marcy's attention.

"She was strong and savage," said the
captain with a laugh, "and for a time it
looked as though she would get the better of
both of us.   If she didn't do that, I was afraid
she would make such a fight that you would
hear it and dig out ; but fortunately two of
my men came to our aid just in the nick of
time."

"I hope you didn't hurt her," said Marcy.

"I choked her into silence, you bet,"
replied the corporal, who then stated that the
firing began when the Confederates rose to
their feet and tried to capture Marcy's friends.
They got more bullets than captives, however,
and the captain had four less men under his
command now than he had when the fight
commenced.

"You have wagons on the place, I suppose?" said the captain to Marcy, when the corporal intimated by a salute that his report was ended. "Very well. We'll have to borrow one of them to take the bodies to Williamston. I did intend to visit two other houses to-night, but I shouldn't make anything by it now, for of course the whole settlement has been alarmed by the firing. Go and see about that wagon, corporal."

As the non-commissioned officer disappeared through one door Marcy's mother came in at another, carrying a well-filled valise in her hand. It was not locked, and she opened and presented it for the captain's inspection.

"There is nothing in it except a few articles which I know will be useful to my boy while he is in the army," said she.

"That assurance is sufficient," replied the captain. "Now, as soon as the corporal reports that wagon ready, we will rid your house of our unwelcome presence. I am sorry indeed that I had this work to do, but the Yankees are to blame for it. If they hadn't shot me almost to death in the last battle I was in, I should now be at the front where I

21

belong. I wish your son might have got away, but I was ordered to take him and I was obliged to do it."

"We have seen enough of this war to know that a soldier's business is to do as he is told, no matter who gets hurt by it," said Marcy, speaking for his mother, who seated herself on the sofa by his side and looked at him as though she never expected to see him again. "I don't mind telling you, captain, that if I could have had my own way, I should have been fighting under the Old Flag long ago."

"So I have heard; and there are a good many men in our army who think as much of the Union as Abe Lincoln does," answered the captain truthfully. "But don't say that again unless you know who you are talking to."

"Have you any idea where Marcy will be sent?" asked Mrs. Gray, speaking with an effort.

"Of course I don't know for certain, but my impression is that he will have to do guard duty somewhere. The authorities used to send conscripts from this State to fill out North Carolina regiments in the field, but they don't trouble themselves to do it now. They put them on guard duty wherever they want them, and send volunteers to the front."

"Let that ease your mind, mother," said Marcy, with an attempt at cheerfulness. "If I am to stay in the rear I shan't have such a very hard time of it."

The captain opened his eyes, smiled incredulously, and once or twice acted as if he were on the point of speaking ; but he thought better of it, and just then the corporal returned to report that the men had been called in and the wagon was waiting at the door. Captain Fletcher went into the hall while Marcy took leave of his mother, and this gave the latter opportunity to whisper in his ear, as her head rested on his shoulder :

"Be careful of that valise, and the first chance you get take the money out of it. You will find one vest in there, and the gold is in the right-hand pocket. O Marcy, this blow will kill me."

"You mustn't let it. I shall surely return, and when I do I want you and Jack here to welcome me."

The leave-taking was not prolonged,—it would have been torture to both of them,—and when Captain Fletcher reached the carriage porch, where the corporal stood holding three horses by the bridle, Marcy was at his side.

"Mount that horse and come on," said the captain. "When we overtake the wagon you can put your valise in it."

But that valise was much too valuable to be placed in the wagon, or anywhere else that a thieving Confederate could get his hands on it, so Marcy replied that if it was all the same to the captain he would tie it to the horn of his saddle, where he could keep an eye on it. He mounted the horse that was pointed out to him, kissed his hand to his mother, said a cheery good-by to the weeping blacks, who had at last found courage to come into the house, and rode on after the wagon, which had by this time passed through the front gate into the road. Marcy was the only prisoner the Confederates captured that night, and he had cost them the lives of four men. The soldier who had once owned the horse he was riding was one of the unfortunates. Marcy would have given much to know whether Ben Hawkins and his comrades escaped unscathed, but that was something he never expected to hear, for he was by no means as sure that he would come back to his home as he pretended to be. Others had been killed, and what right had he to assume that he would escape?

"This scout hasn't amounted to a row of pins," observed Captain Fletcher, when he and Marcy came up with the wagon and rode behind it. "I expected to find the country alive with Yankee cavalry and to fight my way against a small army of refugees, who would ambush me from the time I left Williamston till I got back. That is the reason I brought so large a squad with me. I have been out four days, and what have I to show for my trouble? Four dead men and three prisoners. I don't like such work, and shall get back to Virginia as soon as I can."

The captain relapsed into silence, and during the rest of the journey Marcy was at liberty to commune undisturbed with his own gloomy thoughts.

CHAPTER XIII.

IN WILLIAMSTON JAIL.

"FRESH fish! where did you come from? Are you a deserter or a conscript?"

It was about two o'clock in the afternoon. Marcy Gray was in Williamston jail at last, and this was the way he was welcomed when the heavy grated door clanged behind him. Much to his relief he was not thrust into a cell as he thought he would be, but into a large room which was already so crowded that it did not seem as though there could be space for one more. The inmates gathered eagerly about him, all asking questions at once, and although some of them affected to look upon their capture and confinement as a huge joke, Marcy saw at a glance that the majority were as miserable as he was himself. While he told his story in as few words as possible he looked around for the two foragers who had been captured on the night that Ben Hawkins was surprised in his father's house, and failing to discover them he shouted out their names. They had had a few days' experience as prisoners, and could perhaps give him some needed advice.

"Oh, they're gone," said one.

"Gone where?" inquired Marcy.

"Nobody knows. This room was cleaned out on the very day they were brought in, and your two friends went with the rest to do guard duty somewhere down South. All of us you see here have been captured during the last two or three days."

"How long do you think it will be before we will be shipped off?"

"It won't be long," said the prisoner, "for this room is about as full as it will hold. What are you anyway? Union or secesh?"

Before Marcy could make any reply to this unexpected question, someone who stood behind him gave him a gentle poke in the ribs. He took it for a warning, as indeed it was intended to be, and turned away without saying a word. The incident frightened him, for it proved that there were some among the

prisoners whom their companions in misery
were afraid to trust.   He began to wonder how
it would be possible for him to secure possession of the gold pieces which his thoughtful
mother had placed in his vest pocket.   There
were some hard-looking fellows among the
prisoners, men of the Kelsey and Hanson
stamp, and Marcy was not far wrong when he
told himself it would never do to let them
know or suspect that he was well supplied
with good money.   Holding fast to his blanket
and valise he freed himself from the crowd as
soon as he could, and taking his stand by an
open grated window, began looking about in
search of a face whose owner seemed to him
worthy of confidence ; for Marcy felt the need
of a friend now as he had never felt it before.
As good fortune would have it, the first man
who attracted his notice was Charley Bowen,
and he turned out to be the one who had
given him the warning poke in the ribs.   His
was an honest face if there ever was one, and
Marcy liked the way the man conducted himself.   He took no part in the joking and
laughing.   He looked as serious as Marcy felt,

but did not seem to be utterly cast down, as many of the prisoners were, because he knew he was going to be forced into the army. When he saw that Marcy's eyes were fixed upon him with an inquiring look, he gradually worked his way out of the crowd and came up to the window.

"You look as though you had been used to better quarters than these and better company, too," was the way he began the conversation.

"And so do you," replied Marcy.

"I never was shut up in jail before, if that is what you mean. You see I don't belong in this part of the country. I got this far on my way up from Georgia, intending to get outside the Confederate lines if I could, but I was gobbled at last, and within sight of the Union flag at Plymouth."

"That was hard luck indeed," answered Marcy. "You earned your freedom and ought to have had it. Why, you must have travelled four or five hundred miles. What excuse did the rebels make for arresting you?"

"Don't use that word here," said the man

hastily. "It's dangerous. We have the best of reasons for believing that there are spies among us searching for deserters, and they will go straight to the guards with every word you say. The man who asked if you are Union or secesh is one of them."

"Why are they so anxious to find deserters?" asked Marcy.

"To make an example of them, I suppose. At any rate the guards took a deserter out of this room on the day I came, and we've never seen him since. The men who captured me did not make any excuse for holding me, if that was the question you were going to ask. They simply said that I couldn't be of any use to the Yanks in Plymouth, but could be of a good deal of use in the Confederate army, and so they brought me along. Who are you? and what's your name?"

Marcy had not talked with the man very long before he made up his mind that he had found the friend he needed ; but still he was afraid to trust him too far on short acquaintance. He told Bowen that he was neither a deserter nor a conscript, but a refugee, and owed his capture to personal enemies, who would be sure to suffer for it sooner or later; but he did not say that he intended to escape if his captors gave him half a chance, or that he had some good money in his valise. Consequently he was not a little surprised and alarmed when Bowen turned his back to the rest of the prisoners, and said in an earnest whisper:

"Have you been searched?"

"No," answered Marcy. "What will I have to be searched for? My mother presented my valise for Captain Fletcher's inspection, but he was gentleman enough to say he wouldn't look into it."

"Well, you'll be searched, and that too just as soon as old Wilkins learns something of the circumstances under which you were captured," continued Bowen in the same earnest whisper. "It don't stand to reason that your mother would have packed your carpetbag without slipping in a little money, if she had any, and Wilkins is hot after money."

"Who is Wilkins, anyhow?"

"The Confederate captain who commands here, and he's a robber. He goes through every man who comes into the jail, and you will not escape. Why, he was mean enough to take three dollars in scrip from me. He said I would have no use for money, for the government would furnish me with grub and clothes. If you've got anything you want to save you'd better let me have it."

"But how do I know that it will be any safer with you than it is with me?" demanded Marcy. "What assurance have I that you will give it back when I want it?"

"You haven't any. You'll have to take my word for it."

This was honest at any rate, and something prompted Marcy to take out the key of his valise and slip it into Bowen's hand.

"Look for my vest and feel in the right-hand pocket," he whispered; and then he turned around to engage the nearest of the prisoners in conversation and draw their attention away from Bowen if he could. It looked like a hopeless task. The room was so full that it did not seem possible that any of its inmates could make a move without being seen by somebody ; but as soon as he showed a disposition to talk he found plenty ready and eager to listen, for he was the last arrival and brought the latest news from the outside world. He kept as many as could crowd around him interested for perhaps five minutes, and then his narrative was brought to a close by a commotion in the farther end of the room and the entrance of a Confederate corporal, who elbowed his way into the crowd, calling for Marcy Gray.

"Here!" replied the owner of that name. "What do you suppose he wants of me?" he added in an undertone.

"Most likely he wants to take your descriptive list," said one of the prisoners, with a wink at his companions.

"But that was done when I came in," said Marcy.

"Did old Wilkins do it?" said the conscript. "I don't reckon he did, for he has been off somewhere since morning. If he's got back he will want to see you himself."

That somebody wanted to see him was made

plain to Marcy in a very few seconds, for the
corporal worked his way through the crowd
until he caught sight of the new prisoner, who
was ordered to pick up his plunder and "come
along down to the office"; and, what was
more, the corporal watched him to see that
he did not leave any of his "plunder"
behind.

"That proves that the descriptive list of
your valise hasn't been taken," whispered one
of the prisoners, as Marcy followed the corporal toward the door.

When he picked up his valise he noticed
that the key was in the lock, and of course
Bowen must have put it there; but whether
he had had time to examine the vest and find
the precious gold pieces was a question that
could not be answered now. "Old Wilkins"
would no doubt answer it in about five
minutes, was what Marcy said to himself, as
he followed his guide down a flight of stairs
into a wide hall, which was paved with brick
and lined on both sides with dark, narrow
cells. Marcy shuddered when he glanced at
the pale, hollow-eyed captives on the other

side of the grated doors, who crowded up to look at him as he passed along the hall.

"Who are these?" he whispered to his conductor.

"Deserters and the meanest kind of Yankee sympathizers," was the answer. "Men who give aid and comfort to the enemy while honest soldiers are risking their lives at the front."

"What's going to be done with them, do you know?"

"The deserters will be shot, most likely, and every one of the rest ought to be hung. That's what would be done with them if I had my way."

Marcy's heart sank within him. If the corporal could have his way what would be done with *him?* was the question that came into his mind. He had not only given aid and comfort to the Federals but had served on one of their gunboats; and how did he know but that the commander of the prison would order him into one of those crowded cells after he had taken the descriptive list of his valise, or, in plain English, had robbed it of everything of value? While Marcy was thinking about it the corporal pushed open a door and ushered him into the presence of Captain Wilkins, who sat tilted back in a chair, with his feet on the office table and a cob pipe in his mouth. Although he was resplendent in a brand-new uniform he did not look like a soldier, and Marcy afterward learned that he wasn't. He was a Home Guard, and would have been a deserter if he had seen the least prospect before him of being ordered to the front.

"Private Gray, sir," said the corporal, waving his hand in Marcy's direction.

His interview with Captain Wilkins, of whom he had already learned to stand in fear, was not a long one, but it did much to satisfy Marcy that the man was not as well acquainted with his history as he was afraid he might be. His first words, however, showed that he knew all about the fight that had taken place in Mrs. Gray's door-yard when the boy was captured.

"So you are the chap who cost the lives of some of my best men, are you?" said he, after he had given Marcy a good looking over. "Do you know what I have a notion to do with you?"

Marcy replied that he did not, being careful to address the captain as "sir," for he knew it would be folly to irritate such a man as he was. He expected to hear him declare that he would put him into the dungeon and keep him there on bread and water as long as he remained in the jail; but instead of that the captain said:

"I would like to send you to the field without an hour's delay, so that the Yankees could have a chance at you. There's where such cowards as you belong. Why didn't you come in when you knew you had been conscripted and save me the trouble of sending for you?"

"I didn't know it, sir," replied Marcy.

"Well, it was your business to know that every able-bodied man in the Confederacy has been placed absolutely under control of our President while the war lasts," continued the captain. "You were mighty good to yourself to stay at home living on the fat of the land,

22

while your betters are fighting and dying for
the flag, but I'll put you where you will see
service; do you hear? How many more men
are there in that camp of refugees up there?"

"About twenty, sir," answered Marcy.

"Twenty more cowards shirking duty!"
exclaimed the captain, taking his feet off the
table and banging his fist upon it. "But I'll
have them out of there if it takes every man
I've got; do you hear? I say I'll have them
out of that camp and into the army, where
they will be food for powder. Let me see
your baggage."

As Captain Wilkins said this he nodded to
the corporal, who seized Marcy's valise and
turned its contents upon the floor. There
were not many things brought to light—only
an extra suit of clothes, two or three handker-
chiefs, as many shirts and pairs of stockings,
and a pair of shoes; but each of these articles
was carefully examined by the corporal, who
went about his work as though he was used
to it, as indeed he was. He had examined a
good deal of luggage for the captain, who had
nothing to say when he saw him confiscate

any article of clothing that struck his fancy, or which he thought he could sell or trade to his comrades of the Home Guards. Marcy caught his breath when he saw the corporal run his fingers into the right-hand pocket of the vest in which his mother had placed the gold pieces, and felt much relieved when the soldier did not pull out anything. Then his blanket, which Marcy had rolled up and tied with strings so that he could sling it over his shoulder, soldier fashion, was shaken out, but there was not a thing in it to reward the corporal's search. The latter looked disappointed and so did Captain Wilkins, who commanded Marcy to turn all his pockets inside out. He did so, but there was nothing in them but a broken jack-knife that was not worth stealing.

"You must be poor folks up your way," said the captain. "Where's your scrip?"

"I haven't a dollar's worth of scrip, sir," said Marcy truthfully. "In fact I've seen little of it during the war."

It never occurred to Captain Wilkins to ask if Marcy had seen any other sort of money, for gold was something he had not taken from the pockets of a single conscript. He put his feet on the table again, touched a lighted match to his pipe, and told Marcy that he could go back upstairs. Glad to escape so easily the boy tumbled his clothing into his valise, gathered up his blanket, and went ; and the sentry who stood in the hall at the head of the stairs opened the door for him.

"What did you have ? What did you lose?" were the questions that arose on all sides when he entered the room he had left a few minutes before.

"Not a thing," answered Marcy, glancing at Charley Bowen, who stood among the prisoners, looking as innocent and unconcerned as a man could who had almost a hundred dollars in gold in his pocket. "And they gave my things a good overhauling, too."

"What did you do with your scrip, any-way ? Put it in your shoe ?"

"I didn't have any," said Marcy. "If I had the corporal would have found it sure, for he turned everything inside out."

Marcy elbowed his way to the nearest window to roll up his blanket and repack his valise, and after a while Bowen came up.

"If it hadn't been for you they would have stolen me poor," Marcy found an opportunity to whisper to him. "They are nothing but robbers."

"What did I tell you?" replied Bowen. "Put your hand into my coat-pocket, and you will find it safe; but I warn you that you will lose it if you don't watch out. There are some among the prisoners who would steal it in a minute if they got a good chance. What do you intend to do with it anyway?" he added, after Marcy had transferred the gold coins to his own pocket without attracting anybody's attention. "The first time you try to spend any of it, someone will rob you."

"It may come handy some day," whispered Marcy. "Since you have showed yourself to be a true friend I don't mind telling you that I don't mean to serve under the rebel flag a day longer than I am obliged to."

"Are you going to make a break?" said Bowen eagerly.

"I am, if I see the ghost of a show."

"You're a boy after my own heart, and if you want good company I will go with you."

Nothing could have suited Marcy Gray better. The fact that Bowen had travelled hundreds of miles through a country that was in full possession of the enemy, and had even come within sight of the Union lines before he was captured, proved that he was not only a brave and persevering man, but that he was skilled in woodcraft as well ; and such a man would be an invaluable companion if they could only manage to escape at the same time. Bowen said it would be impossible for them to escape from the jail, for in addition to the sentry, who stood in the hall and could look through the grated door into the room and see every move that was made among the prisoners, the building was surrounded by guards every night. It would be folly for them to make the attempt until they were certain of success, for no man in the rebel army ever deserted more than once.

"But whether we escape in one month or two we'll have something to think about and live for, so that our minds will not be constantly dwelling upon our misfortunes ; and that's a great thing in a case like this, I tell you," said Bowen. "We must keep up a brave heart by thinking about pleasant things, or else it will not be long before we shall be moping like those poor fellows over there in the corner. They're all the time worrying, and the first they know they will be down sick."

"I suppose that is the right way to do, but it is awful hard for a conscript to be jolly," said Marcy, who was thinking of his mother and of Jack, whom he might never see again.

" I know it ; but it is the only way for us to do if we want to keep on our feet."

When five o'clock came and the long table which occupied the middle of the room had been cleared of the men who had been sitting and lying upon it, and the supper was brought in, Marcy Gray began to realize that being shut up in jail meant something. While Bowen talked he had been slowly working his way through the crowd toward the table, and now Marcy saw what his object was in doing it. The supper, which consisted of bean soup and corn bread, was brought in in small wooden tubs which were placed upon the table, together with a sufficient number of pans and spoons to accommodate about half the prisoners at once. No sooner had these pans and spoons been set on the table than Bowen seized two of them as quick as a flash, and filled the pans with soup with one hand, while he passed Marcy a generous piece of corn bread with the other.

"Now get over there by the window before somebody jostles you and spills it all," said he; and although Marcy, acting upon the suggestion, succeeded in reaching the window without losing his supper, it was not owing to any consideration that was shown him by the prisoners, who made a regular charge upon the table, pushing and crowding, and acting altogether like men who were more than half famished. Marcy said, in a tone of disgust, that they reminded him of a lot of pigs.

"I don't know's I blame them," said Bowen, swallowing a spoonful of his soup with the remark that it was somewhat better than common. "You will soon learn to push and shove with the rest."

"I hope not," replied Marcy.

"Then you'll have to eat out of a dirty dish; that's all."

"Do you mean to say that someone will have to use this pan and spoon after I get through with them?"

"That's just what I mean. You see there are not more than half enough to go around."

"Well, why don't they wash them?"

"Too much trouble, I suppose. And besides, anything is good enough for a conscript."

Marcy did not in the least enjoy his supper. The soup was so badly smoked that it was not fit to eat, and the corn bread was not more than half baked. More than that, one of the prisoners urged him to make haste and "get away with that soup," for he wanted the pan as soon as he could have it.

"Don't mind him," said Bowen. "Take your time. That's the way they will all serve you when you get left."

Up to this time Marcy Gray had not been troubled very much with the pangs of homesickness. One seldom is when the bright sun

is shining and he can see what is going on
around him. It is when the quiet of night
comes and everybody else is asleep that the
young soldier thinks of home and the friends
he has left behind him. It was so with Marcy
Gray at any rate. When the supper dishes
had been removed, and somebody had touched
a match to a couple of sputtering candles
which threw out just light enough to show
how desolate and cheerless the big room really
was, and the prisoners began arranging their
blankets and quilts, and the joking and laughing ceased, then it was that Marcy's fortitude
was put to the test. He thought of his
mother, of Jack, and Ben Hawkins, who had
proved so stanch a friend to him, and told
himself that he would never see them again.
He had heard that nostalgia (that is the name
the doctors give to homesickness) killed people
sometimes, and he was sure it would kill him
before the month was ended.

"What are you doing at that window?"
demanded Bowen, breaking in upon his
revery.

"I am watching the sentry in the yard below," answered Marcy. "I wish I was in his place. It wouldn't take me long to slip away in the darkness and draw a bee-line for home."

"Well, you just let that sentry alone and come here and lie down," said Bowen.

"What's the use? I can't go to sleep."

"You can and you must. Sleep and eat all you can, hold your thoughts under control, and so keep up your strength. Come here and lie down."

Marcy knew that Bowen's advice was good, but it was hard to follow it. Reluctantly he stretched himself upon the man's blanket,— there was no room on the floor for him to spread his own,—pulled his valise under his head for a pillow, and listened while Bowen told of some exciting and amusing incidents that had fallen under his observation while he was trying to reach the Union lines. On three occasions, he said, he had acted as guide to small parties of escaped Federals who were slowly working their way out of Dixie, but somehow he never could induce them to remain very long in his company.

"They had the impudence to tell me that I

didn't know anything about the geography of my own State," said Bowen in an injured tone.

"That's what I think myself," replied Marcy. "Whatever put it into your head to come away up here to North Carolina, when you might have taken a short cut to the coast?"

"There you go just like the rest of them," said Bowen. "It shows how much you know of the situation down South. The Confederacy is like an empty egg-shell. There's nothing on the inside—no soldiers to be afraid of— nothing but niggers, who are only too glad to feed and shelter a Union man. You're safe while you stay on the inside, but the minute you try to get out is when the danger begins, for there's the shell in the shape of the armies by which the Confederacy is surrounded. There was no need of my being captured, and that's what provokes me. When I caught sight of the Union flag in Plymouth I thought I was safe and so, instead of keeping to the woods, I came out and followed the road ; and here I am. If I had held to the course that I followed all through my long journey, I'd have been among the boys in blue now instead of being shut up in jail."

"Did old Wilkins conscript you?"

"The minute I struck the jail. He took my descriptive list, robbed me of the little money I had left, and told me I could make up my mind to fight until the Confederates gained their independence."

"You'll die of old age before that day comes," said Marcy.

"That's what I think, and it's what more than half the people down South think. There are men and boys in the Confederate army who are as strong for the Union as Abe Lincoln is; but if they said so, or if they shirked their duty, they would be shot before they saw another sun rise. Now, if they put you and me on guard duty at one of their prison pens we'll not stay there any longer than we feel like it."

Bowen continued to whisper in this encouraging strain until long after the rest of the prisoners were wrapped in slumber; and finally Marcy's eyes grew heavy and he fell asleep himself.

CHAPTER XIV.

THE PRISON PEN.

WHEN Marcy Gray awoke the next morning he made the mental resolution that from that time forward, no matter what happened or how homesick he might be, he would follow Bowen's advice and example to the letter, eat and sleep all he could and keep up a brave heart, so as to be in readiness to improve the first opportunity for escape that presented itself. Fortunately some things occurred that made it comparatively easy for him to hold to his resolve for a few days at least. After some more smoked bean soup and half-baked corn bread had been served for breakfast (and this time Marcy did just what Bowen said he would, and pushed and crowded with the rest in order to get a clean pan to eat from), the grated door that led into the hall was thrown open and the commander of the prison appeared on the threshold with Captain Fletcher at his side. The latter held in his hand the book in which Marcy had seen his name and descriptive list entered the day before. A hush of expectancy fell upon the prisoners, who surged toward the door in a body. Something out of the ordinary was about to happen, and they were impatient to know what it was.

"Get back there!" shouted Captain Wilkins. "You seem to be in a mighty hurry to leave these good quarters, but some of you will wish yourselves back here before many days have passed over your heads."

These words had a depressing effect upon some of the prisoners, but they were very cheering to Marcy Gray and his friend Bowen. The captain made it plain that they were to be sent off in some direction, and anything was better than being shut up in that gloomy jail.

"As fast as your names are called pick up your plunder and go down into the yard and fall in for a march of seventy-five miles," continued the captain. "That will be your first taste of a soldier's life."

"Seventy-five miles," repeated Marcy.

"We must be going to Raleigh, and from there it is about a hundred miles by rail to Salisbury. By gracious, Bowen, if they send us there I'll not be much over two hundred miles from home."

"I hope they'll not separate us," was the reply. "That's what I am afraid of now."

Captain Fletcher called off the names as they were written in his book, and the prisoners one after another disappeared down the stairs. Some responded with a cheerful "here," and walked as briskly as though they were going home instead of into the army, while others answered in scarcely audible tones and moved with slow and reluctant steps. When Bowen's name was called he lingered long enough to give Marcy's hand a friendly squeeze, and when he passed through the door out of sight he seemed to have taken all the boy's courage with him; but when his own name was called a few minutes later, Marcy was himself again. He went into the jail yard and fell into the line that was being formed there under command of an officer he had not seen before. On the opposite side of

the yard was a company of soldiers, veterans
on the face of them, who were standing at
"parade rest," and Marcy straightway concluded that they were the men who were to
guard the prisoners during the march. Marcy
hoped they would continue to act in that
capacity as long as an escort was needed. He
wasn't afraid of veterans, but he did not want
any Home Guards put over him.

"What have you got in your grip?"
inquired the officer, as Marcy fell into his
place in line.

"Clothing, sir," answered the boy, holding
out the valise as if he thought the officer
wished to inspect it.

"I am willing to take your word for it,"
said the latter, who no doubt knew that Captain Wilkins had given the valise a thorough
examination. "I was going to suggest that
you had better wrap its contents in your
blanket and leave the grip behind. It will
only be in your way, and you don't want too
much luggage on the march."

Marcy thought the suggestion a good one,
and with the officer's permission he fell out

23

long enough to act upon it. By the time he took his place in line again the prisoners who were to be sent away were all assembled in the yard, and the commander and Captain Fletcher had come out of the jail. The few unfortunates who remained behind were suspected of being deserters, and they were to be detained until their record could be investigated. Captain Fletcher handed his book to the strange officer, who proceeded to call the roll a second time, for he had to receipt for the men committed to his care as if they had been so many bags of corn. When this had been done the prisoners were marched through the gate into one of Williamston's principal streets, the guards with loaded muskets on their shoulders fell in on both sides of them, and their weary journey, which was to end at a point more than three hundred miles away, was fairly begun.

They were nearly three weeks on the road, and during that time not an incident happened that was worthy of record. Marcy afterward said that all he could remember was that he was hungry all the time, and too tired and sleepy to think of escape, even if it had been safe to attempt it. Their veteran guards, who accompanied them no farther than Raleigh, told them that from that point they would travel by rail, and so they did as far as the rails went; but miles of the road-bed had to be traversed on foot because the road itself had been torn up by raiding parties of Union cavalry, who, after heating the rails red-hot, had wrapped them around trees or twisted them into such fantastic shapes that nothing but a rolling-mill could have straightened them out again.

At Raleigh a company of militia took charge of the conscripts (that was what everyone called them and what they called themselves now), and then their sufferings began. Their new guards were absolutely without feeling. The commanding officer either could not or would not keep them supplied with food, nor would he permit them to leave the ranks long enough to get a drink of water. Marcy, who found it hard to keep up under such circumstances, wanted to try what power there might be in one of his gold pieces, but Bowen would not listen to it.

"Not for the world would I have these ruffians know that you have good money in your
pocket," said he earnestly. "They would
make some excuse to shoot you in order to get
it. Hold fast to every dollar of it, for you will
see the time when you will need it worse than
you think you do now."

It was not until they arrived within a few
miles of their destination that Marcy and his
companions learned where they were going,
and what they were expected to do when they
got there. Some of the militia who were
doing guard duty at the Millen prison pen had
been ordered to Savannah, and the conscripts
were to take their places; but beyond the fact
that Millen was situated somewhere in the
eastern part of Georgia, a few miles south of
Waynesborough, their ignorant guards could
not tell them a thing about it.

"It must be pretty close to the coast, and
that's the way we'll go when we get ready to
make a break," said Marcy.

"And what would we do if we succeeded in
reaching the coast?" demanded Bowen. "It
would be the worst move we could make, for

it would take us right into danger. There are
no Union war ships stationed off the Georgia
coast, and even if there were, how could we
get out to them? No, sir. We'll go the other
way and strike for the Mississippi."

"And cross three States?" exclaimed Marcy,
astounded at the proposition. "Why, it must
be four or five hundred miles in a straight
line."

"No matter if it's a thousand," said Bowen
obstinately. "We'll be safe if we go that way,
and we'll be captured and shot if we go the
other. If we can only pass Macon I'll be
among friends."

"And if we can strike the Mississippi about
Baton Rouge *I* would be among friends," said
Marcy. "But across three States that are no
doubt infested with Home Guards and bloodhounds! Bowen, you're crazy."

"Not so crazy as you will show yourself to
be if you try to reach the coast," was the reply.
"But we haven't started yet, and you will
have plenty of time to think it over and decide
if you will go with me or strike out by yourself."

This conversation had a disheartening effect upon Marcy, who knew that if his clear-headed companion left him to take care of himself, his chances for seeing home and friends again were very slim indeed. While he was thinking about it, and trying to grasp the full meaning of the words "across three States infested with Home Guards and bloodhounds," the train stopped at Millen Junction and the conscripts were ordered to disembark. As fast as they left the cars they were drawn up in line near the depot, which was afterward burned by Sherman's cavalry, and the roll was called. After that they were formally turned over to the commander of the prison, who was there to receive them, and marched out to the stockade. Marcy had just time to note that it was a gloomy looking place and that a deep silence brooded over it, before he was marched into the fort, whose cannon commanded the prison at all points. There they were divided into messes and assigned to quarters, with the understanding that they were to go on duty the next morning at guard-mount. The barracks were crowded when Marcy first went into them, but some of the militia were ordered to Savannah that afternoon, and when they were gone he and Bowen were able to find a bunk. They had managed to be put into the same mess, and that was something to be thankful for.

So far the conscripts had nothing to complain of. Their supper was abundant and passably well cooked, and it was delightful to know that they could get a drink of water when they wanted it, without asking permission of some petty tyrant who was quite as likely to refuse as he was to grant the request. But Marcy looked forward with some misgivings to guard-mount the next morning. The idea of putting raw recruits through that complicated ceremony was a novel one to him, and although he had no fears for himself, he was afraid that the awkwardness of some of his companions would bring upon them the wrath of the adjutant ; that is, if the latter was at all strict, and liked to see things done in military form. Before he went to his bunk, however, he found that he had little to fear on that score. A sergeant came into the barracks with

a paper in his hand, and began warning the recruits for guard duty the next day, ordering
them to fall in line in front of him as fast as
their names were called. Marcy's was one of
the first on the list, and when it was read off
he stepped promptly to his place, dressed to
the right, and came to a front. The sergeant,
who knew a well-drilled man when he saw him,
was surprised. He looked curiously at Marcy
for a moment, and then went on calling off the
names of the guard.

"I'll bet I made a mistake in showing off
that way," thought Marcy. "As soon as this
company is organized they will take me out
of the ranks and make me a corporal or something, and that would be a misfortune, for I
shouldn't have half the chance to talk to
Bowen that I've got now."

There were forty recruits warned for duty,
and when they were all standing before him
the sergeant said that when they heard the
bugle sound the adjutant's call at nine o'clock
in the morning, they would be expected to
assemble on the parade ground, and when
they got there they would be armed and

told what to do. Then, having performed his duty, the sergeant faced them to the right and broke ranks, at the same time looking hard at Marcy and jerking his head over his shoulder toward the door. Marcy followed him when he left the barracks, and when they were out of hearing of everybody the sergeant said:

"Where have you been drilled?"

"At the Barrington Military Academy. I was there almost four years. But don't say anything about it, will you?"

"You're sure you're not a deserter?" continued the sergeant.

"No!" gasped Marcy. "I am a refugee. I haven't even been conscripted. I was arrested in my mother's presence and shoved into Williamston jail; and if I were a deserter, don't you suppose Captain Wilkins would have known it? What put that into your head?"

"Oh, I saw you had been drilled somewhere, and I didn't know but it was in the army. If that was the case you would be in a bad row of stumps among these Home Guards. If one of them could prove that you are a deserter he would get a thirty days' furlough."

"And what would be done with me?"

"I am sure I don't know, but nobody would ever see you again after General Winder got his hands on you."

"Who is General Winder?" inquired Marcy.

"He is the officer who has charge of all the Southern prisons, and it is owing to him that the Yanks are starving and dying by scores right here in this stockade," said the sergeant bitterly.

"Starving and dying by scores!" ejaculated Marcy, who had never heard of such a thing before.

"That's what I said. There were twenty-three bodies brought through that gate yesterday, and eighteen this morning."

"Why, that's brutal! it's downright heathenish!" exclaimed Marcy.

"Well, we can't give them what we haven't got, can we?" demanded the sergeant. "Winder could send us grub if he wanted to——"

"I know he could," interrupted Marcy. "There's plenty of it along the road between here and Raleigh. I saw it."

"But as long as he doesn't see fit to forward it we can't issue it to the prisoners," added the sergeant. "You don't want some Home Guard to report to him that you are a deserter, do you?"

"I should say not," exclaimed Marcy. "If that's the sort of a brute he is, I would stand no show at all with him. But no one can prove that I have ever been in the army before."

"They might put you to some trouble to prove that you haven't, and my object in bringing you out here was to warn you that you'd better not throw on any military airs while you stay in this camp."

"I am very grateful to you," replied Marcy, who did not expect to find a sympathizing friend in a rebel non-commissioned officer. "You are not a Home Guard?"

"Not much. I was one of the first men in our county to volunteer, but I couldn't stand hard campaigning, and so I asked to be put on light duty, and I had influence enough to carry my point. But I would have stayed in the army till I died if I had dreamed that I would be sent to help guard a slaughter-house; for that is just what this stockade is. The commander is nothing but a Home Guard, but he hates conscripts as bad as he does Yankees, and you want to watch out and do nothing to incur his displeasure."

"I don't know how to thank you——" began Marcy.

"That's all right. I knew as soon as I looked at you that you are as much out of place here as I am, and I don't want to see you get into trouble. Of course you won't repeat what I have said to you."

"Not by a long shot. You have done me too great a favor."

The two separated, and Marcy went into the barracks and sought his bunk, feeling as if he were in some way to blame for the sufferings of the Union soldiers who were confined within the stockade. That they should be allowed to perish for want of food, when there was an abundance of it scattered along the line of the railroad within easy reach of the prison, seemed so terrible to Marcy that he could not dismiss it from his mind so that he could go to sleep. He did not then know that the Confederate commissary was the worst managed branch of the army, and that General Bragg's men had been on short rations while in Corinth there was a pile of hard tack as long and high as the railroad depot that was going to waste. Our starving boys in Libby prison could look through the grated windows upon the fertile fields of Manchester, "waving with grain and alive with flocks and herds," and General Lee wrote that there were supplies enough in the country, and if the proper means were taken to procure them there would not be so many desertions from his army. Every Union soldier who died for want of food in Southern prison pens was deliberately murdered, and the Richmond papers declared that General Winder was to blame for it. If the latter had not been summoned by death to answer before a higher tribunal, there is no doubt but that he would have been hanged by sentence of court martial as Captain Wirz was.

Marcy Gray scarcely closed his eyes in slumber that night, and when he did, his sleep was disturbed by horrible dreams in which starving prisoners and unfeeling Confederate officers bore prominent parts. He arose from his bunk as weary and dispirited as he was when he got into it, breakfasted on a cup of sweet potato coffee and a small piece of corn bread, and when the adjutant's call sounded was one of the first to appear on the parade ground ; but he did not take as much pains to fall in like a soldier as he did the day before.   On the contrary he seemed to be the greenest one among the conscripts, for when he was commanded to "dress up a little on the right centre" he did not move until the adjutant shook his sword at him and asked if he were hard of hearing.

In only one particular did this guard-mount resemble those in which Marcy had often taken part at the Barrington Academy.   The guard, which was composed of an equal number of Home Guards and conscripts, was divided into two platoons with an officer of the guard in command of each, and an officer of the day in command of the whole, and there all attempts to follow the tactics ceased except when the adjutant saluted the new officer of the day and reported, "Sir, the guard is formed." There was no band to sound off and no marching in review. Instead of that the officer of the day said to one of his lieutenants, "Go ahead, Billy, and fill up the boxes," and in obedience to the order, the same sergeant who had warned the conscripts for duty the night before placed himself at the head of the first platoon, to which Marcy belonged, and marched them to the commander's headquarters, where they were supplied with old-fashioned muskets and cartridge-boxes.

"Give me that gun!" shouted the sergeant, who was out of all patience when he saw that some of the conscripts held their pieces at trail arms, and that others placed them on their shoulders as they might have done if they had been going to hunt squirrels in the woods. "Now watch me. This is shoulder arms. Put your guns that way, all of you, and keep them there."

So saying he marched the platoon away to

relieve the sentries on post. Marcy was No. 6, and this brought him to a station about the middle of the eastern side of the stockade. When his number was called he followed the sergeant up a ladder and into a box from which a grizzly Home Guard had been keeping watch during the morning hours. The latter, instead of bringing his musket to arms port, as he ought to have done when passing his orders, dropped the butt of it to the floor and rested his chin on his hands, which he clasped over the muzzle.

"There aint nothing much to do but jest loaf here and keep an eye on them abolitionists," said he, jerking his head toward the stockade. "Do you see that dead-line down there ? Well, if you see one of 'em trying to get over or under it shoot him down ; and don't stop to ask him no questions, neither. I'd like mighty well to get a chance to do it, kase I want thirty days home. I reckon that's all, aint it, sard ?"

The sergeant said he reckoned it was, and when the two went down the ladder Marcy stepped to the side of his box and took his first

view of the inside of a Southern prison pen.
He had seen a picture of Camp Douglas in an
illustrated paper which Captain Burrows gave
him one day when he was in Plymouth, and
had taken note that the Confederate prisoners
there confined were provided with comfortable
quarters, into which they could retreat in
stormy weather, and where they could find
shade when the sun grew too hot for them;
but there was nothing of the kind inside this
stockade. There was no shelter from sun or
rain except such as the prisoners had been able
to provide for themselves. There were multi-
tudes of little tents made of blankets, which
were hardly high enough for a man to crawl
into, and scattered among them were mounds
of earth that looked so much like graves that
Marcy was startled when he saw a ragged,
emaciated apparition, which had once been an
able-bodied Union soldier, slowly emerge from
one of them and throw himself down upon the
ground as if he didn't care whether he ever got
up again or not. The stockade was crowded
with just such pitiful objects, who dragged
their skeleton forms wearily over the sun-

24

baked earth, or lay as motionless as dead men under the shelter of their little tents. It was a spectacle to which no language could do justice, and Marcy turned from it sick at heart to make an examination of the stockade itself. It was built of pine logs set upright in the ground and scored on each side so that they would stand closely together, and they were held in place by heavy planks which were spiked across them on the outside near the top. Built upon little platforms, located at regular intervals around the top of the stockade, were sentry boxes like the one Marcy now occupied, to which access was gained by ladders leading from the ground outside. On the inside of the stockade, about fifteen feet from it and running parallel to it all the way around, was a railing three feet high made by nailing strips of boards to posts that had been firmly set in the ground. It was an innocent looking thing, but it had sent into eternity more than one brave man who had incautiously approached it. It was the dead-line.

"But it will never be the death of anybody while I am on post," thought Marcy, wonder-

ing how any man could want a furlough bad
enough to shoot a fellow being down in cold
blood. "I never could look my mother or
Jack in the face if I should do a deed like
that, and I'd never have a good night's rest.
Heaven will never smile upon a cause upheld
by men who are as cruel as these rebels are.
They ought to be whipped."

Long before the time arrived for him to be
relieved Marcy became so affected by the sight
of the misery and suffering he had no power
to alleviate that he wanted to drop his
musket and take to his heels; and he would
have welcomed a cyclone or an earthquake, or
any other convulsion of nature, that would
have shut it out from his view forever. On
several occasions some of the thirsty wretches
approached within a few feet of the dead-
line, with battered, smoke-begrimed cups or
pieces of bent tin in their hands, to drink
from the sluggish stream that flowed through
the pen—for the water was clearer there
than it was anywhere else—and then it was
that the fiendish nature of the sentry in the
next box on the right showed itself. As

often as a prisoner drew near to the stream
with a dish in his hand, this man would cock
his musket, bring it to a ready, and crane his
long neck eagerly forward, as if he hoped that
the soldier might forget himself and approach
close enough to the fatal line to give him an
excuse for shooting. Once or twice Marcy
was on the point of warning the boys in blue
to keep farther away, but he remembered in
time that he had been told to ask no questions, and that was the same as an order for-
bidding him to speak to the prisoners. To his
great joy the sentry who was so anxious to
have a furlough did not earn it that day. At ·
length Marcy saw the relief approaching, and
then he took the first long, easy breath he had
drawn for four miserable hours. He passed
his orders in as few words as possible and
hurried down the ladder, feeling as if he had
just been released from prison himself. He
marched around the stockade with the relief,
and was surprised to see how extensive it was.
It was not crowded like Andersonville, nor
were the sanitary conditions quite so bad ; but
they were bad enough, and the mortality was

just as great in proportion to the number of
prisoners confined in it. When they reached
the barracks the platoon to which he belonged
was drilled for half an hour at stacking arms,
and it was not until the movement was accomplished to his satisfaction that the officer of
the guard allowed them to break ranks and go
to dinner.

"You look as though you had had a spell
of sickness," were the first words his friend
Bowen said to him, when the two found
opportunity to exchange a few words in
private. "What's the matter?"

"Wait until you have stood in one of those
boxes for four hours, and see if you don't feel
as bad as I look," answered Marcy. "It's
awful, and I don't see how I can go there again.
Why, Charley, the sentry who stood next to
me fairly ached to shoot one of those poor
fellows. I never saw a quail hunter more
eager to get a shot than he was."

"Did the prisoner come near the dead-
line?"

"There must have been fifty or more of
them who came to the bayou to get a drink;

but they were not within ten feet of the dead-line."

"And what did you do?"

"I? I didn't do anything."

"Well, the next time that thing happens, I would make a little demonstration, if I were in your place," said Bowen. "You can act as if you were going to shoot, but of course you needn't unless you have to."

"Do you want me to understand that I will be reported if I don't?"

"That's what I mean. I have had a talk with some of these Home Guards this morning, and have found out what sort of chaps they are. If you are too easy with the prisoners you'll get them down on you, and then they'll tell on you whether you do anything wrong or not. And you want to keep out of the clutches of the captain, for he's a heathen."

Marcy afterward had occasion to remember this warning.

CHAPTER XV.

THE life that Marcy Gray led during the next three weeks can be compared to nothing but a nightmare. His duties were not heavy, but the trouble was that when he tried to go to sleep he saw the inside of the prison pen as plainly as he did while he was standing in his box. He saw long lines of dead men carried out, too, and tumbled unceremoniously into the trenches outside the stockade, where they were left without a head-board to show who they were or where they came from. All this while he was losing flesh and strength as well as courage, and Bowen declared that, if they did not "make a break" very soon, Marcy would have to go into the hospital.

"I feel as though I ought to go there now," said the latter wearily. "To tell the honest truth, I haven't pluck enough to make a break for liberty ; we are too closely watched.

When I am on post after dark, I notice that an officer or a corporal comes around every hour to see if the guard is all right."

"That happens only on pleasant nights; but I have noticed that on stormy nights the officer of the guard hugs his comfortable quarters as closely as we do our boxes," replied Bowen. "You'll pick up and be yourself again as soon as we are out of reach of this place, and you mustn't give way to your gloomy feelings. The next rainy night that we are on post together we'll skip. I have been making inquiries about the country west of here, and know just how to travel in order to reach my home. All you've got to do is to be ready to move when I say the word, and I will take you safely through."

It would have been very comforting to hear Bowen talk in this confident way, if Marcy had only been able to believe that the man could keep his promise; but unfortunately he could not get up any enthusiasm. The spiritless prisoners inside the stockade were not more indifferent to their fate than he was to his. There had been no attempts at escape that

Marcy knew anything about, but two unfinished tunnels had been discovered and filled
up, and the pack of "nigger dogs" that the
commander used in tracking fugitives had
been brought into the pen and exhibited to the
prisoners, so that they might know what they
had to expect in case they succeeded in getting outside the stockade. But Bowen declared that the hounds would not bother him
and Marcy. If they escaped during a storm
the rain would wash away the scent so that
they could not be tracked.

It was while Marcy was in this unfortunate
frame of mind that something occurred to
arouse him from his lethargy and drive him
almost to desperation. It was on the morning
following the day on which a fresh lot of
prisoners had been received into the pen.
Marcy stood near the gate when they went in,
and noticed that there were not more than
half a dozen blankets in the party, that some
of them were barefooted, and others destitute
of coats and hats.

"Them Yanks haint got nothin' to trade,"
said a Home Guard who stood near him.

"Whose fault is it?" replied Marcy. "They never looked that way when they were captured."

"No, I don't reckon they did. Them fellars up the country have went through 'em good fashion. But I don't blame 'em for that. I only wish I could get the first pull at a Yank who has a good coat or a pair of number ten shoes onto his feet. I wouldn't be goin' around ragged like I am now, I bet you."

It was one of these fresh prisoners who caused Marcy Gray to fall into the clutches of the commander of the prison, whom Bowen had denounced as a "heathen." He went on post at twelve o'clock the next day, Bowen occupying the box on his right, while the Home Guard who said he would like to have a chance to steal a coat and a pair of shoes stood guard in the one on his left. The new prisoners had had time to take in the situation, and to learn that if they preferred a shelter of some sort to the bare ground, or cooked rations instead of raw ones, they were at liberty to provide themselves with these luxuries if they could, for their captors would not

furnish them. But how could they be expected to build dug-outs when they did not
have even pocket knives to dig with? and how
could they bake corn bread when every flat
stone and piece of board that could be found
was in the possession of someone who would
not part with it for love or money? There
was a treasure lying on the ground in front of
Marcy's box, and directly under the strip of
board that marked the inner edge of the dead-
line. It was a battered tin cup. How it
came there, and why someone had not tried
to obtain possession of it, was a mystery; but
it had been discovered by a party of new-
comers, perhaps a dozen of them in all, who
looked at the cup with longing eyes and then
glanced apprehensively at Marcy, who leaned
on his musket and looked down on them.
One of the most daring of the party seemed
determined to make an effort to secure the
cup, but as often as he bent forward as if he
were about to make a dash for it, his comrades seized him and pulled him back.

"Poor fellow," thought Marcy, who ad-
mired the prisoner's courage. "He little

knows how glad I would be to tell him to come and get it. The cup isn't inside the dead-line anyway, and if he makes a grab for it he can have it for all I will do to stop him."

The result of this mental resolution was the same as though Marcy had announced it in words. As quick as thought the daring soldier made a jump for the dead-line, snatched the cup from the ground, and in a second more was back among his comrades, who closed around him in a body, effectually covering him from the three muskets, Marcy's, Bowen's, and the Home Guard's, that were pointed in his direction. They ran among the tents and dug-outs and mingled with the other prisoners, so that it would have been impossible for the guards to identify a single one of them.

"Good for the Yank!" thought Marcy. "That's what I call pluck. He'll have something to dig with at any rate, and perhaps he can straighten that cup out so that he can cook his corn meal in it."

If Marcy and Bowen had fired at the man it would have been with the intention of missing him, but not so with the Home Guard on the

left, who would have drawn a fine bead in the
hope of winning a thirty days' furlough. The
latter was fighting mad. He shook his fist at
Marcy and shouted in stentorian tones :

" Corporal of the guard, number 'leven ! "

" By gracious ! " gasped Marcy. " He's
going to report it."

He glanced toward Bowen's box, and knew
by the way his friend shook his head at him
that there was trouble in store for somebody ;
but how could he be blamed more than anyone else ? than the Home Guard, for instance,
who had as fair a chance to shoot as any
blood-thirsty rebel could ask for ? The corporal came promptly and went into the Home
Guard's box, and Marcy could see the angry
man pointing out the position of the cup and
flourishing his clenched hand in the air to give
emphasis to something he was saying. After
the corporal had heard his story he descended
the ladder and came into Marcy's box.

" Sentry, what were you put here for, anyway ? " were the first words he spoke. " Why
didn't you shoot that man ? "

" There were two reasons why I didn't do

it," answered Marcy. "My orders are to shoot if I see a prisoner trying to get over or under the dead-line, but that man didn't try to get over or under, for the cup wasn't inside. It was under that strip of board."

"No matter. It was *at* the dead-line, and it was your business to pop him over," said the corporal. "I am afraid the old man will give you a taste of military discipline when you come off post."

"Why should he? I haven't disobeyed any order. And the other reason why I didn't shoot was because I didn't have time. That Yank was as swift as a bird on the wing, and before you could wink twice he was back among his friends, and I couldn't see him."

"Then why didn't you shoot into the crowd?" demanded the corporal.

"And kill or wound somebody who hadn't done a thing?" exclaimed Marcy.

"Why, what's the matter with you? I shall begin to think pretty soon that you are a Yank yourself. Of course you ought to have fired into the crowd and made an example of somebody. What's one Yank more or less, anyway? I believe in shooting everyone who comes down here."

"Why didn't that man in the next box shoot?" inquired Marcy. "He had the same chance I had, and is as much to blame because that Yank made a dash to the dead-line and got the cup."

"Not much he aint. The thing happened directly in front of your post, it was your duty to kill that man, you disobeyed orders by not doing it, and of course I shall have to report you."

"If I get into trouble by it I shall shoot at the next man who comes within twenty feet of the dead-line," said Marcy.

"You'll be sorry you didn't make that resolution long ago," replied the corporal, as he backed down the ladder. He went into Bowen's box to hear what he had to say about it, and then went back to headquarters; and two hours later the relief came around.

"If I had been in your box I would have been on my way home by this time to-morrow," said the Home Guard, as he and Marcy and Bowen fell into their places in the rear of the line. "You'll never have another chance like that to earn a furlough. Why didn't you shoot that there Yank?"

"Why didn't you?" retorted Marcy. "You had as good a show as I."

"Not much, I didn't. He was closter to you nor he was to me, and besides I didn't have time."

"Neither did I. I never could hit a moving object with a single bullet."

"You could have showed your good will if you had been a mind to. That's what I think, and less'n the old man has changed mightily sense I jined his comp'ny, it's what he'll think about it, too."

The unhappy Marcy had made up his mind that he would have to stand punishment of some sort for permitting a prisoner to put his hand under the dead-line; and his worst fears were confirmed when he came within sight of the barracks and saw all the officers of the guard and the commander of the prison standing there, and three Home Guards stationed close by, with muskets in their hands. When the platoon was halted before the door and brought to a front, the captain said:

"No. 12, step out here."

As that was the number of the post from which Marcy had just been relieved, he moved one pace to the front and saluted.

"So you are the low-down conscript who presumes to set my orders at defiance, are you?" continued the captain. "What were you put in that box for? Why did you allow that prisoner to come to the line?"

"Sir, my orders were——" began Marcy.

"Shut up!" shouted the captain, growing red in the face. "If you talk back to me I'll put a gag in your mouth. Trice him up, and leave him that way till he learns who's boss of this camp."

Without saying a word, one of the three Home Guards before spoken of took Marcy's musket from his hand, while another unbuckled the belt that held his cartridge-box. Then they laid hold of his arms, and with the officer of the guard marching in front and the third soldier bringing up the rear, led him to a tree that stood before the door of the cap-

25

tain's quarters. It did not take them more than two minutes to do their cruel work, and when it was over and the officer of the guard moved away with two of his men, leaving the other to keep watch over the culprit with a loaded musket, Marcy Gray was standing on his toes, and his arms were drawn high above his head by a strong cord which had been tied around his thumbs and thrown over a limb of the tree. The pain was intense, but the boy shut his teeth hard and gave no sign of suffering till his head fell over on his shoulder and he fainted dead away. When he came to himself he was lying in his bunk, his wounded hands were resting in a basin of hot water which Bowen was holding for him, and another good-hearted conscript was keeping his head and face wet with water he had just drawn from the well. Their countenances were full of sympathy, and there were signs of rage to be seen as well.

"This is rough on me, boys," groaned Marcy.

"While you were hanging to that tree I asked some questions about Captain Denning," whispered Bowen, "and now I know who he is, and where he hails from. He owns a fine plantation about twenty miles from where I live when I am at home, and we shall pass it on our way to the river."

"O Charley, let's go to-night," murmured Marcy. "I shall die if I stay here any longer."

"That's what I have thought all along, and I am with you when we go on post at twelve o'clock. It's going to rain like smoke in less than half an hour, and when it begins it will keep it up for a day or two. I am glad if you have been waked up, but sorry it had to be done in this way."

"Captain Denning will be sorry for it, too," said Marcy.

In spite of the agony he was in, but one thought filled Marcy Gray's mind, and that was that under no circumstances would he pass another day alive in that camp. No matter how great the danger might be, he would escape that very night. He would go with a musket in his hand and a box of cartridges by his side, and if he were recaptured, it would be after every bullet in those cartridges had found a lodgement in the body of some Home Guard. He did not have very much to say, but Bowen knew by the expression on his face that Marcy was thoroughly aroused at last.

Marcy did not want any supper, but managed to eat a little, and to slip a generous piece of corn bread in his pocket for the lunch he knew he would need before morning. The storm did not come in half an hour, as Bowen had predicted, but it came a little later, and when the two went on post at twelve o'clock, the night was as dark as a pocket, and the rain was falling in torrents.

"Splendid weather," Bowen found opportunity to whisper to Marcy. "It couldn't be better. Listen for my signal, for we must start as soon as the guard is out of the way."

"You'll take your gun?" said Marcy.

"Of course, and I'll use it too, before I will allow myself to be brought back here."

If it was a splendid night for their purpose it was a terrible one for the prisoners, especially for the new-comers who had not had time to finish their dug-outs. To make matters worse for them there had been a sudden and noticeable change in the temperature. It was almost freezing cold, and protected as he was by the walls of his box, and by his warm blanket, which he had tied over his shoulders like a cloak, Marcy shivered as he stood with his musket in the hollow of his arm and his aching, bandaged hands clasped in front of him. He stood thus for ten minutes when he heard a gentle tapping at the foot of his ladder. That was the signal agreed upon between him and Bowen, and without a moment's hesitation Marcy wheeled around and backed to the ground.

"Is this you, Charley?" he whispered. "I can't see a thing."

"No more can I," was the answer, "but I know where we are and which way we want to go, and that's enough. Grab hold of the tail of my blanket and I will pilot you to the railroad track. Mark my words: We'll never hear a hound-dog on our trail. They'll think we have struck for the coast, and that's the way they'll go to find us."

If we were to write a full history of the long
tramp these two fugitives made before they
found themselves safe at Rodney Gray's home,
as we have described in a former chapter, it
would be to repeat the experience of hundreds
of escaped Union prisoners whose thrilling
stories have already been given to the world.
Captain Denning's "nigger dogs" never once
gave tongue on their trail, and at no time were
they in serious danger of falling into the hands
of their enemies. Of course there were other
Home Guards and other dogs in Alabama and
Mississippi, and more than once they were pursued by them ; but every negro they met on
the road was their friend, and, believing Marcy
and Bowen to be escaped Federals, took big
risks to help them on their way. During the
three days they rested at Bowen's home in
Georgia they were in more danger than at any
other time, for Bowen's neighbors were all
rebels. They knew that he had been forced
into the army, and if they had suspected that
he was hiding in the loft of his father's cotton
gin, they would have left no stone unturned to
effect his capture. But outside of Bowen's

family no one knew it except one or two faithful blacks, who could be trusted, and after they had made up for the sleep they had lost, and some of Marcy's money had been expended for clothing, shoes, and blankets, the fugitives set out to pay their respects to the commander of the prison from which they had escaped. They remained on his plantation a part of one night, and when they left, everything that would burn was in flames. It was a high-handed proceeding, and many a soldier not wanting in courage would have hesitated about taking chances so desperate ; but fortunately another rain storm washed out their trail and if they were pursued they never knew it.

"There's one thing I am sorry for," said Marcy, as he and Bowen halted for a moment on the summit of a little rise of ground from which they had a fair view of the destructive work that was going on on the plantation they had just left. " I am not revengeful, but I do think Captain Denning ought to be punished for giving me these hands that I may not be able to use for months, and I wish he could know that I had a hand in starting that fire."

Marcy's hands certainly were in a bad way. They needed medical attention, but if there was a surgeon in the country they had not been able to find it out. Bowen gave them the best care he could, but Marcy was so nearly help-less that he could not even carry his musket. He took no note of time or of the progress they made, but left everything to his friend Bowen, who could always tell him where they were, how many miles they had made that day, and how far they would have to travel before they could get something to eat. If he sometimes drew on his imagination, and shortened the distance to the Mississippi by a hundred miles or so, who can blame him? He knew that everything depended on keeping up Marcy's courage.

At last, when the homesick boy became so weary and foot-sore that he could scarcely drag himself along the dusty road, he noticed with a thrill of hope that the negroes who befriended him and Bowen no longer spoke of "Alabam'" but had a good deal to say about "Mississipp'"; and this made it plain to Marcy that they were slowly drawing near to the end of their journey, and that his companion had been deceiving him.

"If you are as well acquainted with the country as you pretend to be, how does it come that you didn't know when we passed the boundary line into the State of Mississippi?" said he. "But I don't care. I remember enough of geography to know about where we are now, and that we will save time and distance if we strike a straight southeast course, for that is the way Baton Rouge lies from here."

Bowen, who had long been out of his reckoning, was quite willing to resign the leadership, and it was a fortunate thing for them that he was; for the course Marcy marked out brought them in due time to the Ohio and Mobile Railroad a few miles north of Enterprise. A night or two before they got there (they always traveled at night and slept during the daytime), they were kept busy dodging small bodies of Confederate soldiers who were journeying along the same road and in the same direction with themselves. They were evidently concentrating at some point in advance, but where and for what purpose the fugitives could not determine until some negroes, to whom they appealed for assistance, told them of Grierson's raid.

"Dat Yankee come down hyar from some place up de country, an' he whop an' he burn an' he steal eberyting he see," said one of the blacks gleefully. "But de rebels gwine cotch him at Enterprise, an' you two best not go da'."

This glorious news infused wonderful life and strength into Marcy Gray. He forgot his aching hands and feet, and from that time carried his own musket and moved as if he were set on springs. He would hardly consent to halt long enough to take needed rest, for he was anxious to intercept Grierson if possible, and warn him that the rebels were concentrating to resist his further advance.. But as it happened Colonel Grierson was miles away, and it was Captain Forbes, with a squad of thirty-five men, who had been detached from the main body to cut the telegraph north of Macon, that the fugitives found and warned. They ran upon them by accident, and at

first thought they had fallen into the hands
of the rebels.   One bright moonlight night
they were hurrying along a road which ran
through a piece of thick timber, when all on a
sudden they were brought to a standstill by
four men, who stepped from the shade of the
trees and covered them with their guns before
they said a word.   They were soldiers, for their
brass buttons showed plainly in the dim light;
but whether they wore the blue or the gray was
a momentous question that the fugitives could
not answer.   When one of them spoke it was
in a subdued voice.

"Who comes there?" he demanded.

"Friends," replied Marcy in tones just
loud enough to be heard and understood.
Then, believing that the truth would hold
its own anywhere, he added desperately;
"We are escaped conscripts on our way to
the Mississippi, and we want to see Grierson."

"Advance, friends, but be careful how you
take them guns from your shoulders," was the
next order; and when Marcy drew nearer and
saw that the speaker wore the yellow *chevrons*

of a corporal of cavalry on his arms, his joy knew no bounds. When he and Bowen had been relieved of their muskets and cartridge-boxes the corporal inquired :

"Where are the rest of you ?"

"There are no more of us," answered Marcy. "We are alone."

"Mebbe you are and mebbe you aint," said the corporal. "Jones, you take 'em down to the captain and hurry back as quick as you can, for we may need you here."

The corporal was suspicious and in bad humor about something, and so was the captain when they found him. He had been riding hard all day, and had halted in the woods to give his jaded men and horses an hour or two of rest. He knew that he had been led into a trap by false information, and by a treacherous guide who managed to escape amid a shower of bullets that was rained upon him as soon as his treachery was discovered ; and while his men slept the captain rolled restlessly about on the ground, trying to think up some plan by which he could save his small command from falling into the hands of the

Confederates, who were making every effort to cut him off from Grierson's column. He had been assured that the way to Enterprise was clear, and that if he went in any other direction he would have to fight his way through, and now came these two escaped conscripts with a different story. It was little wonder that Captain Forbes did not put much faith in what they had to say, or that he spoke sharply when he addressed them.

"How do you know that the Confederate troops you say you saw along the road were striking for Enterprise?" he inquired.

"Because the negroes told us so, and during our journey we have always found that the negroes told us the truth," answered Marcy, who did most of the talking.

"And you say you have come from Millen?"

"Yes, sir. We were on post there when we escaped."

"Do you know where Millen is?"

"Of course we know where it is."

"Well, now, what I want to know is this:

Why did you take such a long tramp through the country when you were within less than a hundred miles of the coast?"

Bowen answered this question, giving their reasons as we have given them to the reader, but the captain acted as though he did not believe a word of it. Marcy tried to help him out by telling of the relatives he expected to meet when he reached the Mississippi River, and the story was so improbable that the captain told them bluntly that he believed they were spies, that they had come into his camp to see how many men he had under his command, and that they hoped to escape to their friends with the information. Marcy was surprised and hurt to find himself suspected by the officer he wanted to help.

" I assure you, sir——" he began.

"I've had that trick played on me twice during this scout, and if it is played on me again it will be my own fault," interrupted the captain. "Consider yourselves in arrest."

He ordered a sentry to be placed over them at once, and we may add that Marcy and his friend were under suspicion all the time, and under guard most of the time they remained with Grierson's men.

The next morning at daylight Captain Forbes resumed his rapid march, and in two hours' time arrived within sight of Enterprise, which, to his amazement and alarm, he found to be filled with rebel soldiers. There were three thousand of them. They were in motion too, and that proved that they were aware of his coming and making ready to attack him. A fight meant annihilation or capture, and there was but one way to prevent it. Halting his men in the edge of a piece of woods out of sight of the enemy, Captain Forbes called a single officer to his side and galloped boldly toward the town. He was gone half an hour, and when he returned he placed himself at the head of his squad and led it in a headlong retreat, which did not end until the captain reported to Colonel Grierson at Pearl River. In speaking of this dashing exploit history says: "The captain, understanding his danger, tried to bluff the enemy and succeeded. He rode boldly up to the town and demanded the instant surrender of the place to Colonel Grierson. Colonel Goodwin, commanding the Confederate force, asked an hour to consider the proposition, to which request Forbes was only too willing to accede. That hour, with rapid riding, delivered his little company from its embarrassing situation."

That rapid retreat was about as much as Marcy and Bowen could stand after their long walk across the country. They were given broken-down plough-mules to ride, and these delightful beasts, which took every step under protest and "bucked" viciously when pressed too hard, had well-nigh jolted the breath out of them by the time they reached the main column at Pearl River. But they journeyed more leisurely after that, all the most dangerous places along their line of march having been left behind, and when the fugitives learned that they were within forty-eight hours' ride of Baton Rouge, and that the column would pass through Mooreville on the following day, they asked and obtained permission to accompany the scouts that were sent on ahead the next morning. That was the way they came to ride into Rodney Gray's dooryard as we have recorded.

"You have heard my story," concluded Marcy, settling contentedly back among the pillows. "Now, who is going to give me a drink of water?"

"How you must have suffered," said his aunt, with tears in her eyes.

"It's all over now," replied the young hero cheerfully, "and I am anxious to send word to mother. I wish one of you would write to her at Plymouth, care of Captain Burrows, and I am sure he will have the letter delivered."

"Do you know that you slept for eighteen straight hours?" replied Rodney. "Well, that gave me time to write the letter and take it to Baton Rouge and mail it to the address Jack gave me before he went home. Now that you are safe I don't see what there is to hinder Jack from carrying out his plan of becoming a cotton trader. If he wants to pay back to his mother every dollar she is likely to lose by this war, I don't know any better thing for him to do."

"Did you say as much in your letter?"

26

"I said all that and more. I am sure he will come, if it is only to see you."

"Rodney, you're a brick," exclaimed Marcy. "But I wish you could tell me more about Tom Allison and Mark Goodwin."

But Rodney couldn't, for the very good reason that all Jack said about it was that they had been bushwhacked; and with this meagre information Marcy was obliged to be satisfied.

CHAPTER XVI.

IT was a long time before Marcy Gray could bring himself to believe that he was not dreaming, and that he would awake to find himself a conscript guard at the Millen prison pen, but this uncertainty did not prevent him from making long strides toward recovery. His faithful friend Bowen declared that he could *see* him getting well. In less than a week he was strong enough to ride to Baton Rouge with Rodney. He reported to the provost marshal, who listened in amazement to his story, and gave him and Bowen a standing pass in and out of the Union lines. At the end of two weeks he began to wonder why he did not hear from Jack, and at the end of three that wished-for individual presented himself in person, much to the delight of all his relatives. He rode into Rodney's yard in company with Mr. Gray, as he had done on a

former occasion, and no sooner did his eyes
rest upon Marcy, who sprang down the steps
to meet him, than he began quoting something.

" This accident and flood of fortune
 So far exceed all instance, all discourse,
 That I am ready to distrust mine eyes,
 And wrangle with my reason that persuades me
 To any other trust,"

exclaimed Jack, as he swung himself from his
mule and clasped his strong arms about the
brother he had never thought to see again.
"How are you, conscript?"

"O Jack!" was all Marcy could say in
reply.

"She's pretty well," said the sailor, who
knew that Marcy would have asked about his
mother if his heart hadn't been so full, "and
has grown ten years younger since she heard
you were safe among friends."

He shook hands with Rodney, whom he addressed as "Johnny," and then walked up to
Bowen and fairly doubled him up with one of
his sailor grips.

" You are the man I have to thank for saving my brother's life, are you?" said he in a trembling voice. "I don't know that I shall ever have a chance to show how grateful I am to you, but if you ever need a friend you will always find him in Jack Gray."

It was a happy meeting altogether, and if one might judge by the way he acted, Sailor Jack himself didn't know whether he was awake or dreaming. Marcy's hands still showed the effect of his unmerited punishment, and when his big brother looked at them, an expression came upon his face that might have made Captain Denning a trifle uneasy if he had been there to see it.

"My orders are to bring you home with me, young man," said he. "And, Bowen, you must go, too."

"Don't you think it would be dangerous?" inquired Rodney, who had somehow got it into his head that Marcy would have to live with him as long as the war continued.

"Union people are safer in our country now than they ever were before," answered Jack. "There's been some shooting done up there since I wrote to you."

"O Jack!" exclaimed Marcy. "Were Tom and Mark very badly hurt?"

"Hurt!" repeated the sailor. "Well, I reckon so. They were killed deader'n herrings, and so were Beardsley, Shelby, and Dillon. Buffum, the spy who was the means of getting you captured, was hanged, and so was mother's old overseer, Hanson. I tell you, Rodney, the country is full of Union men, and they have been carrying things with a high hand since Marcy went away."

"I should think they had," said the latter, who had never been more astounded. "I am sorry to hear about Tom and Mark."

"Well, then, why didn't they mind their own business? If they'd had a grain of common sense they would have known that they were bound to get paid off sooner or later. They brought it on themselves, and it is a wonder to me that they were not dealt with long before."

"Jack," said Marcy suddenly. "You had no hand in it?"

"Not a hand. Not a finger, though there's no telling what I might have done if Captain

Denning had been there, and I had known
that he triced you up for nothing. Your
friends, the refugees, didn't need any help
from me. There are eighty or a hundred of
them now, and they have become regular guerillas. They are well armed, and when I came
away were talking of raiding Williamston
and burning the jail. I think you will be safe
at home, for rebel cavalry don't scout through
our section any more."

"How soon do you expect to go?" inquired
Rodney.

"Just as soon as I can fill up the *Hyperion's*
hold," replied Jack. "She is due in New
Orleans week after next, and I want a boat-
load of cotton ready for her when she pulls in
to the wharf. So you can trot out your four
hundred bales as soon as you get ready, and
I will give you twenty-five cents greenback
money for it. I was dead broke when I was
here before, but I'm wealthy now," added
Jack, pulling from his pocket a roll of bills
that was almost as big as his wrist. "Marcy,
that's mother's money."

"I am overjoyed to hear it," said the boy.

"And she was overjoyed to get rid of it, for it has been nothing but a botheration to her ever since she drew it from the bank. Old Morris showed me where you and he buried it on the night you dug it out of the cellar wall, and I brought it to New Orleans and exchanged it for greenbacks at a premium that made me open my eyes. I am first officer of the *Hyperion*, and in partnership with her owners. I do not expect to have time to make more than two or three trips on her before the Mississippi is opened, and then I hope to come back here and run a trading boat on the river."

"Where will I be while you are doing that?" inquired Marcy.

"At home with your mother, where all good boys ought to be. You will get not less than a dollar for your cotton," said Jack, turning to Rodney, "perhaps a dollar ten, minus the freight——"

"You don't mean it!" Rodney almost gasped; for Jack's matter-of-fact way of speaking of the fortune that seemed about to drop into his father's hands took his breath away.

"What's the reason I don't mean it? I hope you don't imagine that I am going to let anyone speculate with your property!" exclaimed the sailor. "Whatever the market price is when your cotton is landed in New York, that you will get, less the freight the *Hyperion* will charge you for taking it there. The twenty-five cents I am authorized to offer you is business; what you will receive over and above that will be owing to kinship. Your father and mine were brothers. Now what shall we do with that man Lambert; send him North for a guerilla or what?"

"I am perfectly willing to buy him off," said Mr. Gray. "I can afford to be liberal, for I really believe we would have lost our cotton if it hadn't been for him and his 'phantom bushwhackers.'"

"I am afraid he'll not let you buy him off for any reasonable sum," said Rodney.

"You might try him the first chance you get and find out what he is willing to do," suggested Jack. "Any way to get rid of him, so that he will not bushwhack the teamsters we shall send into the woods after the cotton."

"I suppose you have a permit this time," observed Rodney.

"Right from headquarters. We didn't ask for military protection, and it isn't likely that we would have got it if we had; but we are at liberty to take as many bales of cotton through the lines as we can buy. General Banks' signature is on our permit, and he is supreme in this Department."

Before Mr. Gray and Jack went home that night a plan of operations had been decided upon. The former were to engage all the wagons and mules that could be found in the neighborhood to haul Mr. Gray's four hundred bales to Baton Rouge, while Rodney was to seek an interview with Lambert and "buy him off" if he could. Rodney declared that he had the hardest part of the work to do, and he set about it, not by going into the woods to hunt up the ex-Home Guard, but by riding to the city to ask the advice and assistance of the provost marshal. As he was about to mount his horse he said to Marcy:

"If that man Lambert comes here while I am gone, please tell him to come again to-morrow morning, for I want to see him on important business. If you question him a little, no doubt you will be surprised at the extent of his information. There's little goes on in the settlement that he doesn't know all about."

Rodney's interview with the marshal must have been in the highest degree satisfactory, for when he came back at night he was laughing all over; but his cousin Marcy looked troubled.

"He's been here," said the latter, without waiting to be questioned, "and he was as impudent as you please."

"It's no more than I expected," replied Rodney. "What did he say?"

"That them fellers might jest as well give up hirin' teams to haul out that cotton till after you had made some sort of a bargain with him," answered Marcy.

"That's all right. Did he say he'd come to-morrow?"

"Yes, he said he would be here to listen to what you have to say, and if you don't talk to suit him he'll start another bonfire."

"That's all right," said Rodney again.

"I was afraid he might take it into his head to start it to-night, in which case I should be under the disagreeable necessity of bushwhacking him before I slept. But if he puts it off till to-morrow, he'll never set any more bonfires. Did you ever hear of such impudence before?"

For some reason or other Rodney Gray was in excellent spirits that evening. He did not go to bed until long after midnight, and when he did, he could not sleep for more than ten minutes at a time. But when morning came he sobered down, and his face took on the determined expression that Marcy had so often seen there during those exciting days at the Barrington Academy, when Dick Graham stole the flag and the Minute-men burned Unionists out of house and home. Just as they arose from the breakfast table Ned Griffin threw down the bars and rode into the yard, and that made four resolute fellows, counting in Charley Bowen, who were ready to see Lambert and talk to him about Mr. Gray's cotton. They all wore sack coats, and in each of the outside pockets was a loaded revolver.

"I am afraid Lambert will weaken when he sees this crowd," said Ned. "Perhaps he'll not come into the yard at all. Wouldn't it be a good scheme for a couple of us to go into the house out of sight?"

"I don't think it would," answered Rodney. "Lambert knows how many there are of us, and if he doesn't find us all on the porch when he comes his suspicions will be aroused. He'll not come alone, you may be certain of that."

And sure enough he didn't. When he rode up to the bars half an hour later he had two companions with him, and they all carried guns on their shoulders. There was something aggressive in the way they jerked out the bars and dropped them on the ground, and Rodney noticed that Lambert did not take the trouble to put them up behind him as he usually did. This was the way he took of showing Rodney that he held some power in his hands, and that he intended to use it for his own personal ends.

"What did I tell you?" said the young master of the plantation, who was angry in an instant. "He's brought Moseley and another

long-haired chap, whose name I do not now
recall, and thinks he's going to ride over me
rough-shod. Of course he will demand a
private interview, and I will grant it. All
you've got to do is to come when you hear me
shoot. I'll show him that I am in no humor
to put up with any more of his nonsense."

"Don't run any risks," cautioned Marcy.
"Your mother says that Lambert is a dangerous man."

"I'll prove to you, before this thing is over,
that he is the biggest coward in the Confederacy," replied Rodney.

The near approach of Lambert and his
friends cut short the conversation. They did
not get off their mules, but rode straight up to
the porch ; and then Rodney knew why they
left the bars down behind them. Their bearing was insolent, and the first words Lambert
uttered were still more so.

"Look a-here, Rodney Gray," said he,
"I'd like to know what them fellers mean by
goin' round the settlement hirin' teams to haul
that cotton outen the swamp without sayin'
a word to me about it."

"I don't know why you should be consulted," was the quiet reply. "Since when has that cotton belonged to you?"

"I've had an intrust in it ever sence I began watchin' it for you an' your paw," said Lambert.

"You never had an interest in it, but my father is willing to pay you for keeping an eye on it, if we can agree upon terms."

"That's what I call business," said Lambert, his face brightening. "How much you willin' to give?"

"What are you willing to take?"

"I can't set no figures till I know how much the cotton is wuth to you," said Lambert. "How much you goin' to get for it?"

"I can't tell until it is sold in New York," answered Rodney, controlling his rising anger with an effort.

"Are you tryin' to make me b'lieve that you are goin' to let some abolitionist run that cotton outen the country without payin' you a cent down for it!" shouted Lambert. "I don't b'lieve a word of it."

"You needn't yell so. I am not deaf."

"Then if you aint you can hear what I've got to tell you," said the man, raising his voice a full octave higher. "I won't have no more foolin'. How much you goin' to get for that cotton?"

"It's none of your business. You understand that, I suppose?"

By this time Lambert had succeeded in working himself into a furious passion, but if he had possessed ordinary common sense he never would have done it. He thought he could frighten Rodney, but should have known better. The boy sat tilted back in his chair, with his feet on the gallery railing and his thumbs hooked in the armholes of his vest, and his very attitude ought to have warned the ex-Home Guard that he was treading on dangerous ground, and that there was a point beyond which Rodney would not be driven. The latter's reply to his insolent question capped the climax.

"Whoop!" yelled Lambert, flourishing his rifle above his head. "It aint none of my business, aint it? I'll make it my business to make a beggar of you this very night. I'll

send that cotton of yourn where I sent Randolph's to pay that no-account boy of his'n
for shakin' his sword at me."

"You have fully made up your mind to
burn my father's cotton, have you?" said
Rodney.

"Yes, I have. It shan't never be hauled
outen them woods less'n I get fifty cents a
pound, cash in hand, for it. That Yankee
cousin of yourn is goin' to run it up North an'
get a dollar for it. I heered all about it an'
you needn't think to fool me. Will you give
it or not?"

"I certainly will not."

"You hearn what he says, boys," said Lambert to his companions. "I always said that
this was a rich man's war an' a poor man's
fight, didn't I; an' now you see it for yourselves, don't you? Let's go right back to the
woods an' set her a-goin'."

"Bang!" said one of Rodney's revolvers,
and to Marcy's inexpressible horror Lambert
dropped his rifle and fell headlong from his
mule, which set up a sonorous bray and
started for the bars at top speed. "Bang!"

27

said the other revolver an instant later, and
Moseley let go his hold upon his gun and
clung to his mule with both hands. The result of the next shot was still more terrifying.
The third man made a frantic effort to turn
his beast toward the bars ; but before he could
put him in motion a bullet passed through the
mule's head, and he and his rider came to the
ground together. It was done in much less
time than it takes to tell it. Rodney's companions jumped to their feet, but before they
could draw their weapons it was all over.

"Rodney, Rodney, what have you done ?"
cried Marcy in great alarm.

"I have simply proved my words," replied
his cousin, walking leisurely down the steps,
pushing his revolver into his pocket as he
went. "Did I not say," he added, picking
up the three guns, one after the other, and firing their contents into the air, " that I would
show Lambert to be the biggest coward in the
Confederacy? Get up, here. It's my turn to
be sassy now. Moseley, dismount."

Moseley obeyed with alacrity, and at the
same time Lambert raised himself on his elbow

RODNEY SURPRISES LAMBERT.

and gazed about him with a bewildered air. Then he felt of his head, and examined his hand to see if there was blood upon it. The third man could not move without assistance, for the mule had fallen upon his leg and pinned him to the ground.

"Get up," repeated Rodney, taking Lambert by the arm and helping him rather roughly to his feet. "Now you and Moseley sit down on the steps till I am ready to talk to you. Lend a hand here, a couple of you."

Hardly able to realize what had taken place before their eyes, Rodney's companions hastened down the steps to roll the dead mule off his rider, so that the man could get up. When he was placed upon his feet he was found to be so weak from fright that he could scarcely stand ; so Marcy and Ned helped him to a seat on the steps. Then they stood back and looked closely at Lambert and Moseley. Their faces were very white, and Lambert was covered with dust from head to foot, but there wasn't the sign of a wound on either of them. It was bewildering.

"Mister Rodney," ventured Lambert, when

he had made sure that he was still alive and had the use of his tongue, "I hope you don't bear me no grudge for them words I spoke to you a while ago."

"Oh, no," replied Rodney cheerfully. "But you have had your say, and I can't waste any more time with you now. Moseley, I believe you would be a harmless sort of rebel if you were out of Lambert's company."

"Yes, I would, sah," whimpered the hog thief. "Every bit of meanness I have done was all owin' to him, sah."

"Jest listen at the fule!" exclaimed Lambert.

"Consequently I think I will let you and your friend here—what's his name?"

"Longworth, sah ; Joe Longworth," replied the owner of the name.

"Ah, yes! I know you now. I believe I will let you two off on one condition. Wait until I get through!" cried Rodney, turning fiercely upon Lambert, who had made several attempts to interrupt him. "You did lots of talking a little while back, and now it's my turn. That condition is, Moseley, that you take your gang out of the woods and keep it out from this time on, unless I tell you to take it back."

"I'll do it, sah," said Moseley earnestly. "Sure's you live——"

"He can't, Mister Rodney," exclaimed Lambert. "There aint nobody but me can do that, kase I'm the captain of 'em."

"You're not the captain of them any longer. They will have to elect someone to take your place, for you are going to start for Baton Rouge in less than fifteen minutes."

When Lambert heard this he almost fell off the step on which he was sitting. Without giving him time to recover himself sufficiently to utter a protest, Rodney again addressed ex-Lieutenant Moseley.

"If you will do that, you can go to my father after our cotton has been shipped, and he will give each of you some money," said Rodney. "I don't know how much, but it will be a larger sum than you ever owned before at one time. It will be good money, too."

"Say, Mister Rodney," faltered Lambert, "what's the reason I can't have a share?"

"But if you don't do it," continued Rodney, "if you interfere in any way with the
teamsters who will go into the swamp to-
morrow to haul that cotton out, the last one
of you will be hunted down and shot, or sent
to a Northern prison to keep company with
Lambert. How many did you leave behind
when you came here?"

"Four, sah," replied Moseley.

"Only seven of you altogether!" exclaimed
Rodney. "Well, I think I can promise you
a hundred dollars apiece in greenbacks, and
that will be equal to six or eight hundred dollars in Confederate scrip."

Moseley's eyes glistened and so did Longworth's; but Lambert's grew dim with tears,
and his face was a sight to behold. The man
had less courage than Rodney gave him credit
for, and the boy wondered what his mother
would think of this "dangerous" person if
she could see him now. He couldn't even talk,
and Rodney was glad of it, for he wanted to
finish his instructions to Moseley and take
down the names of his companions without
being interrupted.

"Longworth, is that your beast?" said Rodney, with a nod toward the dead mule. "I am sorry I had to shoot him, and I shouldn't have done it if you hadn't tried to run off. When you are ready to come out of the woods and put in a crop, I will give you another and better one to take his place ; but I'll not furnish you anything to ride as long as you are playing bushwhacker."

After a little more conversation, and before Lambert had recovered from the stupor into which he had been thrown by Rodney's ominous words, Moseley and Longworth started for the swamp to spread consternation among their companions by telling what a desperate fighter the young overseer was when aroused, and what terrible things he had threatened to do if his demands were not complied with, while Rodney and his cousin went into the house, leaving Ned and Bowen to watch the prisoner.

"I don't see how you could bring yourself to do it," said Marcy.

"Do it ! Do what?" replied Rodney innocently.

" I thought sure you had killed Lambert and wounded Moseley, and when I saw Longworth come to the ground as if he had been struck by lightning——"

"That's nothing," laughed Rodney. "If you could see a platoon of cavalry floored as quickly as he was, perhaps you would open your eyes. As to Lambert, I didn't shoot within a foot of his head, although I shoved my revolver so close to his face that the smoke went into his eyes and blinded him for a minute or two. I shot even wider of the mark when I pulled on Moseley, and no doubt he dropped his gun because Lambert did. It was not my intention to touch either one of them. I thought it would be a good plan to let them understand who they were fooling with and what I could do if I set about it. But I meant to hit that mule. Now, will you ride to Baton Rouge with me?"

"Of course I will; but you are not going to send Lambert up North?"

"That is a matter with which I have nothing to do, but beyond a doubt it's where Lambert will bring up before he is many weeks older. As soon as it becomes known that he is in the hands of the Yanks, the Union people he persecuted so outrageously, while Tom Randolph was captain of the Home Guards, will prefer charges against him, and that will be bad for Lambert."

"I wish you thought it safe to let him go," said Marcy, who could not bear to see anyone in trouble.

"But I don't, you see. Of course he would make all sorts of promises, but he'd burn that cotton of ours as soon as he could get to it."

When the events we have just described became known in the settlement, they created almost as much excitement as did the news of the firing upon Sumter, but of course it was a different sort of excitement. The Union men whom Lambert had robbed and abused went into the city by dozens to bear testimony against him, and then hastened home to repair their wagons and harness so that they could earn the four dollars a day, "greenback money," that Sailor Jack offered them for hauling out his uncle's cotton. Everyone who had cotton to sell and teams for hire, with one exception, was happy; and that exception was Mr. Randolph, who was the most miserable man in the State. He had not only lost the most of his cotton (he had about twenty bales that Jack said he would buy), but since Lambert's arrest he had learned why he lost it. That was a matter which Tom desired above all things to keep from his father's knowledge; but Lambert had told all he knew about him in the hope that, if he were sent to prison, his old captain would have to go with him. Tom himself had some fears on this score, but thus far no one in the settlement had thought it worth while to trouble him. Such treatment as that made Tom angry.

"Nobody pays any more attention to me than if I was a stump-tailed yellow dog," he complained to his mother, who was the only friend he had in the world. "Father will scarcely speak when I am around, and when I go to town, the men who used to go out of their way to salute me and say 'Good-morning, Captain Randolph,' won't look at me. It wasn't so when we were rich."

"That is true," assented his mother. "I

have always heard it said that one's pocket-book is one's best friend, and I believe it. Tommy, don't you think, if you could fix up a wagon and earn a little money, it would be better than idling away your time doing nothing?"

"And drive crow-bait mules and work for Rodney Gray?" exclaimed Tom. "Mother, I am surprised at you. Think what a come-down that would be for one who has been a captain in the Confederate service!"

Mrs. Randolph did not say that it would have been a good thing for the captain if he had been content to remain a civilian, but she thought so.

There were others in the neighborhood who had never performed any manual labor, rich planters before the war, who had nothing to do but spend the money their slaves made for them, but they did not talk as Tom did. They took off their coats and went to work, and never stopped to see whether the shoulder that was under the opposite side of a cotton bale belonged to a white man or a negro. Rodney Gray, who superintended the work while

Sailor Jack went to New Orleans to charter a
river steamer, paid them their greenbacks every
night, and the planters took them home and
hid them for fear that a squad of rebel cavalry
might make a night raid into the settlement
and steal them.   Jack did not ask for military
protection, but he had it, for every day or
two a company of Federal troopers galloped
through the country, ready to do battle
with any "Johnnies" who might try to interfere with the work.   Rodney was always glad
to see them.   He knew that the Confederate
authorities would not permit that cotton to be
shipped if they could prevent it, and he never
left it unguarded.   Moseley and his five companions were in his pay, and earned two dollars
a night by holding themselves ready at all
times to drive off any marauders who might
try to burn it.   On one memorable night they
proved their worth and earned five times that
amount.   Moseley, who seemed to have grown
several inches taller since Rodney last saw
him, proudly reported that he had had a
regular pitched battle about three o'clock
that morning, and that he had driven the

enemy from the field in such confusion that they left their wounded behind them. And, what was more to the point, he produced three injured rebels to show that he told nothing but the truth.

By the time Sailor Jack returned with the steamer he had chartered, Mr. Gray's cotton was all on the levee at Baton Rouge awaiting shipment to New Orleans, and Rodney's teams were hard at work hauling in Mr. Walker's. By this time, too, everyone in the southwestern part of the State knew what was going on at Mooreville, and Union men and rebels, living as far away as the Pearl River bottoms, came to Jack and begged, with tears in their eyes, that he would take their cotton also and save them from utter ruin. Jack assured them that he would be glad to buy every bale, provided they would put it where he could get hold of it without running the risk of being bushwhacked; but there was the trouble. The guerillas became very active all on a sudden, and almost every morning someone would report to Rodney that he "seen a light on the clouds over that-a-way, and jedged that some poor chap had been losin' cotton the night afore." On one or two occasions Rodney saw such lights on the sky, and if his heart was filled with sympathy for the planter who was being ruined by the wanton destruction of his property, there was still room enough in it for gratitude to his sailor cousin, through whose manœuvring his father had been saved from a similar fate.

Jack Gray was a " hustler," and he "hustled" his men to such good purpose that in ten days more his chartered steamer was loaded to her guards, and Mr. Gray and a few of his neighbors were rich and happy, while Rodney was very miserable and unhappy, for his cousin and Charley Bowen were going away. Jack had been told to take Marcy home with him, and Jack's rule was to obey orders if he broke owners. Anxious to remain with Marcy as long as he could, Rodney accompanied him to New Orleans and saw his father's cotton loaded into the *Hyperion's* hold. A few days afterward he waved his farewell to Marcy as the swift vessel bore him down the river, and then turned his face homeward to

wait for Grant and Banks to open the Mississippi. But his patience was sadly tested, for
it was not until July 4 that Grant's army
marched into Vicksburg. After an active campaign of eighty days the modest man who afterward commanded all the Union armies "gained
one of the most important and stupendous vic-
tories of the war," inflicting upon the enemy a
loss of ten thousand in killed and wounded,
capturing twenty-seven thousand prisoners, two
hundred guns, and small arms and munitions
of war sufficient for an army of sixty thousand
men. General Banks took possession of Port
Hudson on the 9th, and no Northern boy
shouted louder than Rodney Gray did when
he heard of it. The river was open at last,
and Jack Gray and his trading boat could
make their appearance as soon as they
pleased.

But this was not all the glorious news that
Rodney heard about that time. On the 3d of
July, at Cemetery Ridge in far-off Pennsylvania, there had been a desperate charge of
fifteen thousand men and a bloody repulse
that "marked the culmination of the Confed-

erate power." When General Lee saw Pickett's lines and Anderson's fading away before
the terrible fire of the Union infantry, he also
saw "the fading away of all hope of recognition by the government of Great Britain. The
iron-clad war vessels, constructed with Confederate money by British ship-builders and
intended for the dispersion of the Union fleets
blockading Wilmington and Charleston, and
which were supposed to be powerful enough
to send the monitors, one by one, to the bottom of the sea, were prevented from leaving
English ports by order of the British government"; but if Pickett's charge had been successful, those iron-clads would have sailed in
less than a week, and France and England,
who were waiting to see what would come of
the invasion of Pennsylvania, would have
recognized the Confederacy. It is no wonder
that General Lee's soldiers fought hard for
victory when they knew there was so much
depending upon it. The boys in blue who
whipped them at Cemetery Ridge are deserv-
ing of all honor.

We must not forget to say that before these

things happened Sailor Jack ran up from New Orleans to tell what he had done with Marcy, and to make a settlement with his uncle.

"I've made a successful trip," said he gleefully, "and, Uncle Rodney, you have that much to your credit in the Chemical Bank of New York."

As he said this he handed Mr. Gray a certificate of deposit calling for a sum of money so large that Rodney opened his eyes in amazement.

"Of course I had to take Marcy to New York with me," continued Jack, "but two days after we got there Captain Frazier found a Union storeship that was about to sail with provisions for the blockading fleet; and as she had a lot of mail and stuff aboard for Captain Flusser, whom I knew to be serving on the *Miami* in Albemarle Sound, I managed to obtain permission for Marcy to take passage on her, believing that if he could reach the *Miami* he could also reach Plymouth, and from there it would be easy for him to get home. I expect to find a letter from him when I return to New York, and he also prom-

28

ised to write you in care of the provost marshal at Baton Rouge."

There was one thing Jack did before he went
back to New Orleans that at first disgusted
Rodney Gray, though he was afterward very
glad of it. He paid over to Mr. Randolph
every dollar his twenty bales sold for in New
York, not even deducting the *Hyperion's*
freight bill, so that unfortunate gentleman
was not quite as badly off as he thought. He
had a little money with which to make a new
start when the war ended.

CHAPTER XVII.

ONE of the most soul-stirring scenes that Rodney Gray ever witnessed occurred a short time subsequent to the fall of Vicksburg. He and his father and Ned Griffin stood on the Baton Rouge levee and saw the steamer *Imperial* dash by on her way to New Orleans. The swift vessel, which came from St. Louis, moved as if she were a living thing and knew that she was speaking not only to the Confederacy, but to the world. To the Confederates she said that the last vestige of their power and authority had disappeared from the Mississippi forever ; that its waters were free to the commerce of the great West, which should nevermore be interrupted. And to France and England, who had been hoping and plotting for our downfall, she said that "thenceforth the country was to be one nation, under one flag, with Liberty and Union forever."

Exciting and interesting events happened rapidly after that, but we can touch upon but few of them, for our "War Series" ought to end with the war record of the characters that have appeared in it. Rodney, who was waiting impatiently for Sailor Jack to make his appearance, spent the most of his time on the Baton Rouge levee, so as to be the first to welcome him when he came up with his trading boat. On one memorable night he reached home after dark, as he usually did, put his horse into the stable-yard, and went into the house ; and there, just as we found him on a former occasion, seated in Rodney's own rocking-chair, with his feet resting upon the back of another and a book in his hand, was Dick Graham. When Rodney entered the room Dick merely turned his head slightly and looked at him as he might have done if they had parted an hour or two before.

"I always knew you had cheek," exclaimed Rodney, as soon as he could speak. "Dick, old boy, how are you ?"

"Pretty and well, thank you," answered

Dick, dropping the book and jumping to his feet.

We shall not attempt to describe that meeting, for we could not do it justice. Just consider that they have got through gushing over each other, and that they are sitting down quietly, talking like veterans who have seen fifteen months of the hardest kind of service.

"I don't know how I missed seeing you," said Rodney, "for I was on the levee almost all day yesterday, and saw every boat that came in. How did you get home? and where did you leave your folks?"

"I got home easy enough, and left the folks in St. Louis. My discharge from Bragg's army put me on the right side of both rebs and Yanks, and the money you so generously provided brought me all the grub I wanted. I found the folks at home, but they didn't remain there long after I joined them, for there was almost too much guerilla warfare going on in Kansas and western Missouri to make it pleasant for non-combatants. So we dug out for St. Louis, and we've been there ever since. I couldn't get a letter to you, but

I knew I could come myself as soon as the river was opened, and here I am. A pass from the provost marshal took me through the lines, and Mr. Turnbull was kind enough to hitch up a team and bring me to your father's house, where I stopped last night. I heard some astonishing stories about Marcy and that sailor brother of his, and am sorry indeed that Marcy has gone home to stay. I should like much to see him."

"And he would be delighted to see you, but I don't look for him until this trouble is all over. Sailor Jack is liable to come along any day; and Dick, we'll go with him and help him buy cotton."

"Oh, you needn't think that you and Jack are going to have a picnic," replied Dick with a smile. "I talked with some of the officers of the boat on my way down, and they seemed to think that Uncle Sam's tin-clads will have all they can do to keep the river clear of guerillas. They'll not let traders take cotton out of the country if they can help it."

It goes without saying that in Dick Graham's company Rodney was almost as happy as he desired to be. He was blessed with perfect health, his family had in a great measure escaped the horrors of war which fell to the lot of so many others, there was no cotton in the woods for him to worry over, the man Lambert, who was a thorn in his side for so many months, had been sent to Camp Douglas for his merciless persecution of the Union people in the settlement, his father's check was good at the bank for a larger amount than it had ever been before, and one of the few things Rodney had to wish for now was that the war might end with the battle of Gettysburg. Many brave soldiers on both sides declared that would have been the result of the fight if the arrogance of Jeff Davis had not stood in the way. He continued to slaughter men and desolate homes in the vain effort to make himself the head of a new nation. Great battles were yet to be fought to satisfy one man's ambition and desire for power. Hood's army of forty-five thousand men was to be annihilated at Nashville, and Sherman's march to the sea accomplished before the "day of

Appomattox" dawned upon the country. And Sailor Jack was to try his hand at being a trader.

He made his appearance about a week after. Dick Graham did, and quite as unexpectedly, and so the boys were not on the levee to meet him. He secured a pass from the provost marshal, borrowed a horse, and rode out to his uncle's plantation. Dick Graham had never seen him before, but when he got through shaking hands he was willing to believe that the sailor was glad to make his acquaintance.

"If I do say it myself I think I am well equipped for the business," said Jack in response to Rodney's inquiries. "My boat is the *Venango*, which is guaranteed to carry a full deck-load on a heavy dew, my officers are all river men and my deck-hands whites; for I wasn't going to take darkies among the rebels to be captured and sent back into slavery."

"Why, Jack," said Mrs. Gray, "you talk as if you were going into danger."

"Well, I am not as sanguine of keeping out of it as I was a few weeks ago," said the sailor.

"If I can hold fast to the *Venango* until I can load up the *Hyperion* twice, I shall think myself lucky. And I shall make a good thing out of it besides."

Mr. Gray did not raise any objections when Rodney and Dick made ready to accompany Jack to Baton Rouge on the following morning, for he knew that if he were a boy he would want to go himself. He went with them to the city, and stood on the levee when the *Venango* backed away from it and turned her head up the river. When the boys could no longer distinguish him among the crowd which had assembled to see them off, they went into the cabin that Jack occupied in common with the river captain whom he had hired to run the vessel, and sat down to wait for dinner.

"This looks to me like hunting for a needle in a haystack," said Rodney. "How are you going to manage? Do you intend to keep on up the river until someone hails you with the information that he has cotton to sell?"

"Not precisely," laughed Jack. "We don't do business in that uncertain way. My first landing will be at a plantation ten miles

above Bayou Sara, if you know where that is,
and there I hope to find cotton enough to load
this boat about four times."

"Why, how did you hear of it?"

"I received my orders from our agent in
New Orleans, if that is what you mean; but
how he heard of it I don't know, and didn't
think to inquire. I wish this steamer was
four times bigger than she is."

"Why didn't you charter a large one while
you were about it?"

"I couldn't, for their owners were too anxious to have them go back to their regular
trade, which has so long been interrupted by
the blockade at Vicksburg. They can make
more money at it."

After dinner had been served and eaten in
what had once been the *Venango's* passenger
cabin, but which was now given over to the use
of the officers of the boat, the boys walked out
on the boiler-deck and saw a stern-wheeler
coming toward them with a big bone in her
teeth. She was painted a sort of dirt color
that did not show very plainly against the
background of the high bank she was passing,

and it was a long time before the boys could make her out; but they told each other that she was the oddest looking craft they had ever seen. She had no "Texas" (that is the name given to the cabin in which the officers sleep), and her pilot house stood on the roof of her passenger cabin. Her main deck was not open like the *Venango's*, but was inclosed with casemates provided with port-holes, two in the bow and three on the side that was turned toward them. She was following the channel in the right of the bend while the light-draft trading boat was holding across the point of the bar on the opposite side, so that there was the width of the river between them; but when they came abreast of each other, the stranger's bow began swinging around, and in a few minutes she was running back up the Mississippi in company with the *Venango*, and only a few rods astern.

"She must be one of the mosquito fleet—a tin-clad," exclaimed Dick. "They say the river is full of them, but I didn't happen to see one on my way down. She and her kind are intended to fight guerillas."

"That's what she is," said Jack. "And she's the first I ever saw."

"But what is she following us for?" asked Rodney. "Perhaps she wants to see your papers."

"Then why doesn't she whistle five times to let me know that she wants to communicate?" answered Jack. "She is giving us a convoy."

"It's very kind of Admiral Porter, or whoever it was told her to do it," said Rodney. "If we are to be protected in this way we shall never have anything to fear from guerillas. She has six broadside guns, two bow-chasers, and a field howitzer on her roof, nine in all. She ought to make a good fight."

"Oh, she will do well enough for guerillas," said Jack, "but how long do you imagine she would stay above water if a battery should open on her?"

Jack Gray was not the only one who had little faith in tin-clads, but some of the most desperate engagements that were fought in Western waters were fought by these very vessels. If they wanted to go anywhere they did not stop because there was a battery in their way. Take one exploit of the *Juliet* as a fair specimen of what they could do as often as the exigencies of the service demanded it. When this fleet little gunboat was commanded by Harry Gorringe, the man who afterward brought over the Egyptian obelisk that now stands in Central Park, New York, she carried Admiral Porter past a long line of Confederate batteries, which poured upon her a fire so accurate and rapid that thirty-five shells were exploded inside her casemates in less than three minutes. The engineer on watch was killed with his hand on the throttle, but her machinery was not touched; and finding that she had come through the ordeal safe if not sound, she rounded to and went back to help a vessel which had not been so fortunate as herself. The *Venango's* escort kept company with her until she turned in to the plantation where Jack hoped to obtain his first load of cotton, and then turned about and went down the river again, Jack and the boys waving their thanks to the officers who stood on her boiler-deck, and the *Venango's* pilot wishing her good luck and warning the master of the plantation at the same time by giving a long blast on his whistle.

Sailor Jack began his trading at a fortunate time and under the most favorable conditions. Not only was he one of the first to enter the field after Vicksburg fell, but the men with whom his mother's thirty thousand dollars enabled him to form partnership were so influential and shrewd, and had so many ways of finding out things which no one inside the Union lines was supposed to know anything about, that Jack never left port without knowing right where to find his next cargo of cotton. That is to say, he knew it on every occasion except one, and then he was ordered into a trap which he would have kept out of if he had been left to himself.

The cotton he found above Bayou Sara was on what was known as the Stratton plantation, and there was so much of it that he had to make four trips to carry it to New Orleans, where it was loaded into the *Hyperion's* hold. One day when his own deck-hands and all the plantation darkies were busy loading for the last run,

Jack was approached by three men in butter-nut, who wanted to know what he was giving for cotton, whether he paid in greenbacks or Confederate scrip, and if he would be willing to run up the river two hundred miles farther and get a thousand bales that several citizens up there were anxious to sell.

"Which side of the river is the cotton on?" asked Jack.

"Over there," said one of the men, pointing toward the opposite shore.

"Too many rebs," said Jack shortly.

"Thar haint been ary reb in our country fur more'n six months, dog-gone if thar has," replied the man earnestly.

"Well, I can't make any promises. The matter does not rest with me, but with the agent in New Orleans."

"I suppose you pay cash on delivery?"

"Hardly. I don't carry enough money to make it an object for prowling guerillas to rob me."

"What's Stratton got to show fur the cotton of his'n you have tooken down the river?"

"Due-bills, which will be cashed on sight."

"But he'll have to go to New Orleans to have 'em cashed, an' me an' my neighbors dassent go thar. We've been in the Confedrit army."

"Is there no Union man up there whom you can trust to do business for you?"

"Thar aint one of that sort within forty mile of us."

"Then you are in a bad way, and I don't know how you will work it to get greenbacks for your cotton."

"Couldn't you run up there an' buy it out an' out if we gin you a little somethin' for your trouble?"

"No, I couldn't. I am not the only trader there is on the river, and if you watch out you may find somebody willing to take the risk. I am not willing."

"They gave up mighty easy," observed Rodney, as the three men turned away and walked slowly up the bank.

"Don't you know the reason?" replied Jack. "They had no use for me when they found that I don't carry a large sum of money with me. They haven't a bale of cotton, and I doubt if they have been in the rebel army. They are guerillas and robbers like those in Missouri that Dick told us about. No doubt I shall have to go up into that country after this lower river has been cleared of cotton, but I'll tell the captain to keep as far from the Arkansaw shore as the channel will let him go."

This little incident reminded the boys that the war was not yet ended, and that they might hear more about it at any time. They heard more about it when they arrived at New Orleans and found the steamer *Von Phul* lying at the levee with her cabin shot full of holes. She had been fired into by a battery of field-pieces twenty miles below Memphis, but her captain was brave, as most of the river men were, and could not be stopped as long as his engines were in working order. He reported the matter to the captain of the first gunboat he met, and the latter hastened up and shelled the woods until he set them on fire; but the battery that did the mischief was probably a dozen miles away.

29

"There's no telling how long it will be before we shall come here with our boat looking just like that," said Jack. "And the worst of it is, we shall have to take whatever the rebs please to give us without firing a shot in reply. I don't like that pretty well."

But for a long time the *Venango* was a lucky vessel. She was not obliged to go very far out of reach of a gunboat to find her cargoes, for the planters who owned cotton took pains to place it on the river at points where it would be under Federal protection. But the supply was exhausted after a while, and then Jack was ordered into the dreaded Arkansas region, where guerillas were plenty and gunboats and soldiers stationed far apart. Then their troubles began, and Rodney and Dick smelled powder again. On one trip the *Venango* was fired into at three different points, but owing to her speed and the width of the river, which was almost bank full, she escaped without a scratch. On another occasion the rebels shot with better aim, and sent a shell through one of her smoke-stacks and two more through her cabin; but little damage

was done, for the missiles did not explode
until they passed through the steamer and
struck the bank on the opposite side. After
that it was seldom that Jack reported to his
agent without adding: "Of course I was fired
into on the way down," and sometimes he was
obliged to say that he had had men killed or
wounded. But that was to be expected. A
wooden boat couldn't make a business of running batteries at regular intervals without losing men once in a while.

The winter passed in this way, Rodney and
Dick never missing a trip, and all the while
the agent was besieged by planters living
along the Arkansas shore who had cotton to
sell, who had permits to ship it and papers to
prove that they had always been loyal to the
government, and who were ready to stake
their reputation as gentlemen upon the truth
of the statement that the trading boat that
came to their landings would not run the
slightest risk of falling into the hands of
guerillas. When the agent spoke to Jack
about it the latter said:

"If you want to take the responsibility,

why, all right. If you order me to go after that cotton I'll go ; but before you do it, I'd like to have you recall the fact that the trading boats *Tacoma* and *George Williams* were all right and made money until they were sent to the Arkansas shore, and then they went up in smoke. And every shot that has been fired at my boat came from the west bank of the river."

"This cotton is at Horseshoe Bend opposite Friar's Point," continued the agent, "and you will have five or six gunboats within less than a dozen miles of you."

"What of that?" replied Jack. "A party of half a dozen men could set fire to the boat and ride away to Texas before the gunboats would know anything about it. They might as well be a hundred miles away."

"And more," the agent went on, "two of the planters who own this cotton are willing to remain here as hostages, and they say that if anything happens to you or your boat we can do what we please with them."

"What of that?" repeated Jack. "If the *Venango* is burned, who is going to punish those hostages? We have no right to do it, and you do not for a moment suppose that General Banks would interest himself in the matter? He's got government business to attend to, and don't care a cent what happens to us or any other civilians. I'll go after the cotton if you say so, but you'll never see the *Venango* again, and the firm will have to pay for her."

This frightened the agent for a while, and he told Jack to stay on the safe side of the river and let the Arkansaw people get their cotton to market the best way they could. These orders remained in force about three months, and then came a fateful day when the only cotton the agent knew anything about was on the Arkansas side, eight miles above Skipwith's Landing.

"I really think it will be a safe undertaking," said the agent, "for you will be within plain sight of two iron-clads and the ram *Samson*, which are lying at Skipwith's."

"I wouldn't give that for all the help I'll get from the whole of them," declared Jack, snapping his fingers in the air. "They'll not know that trouble has come to me till they see

my boat in flames, and how long will it take
one of those tubs of iron-clads to get up steam
and run eight miles against the current of the
Mississippi? The *Venango* will be in ashes
before one of them will come within shelling
distance of us."

"But there's the *Samson*. She can run
seventeen miles an hour against a four-mile
current."

"And what is the *Samson* but a carpenter
shop, with no guns and a crew of darkies? Do
you want me to go there or not?"

The agent did what Longstreet is said to
have done when General Lee told him to order
Pickett's useless charge at Gettysburg; he
looked down at the ground and evaded a direct
answer.

"We want cotton enough to fill out the
Hyperion's cargo," said he, "and that's the
only batch on the river that I have been able
to hear of."

"Then I'll start after it in less than an hour;
but whether or not I'll get it is another and a
deeper question. Good-by."

Jack walked off whistling, for trouble sat

lightly on his broad shoulders, but the moment he stepped on the *Venango's* boiler-deck and faced the two boys sitting there, they knew what had happened as well as they did when it was explained to them.

"I can see Arkansas written all over you," exclaimed Rodney.

"And can you see that I want you two to be ready to leave the boat at Baton Rouge?" replied Jack. "We'll not make a landing, but just run close enough to give you a chance to jump."

"I never could jump worth a cent," said Dick.

"Look here, Jack, we're not little boys to be disposed of in any such way as you propose. We have seen as much service as you have, and if it is all the same to you we'll stay here. I am not going home to worry my folks with the report that you are going into such danger that you thought it best to drop us overboard," chimed in Rodney.

"If the guerillas catch us they'll only put us afoot," observed Dick. "That's what they did with the *Tacoma's* crew."

Good-natured Jack turned on his heel and walked away, showing by his actions that he did not expect his order to be obeyed. In an hour's time the *Venango* was on her way up the river. She passed Skipwith's Landing the next night after dark, running close enough in to give the boys an indistinct view of the long black hull of the ram *Samson*, lying alongside the repair shops, and the battle-scarred iron-clads at anchor a short distance farther up, and in due time she was whistling for the landing on the Arkansas shore eight miles above. It was dark there, and the boys could see nothing but a dense forest outlined against the sky, and not the first sign of a clearing; but that there was somebody on the watch was made evident a few minutes later, for an iron torch basket filled with blazing "fat wood," such as steamers use when making a landing or coaling at night, was planted upon the levee, and the pilot steered in by the aid of the light it threw out. There were three men on the levee and a few bales of cotton near by.

"Is that all you have?" demanded Jack,

as the *Venango's* bow touched the bank and a couple of deck-hands sprang ashore with a line.

"What boat is that?" asked one of the men.

Jack gave her name, adding the information that he had been sent there for cotton, and there wasn't enough in sight to load a skiff.

"Oh, we've got plenty more back there in the woods," was the answer.

"But I don't want it back there in the woods," shouted Jack, from his perch on the roof. "I want it on the levee where I can get at it."

"We've got teams enough to haul it out faster than you can load it. It's all right, cap'n. I had a long talk with your agent only a few days ago."

"It's all wrong, and you may depend upon it," said Rodney in a low tone.

Jack Gray was of the same opinion, and if he had not been afraid that the men with whom he was associated in business would accuse him of cowardice, he would have cut the bow-line, which had by this time been made fast to a tree on the bank, and backed away with all possible speed. Instead of doing that, he descended the stairs and walked down the gang-plank, while Rodney and Dick drew off to one side to compare notes.

"If it's all right, what's the reason they didn't have the cotton ready for us?" said the latter.

"That's what I'd be pleased to know," said Rodney. "Do you believe there's any cotton here?"

"Not a bale except the few you see on the levee, and which were put there for a blind. Your cousin believes he's in a trap or else his face told a wrong story."

"That's my opinion, too. Now don't you think it would be a good plan for us to put the skiff into the water and go down and tell those gunboats about it?"

"It might, but what shall we tell them? There's been nothing done yet," replied Dick, as he followed Rodney to the main-deck.

That was true, but there was something

done by the time they got the skiff overboard. It was lying bottom up on the guard just abaft the door that gave entrance into the engine-room on the port side, that is, the side away from the bank, and the oars that belonged to it were stowed under the thwarts. Jack was ashore, the mates were on the forecastle, the deck-hands busy with the breast and stern lines, the captain was at his post on the roof, the engineer was at the throttle, slowly turning the wheel to work the boat broadside to the bank, and there was no one to observe their movements. Noiselessly they pushed the skiff into the water, then stepped in and shipped the oars and pulled toward the steamer's bow, edging away a little into the darkness so that they could not be seen by anyone on shore. A subdued exclamation of surprise and alarm burst from their lips when they pulled far enough ahead so that they could look over the bow toward the cotton-bales on the bank. There were a score of men there now, and with the exception of the three who were there when the boat touched the bank, they were all armed and wore spurs.

"Guerillas?" whispered Dick.

"Do you think we will have anything to tell the gunboats?" asked Rodney. "Turn her around and pull the best you know how."

"It looks cowardly to run away and leave Jack," replied Dick, laying out all his strength on his oar.

"We wouldn't do it if we could help him in any other way. But they won't hurt him. It's the boat they're after," said Rodney; but even while the words were on his lips he could not help wondering if the guerillas did not expect to find a large sum of money on the boat, and whether their disappointment would not make them so angry that they would take vengeance on somebody. But there was no way in which he could stop it except by bringing a gunboat to the rescue, and with this object in view he "pulled the best he knew how." He and Dick kept the skiff in the channel in order to get the benefit of the current, and in less time than they thought to do so, brought themselves within hailing distance of one of the iron-clads.

"Boat ahoy !" shouted a hoarse voice from her deck.

"Trading boat *Venango!*" responded Rodney, hoping to give the officer of the deck some idea of the nature of their business.

The latter must have heard and understood, for he told them to come alongside ; and when the order had been obeyed, not without a good deal of difficulty, for the current ran like a mill sluice, and the officer of the deck had listened to their hasty story, he went below to speak to the captain, who, after a long delay, sent word for them to be brought into the cabin. But the sequel proved that he had done something in the meantime. He had told the ensign on watch to arouse the executive, to have two companies of small-arm men called away, and to send word to the *Samson* to raise steam immediately. Being a regular, the captain lost no time. After listening to what the boys had to say, he gave them permission to go aboard the *Samson* with the small-arm men, and in ten minutes more the boat that could run seventeen miles an hour against a four-mile current was ploughing her

way up the river at an astonishing rate of
speed. But the guerillas hadn't wasted any
time either. Before the ram had left the iron-
clads a mile astern, a small, bright light,
which grew larger and brighter every instant,
shone through the darkness ahead, and presently the *Venango* came floating down with
the current, a mass of flame. After robbing
her of everything of value, the guerillas had
applied the torch and turned her adrift. But
where were Jack Gray and her crew? This
question was answered at day-light the next
morning when Rodney and Dick pulled the,
skiff back to the landing, where they found
Jack sitting on a cotton-bale, and whittling a
stick as composedly as though such a thing as
a guerilla had never been heard of. His crew
were asleep behind the levee, and Jack was
keeping watch for a steamer bound down.
The guerillas hadn't bothered him any to
speak of, he said, although they did swear a
little when they learned that he had no money.
They affirmed that if they couldn't make a dollar a pound out of their cotton, the Yankees
shouldn't do it, and they would burn every

trading boat that Jack or anybody else put on the river. But they never burned another boat for Jack. A steamer which came along that afternoon took him and his crew to New Orleans, and there he took leave of the boys, who did not see him again for a long time. But before they parted, however, he showed them a letter from Marcy, in which the latter stated that Charley Bowen had shipped on a Union gunboat at Plymouth. Being a deserter from the rebel army, he was afraid to enlist in the land forces, for if he were captured and recognized he would certainly be shot to death. He thought there would be little danger of that if he went to sea.

The trading business having been broken up Rodney was anxious to see his home once more, and that was where he and Dick started for as soon as they had seen the *Hyperion* drop down the river with Jack Gray on board. Rodney's father and mother had heard of the loss of the *Venango*, but they did not know what had become of her company, and the boys' return was an occasion for rejoicing. At the end of the month Dick Graham also went home, and then Rodney was lonely indeed. If he hadn't had plenty of work and energy enough to go at it, it is hard to tell what he would have done with himself. For want of some better way of passing his leisure moments he made an effort to learn what had become of Billings, Cole, Dixon, and all the other Barrington boys who had promised, with him, to enlist in the Confederate army within twenty-four hours after they reached home. He knew their several addresses, but the only one he heard from was Dixon, the tall Kentuckian who, good rebel as he was, always interfered whenever the hot heads among the academy boys tried to haul down the Old Flag and run the Stars and Bars up in its place. And the reply he received did not come from Dixon himself but from his sister, who told Rodney that her brother had been killed at the head of his regiment while gallantly leading a charge upon a Federal battery. He went into the Confederate army a private and died a colonel.

"Bully for Dixon," said Rodney, with tears in his eyes. "He always was a brave boy."

At last Atlanta fell, Sherman marched to the sea, the battle of Five Forks was fought, the grand result of which was to reduce General Lee's army of seventy-six thousand to less than twenty-nine thousand men, and then came the surrender at Appomattox. A short time afterward came also a joyous letter from Marcy Gray, in which he said that although Plymouth had once been recaptured by the rebels, aided by their formidable iron-clad, the *Albemarle*, which had worsted the Union gun-boats every time they met her, the city did not remain in the hands of the enemy any longer than it took Lieutenant Cushing to blow up the iron-clad with his torpedo; and then, their main-stay being gone, the rebels again surrendered. He and his mother had not been troubled in any way since the night Captain Fletcher took him to Williamston jail. If it had not been for the papers that occasionally came into their hands, they would not have known that dreadful battles were being fought in the next State. There had been peace and quiet in the settlement since Allison, Goodwin, and Beardsley were bushwhacked.

30

It was a terrible thing for Christians to do, but
the refugees had been driven to it, and through
no fault of their own.   The two foragers who
were captured on the night that Ben Hawkins
was surprised in his father's house, and who
were sent South to act as guards at the Andersonville prison pen, had escaped after a few
months' service, and were now at home with
their families.   So were Hawkins and all the
rest of the prisoners who were captured and
paroled at Roanoke Island, and they had
never been molested.   No word had been received from Charley Bowen since he shipped
in the Union Navy, but Marcy hoped to see
him again at no distant day, for he never could
forget that Charley saved his life.   Sailor
Jack had made a "good thing" out of his
trading, and had promised his mother that he
would not go to sea any more.   As a family
they were prosperous and hoped to be happy,
now that the cause of the war was dead and
the war itself ended.   Marcy concluded his interesting letter by saying:

"While I write, the flag my Barrington girl
gave me is waving from the house-top, and

there is not a rebel banner floating to taint the breeze that kisses it. May it ever be so—one flag, one country, one destiny."

"Amen," said Rodney Gray solemnly.

THE END OF THE SERIES.

THE
FAMOUS
CASTLEMON
BOOKS.

BY
HARRY
CASTLEMON.

Specimen Cover of the Gunboat
Series.

No author of the present day has become a greater favorite with boys than "Harry Castlemon;" every book by him is sure to meet with hearty reception by young readers generally. H.s naturalness and vivacity lead his readers from page to page with breathless interest, and when one volume is finished the fascinated reader, like Oliver Twist, asks " for more."

∗ Any volume sold separately.

GUNBOAT SERIES. By Harry Castlemon. 6 vols., 12mo. Fully illustrated. Cloth, extra, printed in colors. In box $7 50

Frank, the Young Naturalist 1 25

Frank in the Woods. 1 25

Frank on the Prairie 1 25

Frank on a Gunboat. 1 25

Frank before Vicksburg 1 25

Frank on the Lower Mississippi 1 25

GO AHEAD SERIES. By Harry Castlemon. 3 vols., 12mo. Fully illustrated. Cloth, extra, printed in colors. In box **$3 75**

Go Ahead; or, The Fisher Boy's Motto 1 25

No Moss; or, The Career of a Rolling Stone 1 25

Tom Newcombe; or, The Boy of Bad Habits . . 1 25

ROCKY MOUNTAIN SERIES. By Harry Castlemon. 3 vols., 12mo. Fully illustrated. Cloth, extra, printed in colors. In box **$3 75**

Frank at Don Carlos' Rancho 1 25

Frank among the Rancheros 1 25

Frank in the Mountains 1 25

SPORTSMAN'S CLUB SERIES. By Harry Castlemon. 3 vols., 12mo. Fully illustrated. Cloth, extra, printed in colors. In box **$3 75**

The Sportsman's Club in the Saddle 1 25

The Sportsman's Club Afloat 1 25

The Sportsman's Club among the Trappers . 1 25

FRANK NELSON SERIES. By Harry Castlemon. 3 vols. 12mo. Fully illustrated. Cloth, extra, printed in colors. In box **$3 75**

Snowed Up; or, The Sportsman's Club in the Mts. . 1 25

Frank Nelson in the Forecastle; or, The Sportsman's Club among the Whalers 1 25

The Boy Traders; or, The Sportsman's Club among the Boers 1 25

BOY TRAPPER SERIES. By Harry Castlemon. 3 vols., 12mo. Fully illustrated. Cloth, extra, printed in colors. In box **$3 75**

The Buried Treasure; or, Old Jordan's "Haunt" 1 25

The Boy Trapper; or, How Dave Filled the Order. 1 25

The Mail Carrier 1 25

ROUGHING IT SERIES. By Harry Castlemon. 3 vols., 12mo. Fully illustrated. Cloth, extra, printed in colors. In box $3 75

George in Camp; or, Life on the Plains 1 25

George at the Wheel; or, Life in a Pilot House . 1 25

George at the Fort; or, Life Among the Soldiers . 1 25

ROD AND GUN SERIES. By Harry Castlemon. 3 vols., 12mo. Fully illustrated. Cloth, extra, printed in colors. In box $3 75

Don Gordon's Shooting Box 1 25

Rod and Gun 1 25

The Young Wild Fowlers 1 25

FOREST AND STREAM SERIES. By Harry Castlemon. 3 vols., 12mo. Fully illustrated. Cloth, extra, printed in colors. In box $3 75

Joe Wayring at Home; or, Story of a Fly Rod . 1 25

Snagged and Sunk; or, The Adventures of a Canvas Canoe 1 25

Steel Horse; or, The Rambles of a Bicycle 1 25

WAR SERIES. By Harry Castlemon. 4 vols., 12mo. Fully illustrated. Cloth, extra, printed in colors. In box 5 00

True to his Colors 1 25

Rodney, the Partisan 1 25

Marcy, the Blockade Runner 1 25

Marcy, the Refugee 1 25

OUR FELLOWS; or, Skirmishes with the Swamp Dragoons. By Harry Castlemon. 16mo. Fully illustrated. Cloth, extra 1 25

ALGER'S RENOWNED BOOKS.

BY HORATIO LGER, JR.

Specimen Cover of the Ragged
Dick Series.

Horatio Alger, Jr., has attained distinction as one of the most popular writers of books for boys, and the following list comprises all of his best books.

∗∗∗ Any volume sold separately.

RAGGED DICK SERIES. By Horatio Alger, Jr. 6 vols., 12mo. Fully illustrated. Cloth, extra, printed in colors. In box $7 50

Ragged Dick; or, Street Life in New York 1 25

Fame and Fortune; or, The Progress of Richard Hunter 1 25

Mark, the Match Boy; or, Richard Hunter's Ward 1 25

Rough and Ready; or, Life among the New York Newsboys 1 25

Ben, the Luggage Boy; or, Among the Wharves . 1 25

Rufus and Rose; or, the Fortunes of Rough and Ready 1 25

TATTERED TOM SERIES. (First Series.) By Horatio Alger, Jr. 4 vols., 12mo. Fully illustrated. Cloth, extra, printed in colors. In box . . . 5 00

(4)

Tattered Tom; or, The Story of a Street Arab . . . 25

Paul, the Peddler; or, The Adventures of a Young
Street Merchant 1 25

Phil, the Fiddler; or, The Young Street Musician . 1 25

Slow and Sure; or, From the Sidewalk to the Shop 1 25

TATTERED TOM SERIES. (SECOND SERIES.)
4 vols., 12mo. Fully illustrated. Cloth, extra, printed
in colors. In box $5 00

Julius; or the Street Boy Out West 1 25

The Young Outlaw; or, Adrift in the World . . . 1 25

Sam's Chance and How He Improved it . . . 1 25

The Telegraph Boy 1 25

LUCK AND PLUCK SERIES. (FIRST SERIES.)
By Horatio Alger, Jr. 4 vols., 12mo. Fully illustrated. Cloth, extra, printed in colors. In box . . . $5 00

Luck and Pluck; or John Oakley's Inheritance . . 1 25

Sink or Swim; or, Harry Raymond's Resolve . . . 1 25

Strong and Steady; or, Paddle Your Own Canoe . 1 25

Strive and Succeed; or, The Progress of Walter
Conrad 1 25

LUCK AND PLUCK SERIES. (SECOND
SERIES.) By Horatio Alger, Jr. 3 vols., 12mo.
Fully illustrated. Cloth, extra, printed in colors. In
box $5 00

Try and Trust; or, The Story of a Bound Boy . . . 1 25

Bound to Rise; or Harry Walton's Motto 1 25

Risen from the Ranks; or, Harry Walton's Success 1 25

Herbert Carter's Legacy; or, The Inventor's Son . 1 25

CAMPAIGN SERIES. By Horatio Alger, Jr. 3
vols., 12mo. Fully illustrated. Cloth, extra, printed
in colors. In box $3 75

Frank's Campaign; or, The Farm and the Camp . 1 25

Paul Prescott's Charge 1 25

Charlie Codman's Cruise 1 25

BRAVE AND BOLD SERIES. By Horatio Alger, Jr. 4 vols., 12mo. Fully illustrated. Cloth, extra, printed in colors. In box **$5 00**

Brave and Bold; or, The Story of a Factory Boy . . **1 25**

Jack's Ward; or, The Boy Guardian **1 25**

Shifting for Himself; or, Gilbert Greyson's Fortunes **1 25**

Wait and Hope; or, Ben Bradford's Motto **1 25**

PACIFIC SERIES. By Horatio Alger, Jr. 4 vols. 12mo. Fully illustrated. Cloth, extra, printed in colors. In box **$5 00**

The Young Adventurer; or, Tom's Trip Across the Plains **1 25**

The Young Miner; or, Tom Nelson in California . **1 25**

The Young Explorer; or, Among the Sierras . . **1 25**

Ben's Nugget; or, A Boy's Search for Fortune. A Story of the Pacific Coast **1 25**

ATLANTIC SERIES. By Horatio Alger, Jr. 4 vols., 12mo. Fully illustrated. Cloth, extra, printed in colors. In box **$5 00**

The Young Circus Rider; or, The Mystery of Robert Rudd **1 25**

Do and Dare; or, A Brave Boy's Fight for Fortune . **1 25**

Hector's Inheritance; or, Boys of Smith Institute . **1 25**

Helping Himself; or, Grant Thornton's Ambition . **1 25**

WAY TO SUCCESS SERIES. By Horatio Alger, Jr. 4 vols., 12mo. Fully illustrated. Cloth, extra, printed in colors. In box **$5 00**

Bob Burton **1 25**

The Store Boy **1 25**

Luke Walton **1 25**

Struggling Upward **1 25**

New Book by Alger.

DIGGING FOR GOLD. By Horatio Alger, Jr. Illustrated 12mo. Cloth, black, red and gold . . . **1 25**

A
New Series
of Books.

———

Indian Life
and
Character
Founded on
Historical
Facts.

Specimen Cover of the Wyoming
Series.

By Edward S. Ellis.

•*• Any volume sold separately.

———

BOY PIONEER SERIES. By Edward S. Ellis.
3 vols., 12mo. Fully illustrated. Cloth, extra, printed
in colors. In box $3 75
Ned in the Block House; or, Life on the Frontier. 1 25
Ned in the Woods. A Tale of the Early Days in
the West 1 25
Ned on the River 1 25
DEERFOOT SERIES. By Edward S. Ellis. In
box containing the following. 3 vols., 12mo. Illus-
trated $3 75
Hunters of the Ozark 1 25
Camp in the Mountains 1 25
The Last War Trail 1 25
LOG CABIN SERIES. By Edward S. Ellis.
3 vols., 12mo. Fully illustrated. Cloth, extra, printed
in colors. In box $3 75

(7)

Lost Trail **$1 25**

Camp Fire and Wigwam 1 25

Footprints in the Forest 1 25

WYOMING SERIES. By Edward S. Ellis. 3
vols., 12mo. Fully illustrated. Cloth, extra, printed
in colors. In box **$3 75**

Wyoming 1 25

Storm Mountain 1 25

Cabin in the Clearing 1 25

NEW BOOKS BY EDWARD S. ELLIS.

Through Forest and Fire. 12mo. Cloth . . . 1 25

On the Trail of the Moose. 12mo. Cloth . . 1 25

By C. A. Stephens.

Rare books for boys—bright, breezy, wholesome and instructive; full of
adventure and incident, and information upon natural history. They blend
instruction with amusement—contain much useful and valuable information
upon the habits of animals, and plenty of adventure, fun and jollity.

CAMPING OUT SERIES. By C. A. Stephens.
6 vols., 12mo. Fully illustrated. Cloth, extra, printed
in colors. In box **$7 50**

Camping Out. As recorded by " Kit " 1 25

Left on Labrador; or The Cruise of the Schooner
Yacht " Curfew." As recorded by " Wash " 1 25

Off to the Geysers ; or, The Young Yachters in Ice-
land. As recorded by "Wade " 1 25

Lynx Hunting. From Notes by the author of
" Camping Out " 1 25

Fox Hunting. As recorded by " Raed " 1 25

On the Amazon ; or, The Cruise of the " Rambler."
As recorded by " Wash " 1 25

By J. T. Trowbridge.

These stories will rank among the best of Mr. Trowbridge's books for the
young—and he has written some of the best of our juvenile literature.

JACK HAZARD SERIES. By J. T. Trowbridge.
6 vols., 12mo. Fully Illustrated. Cloth, extra, printed
in colors. In box **$7 50**